To the three angels who will make my Christmas sparkle –
my beautiful grandchildren Franklin, Jemma and Sophie

Acknowledgements

I knew when I went on a fascinating tour of the Hensley Settlement from the Cumberland Gap National Historical Park it would definitely make its way into one of my books – and our guide genuinely was related to the Hensley family which made it extremely personal. When the story of Black Cherry Retreat began to emerge this captivating area of East Tennessee was the perfect setting and it's possible that nestling in the hills and hollows of this beautiful area Pine Ridge might actually exist!

Thanks go to the Tasting Panel readers who passed this manuscript and made publication a possibility: Heather P, Els E, Melissa C, Jenny W, Linda Sp, Ana A, Alison B, Lizzie D, Jo O, Hannah S, Heidi J, Hrund, Kirsty M, Cindy T, Alma H, Heather S and Linda W.

Chapter One

Getting away from it all was supposed to be good for Fee's health but at this precise moment she was more stressed than ever. She'd spent the last fifteen years working in some of the most dangerous places in the world so a slow meandering drive along the back roads of East Tennessee should be a cinch but the lack of traffic and people made her uneasy. Fee had stopped the car to study the old-fashioned paper map because her cell phone signal had given up five minutes earlier and she couldn't convince herself she was headed in the right direction.

She trailed her finger along the winding curves on the map and guessed it'd be about another five miles. Fee rested her back against the bonnet of her rental car and forced herself to take a good look around, trying to take her London therapist's advice to live in the moment. She sucked in deep breaths of the crisp mountain air which she figured must be better for her lungs than the searing dusty heat of Afghanistan or the recent monsoon season she'd endured in Mumbai. Even to her jaded eyes the fall colours, ranging from a soft buttery yellow to a chilli pepper red were a stunning assault on the senses and a tiny nugget of hope sneaked into her.

Panic attacks. Borderline dependency issues. Insomnia. A stiff left knee thanks to a fall in the Syrian mountains. It wasn't a happy list. The last doctor she saw warned her she wouldn't live to see her fortieth birthday next year if she didn't change her ways. At the time she'd bit back the reply filling her head – that she wasn't sure she cared much either way.

Fee gulped down the last of her Coke and promised herself as soon as she arrived at the isolated cabin she'd condemned herself to for the next month she'd brush her teeth. That way she wouldn't need to add a root canal to her to-do list.

Twenty minutes later she was re-thinking her map reading

prowess. She eased the car around yet another sharp ninety-degree turn and slammed on her brakes.

Black Cherry Retreat. A simple carved wood sign by the side of the road caught her eye and she spotted a narrow track disappearing off into the distance. *My God, they really did mean remote*. She could head back down the mountain and reach the Knoxville airport in about an hour. An overnight flight across the Atlantic and she'd be back in London. Maybe returning to work would be the best cure.

The lingering acid in the base of her stomach stirred up and forced her to swallow hard. Fee's hands shook and eerily familiar waves of panic swept over her.

'Hey, are you all right, honey?'

A man's soft, deep voice penetrated a corner of her brain and she jerked around to stare out of the side window. Fee tried to compose herself as the stranger pushed back the brim of his well-worn, black cowboy hat and peered in at her.

She managed to nod and glanced at the battered white pick-up truck he'd been driving when she came to an abrupt stop in front of him. Thank goodness he was paying attention or he'd have smashed right into her bumper. He gestured for her to roll down the window but she shook her head.

'You goin' up to the cabins?' he asked. Fee didn't answer. For all she knew he could be the local axe-murderer. 'I'm Tom Chambers. I own Black Cherry Retreat. Sorry if I startled you.' He stepped away from her car and hooked his large thumbs in the belt loops of his faded jeans. Fee's gaze ran up over his large, solid frame, noticing the sort of muscles acquired through hard outdoor work.

Most people are decent, Fee, you need to learn to give them a chance.

Doctor Michael's words snaked into her head and with her heart speeding like a Formula One race car she pressed the button to open her window.

'It's not a problem.' Fee was surprised how calm and normal she sounded. It was huge progress from the meltdown she'd have gone into a month ago. 'I'm Fee Winter. We've been in touch by email. I've booked one of your cabins for a month.'

A slow smile crept over his face warming something deep inside her. No one would describe Tom Chambers as conventionally good-looking but his air of quiet confidence would no doubt always catch a woman's eye. He'd obviously been around the block a few times and it was reflected in every fine line and tanned crease of his interesting face. 'I've been into town picking up a few supplies. Follow me on up and I'll get y'all settled in. You sure picked a pretty day to come, of course around here that's mostly what we get.'

'You wouldn't be biased, would you?' she jibed, surprising herself. It'd been a long time since she'd teased a strange man.

'Nah, never. The fact I've lived most of my life within ten miles of the house where I was born and plan to die here, buried next to eight generations of Chambers, has nothing to do with it.'

A pang of envy swamped Fee at the man's casual description of his life. He'd be completely bewildered by her nomadic existence and might even feel sorry for her – something she wholeheartedly detested. 'How unadventurous,' she commented. He didn't reply but a muscle twitched in his clean-shaven, square jaw giving away the fact that her rudeness struck home.

For a couple of seconds they stared at each other until Fee blinked and glanced back down at the steering wheel. She considered apologising, but bit her tongue to stop herself. She had nothing to be sorry for.

'Some might say so.' He pushed his hat back into place and turned away to climb back into his truck, his long legs disappearing inside in one smooth move. Tom fired up his engine and manoeuvred in front of her to head up the road, leaving Fee with little choice but to follow.

Tom checked in the rear-view mirror to make sure he hadn't lost his new guest. Whatever or whoever had put the wind up her had done a top-notch job. Objectively he'd say Fee Winter was a decent-looking woman although a touch too straight up and down for his taste. His preference ran to petite women with soft curves a man could ... He stopped his mental rambling right there. He wouldn't be investigating his new guest in any way, shape or form.

Once a cop always a cop, bro. His older brother's casual remark last time they were together popped back into his head. Tom silently used the same expletive he'd shut Sandy up with. The past was the past. Line drawn. End of story.

Tom slowed down and drove along the narrow gravel road skirting Black Cherry Lake. He stopped outside his own cabin where he'd taken one room as the resort office and jumped out. Slamming the truck door he waited for Fee to park and join him.

'The six guest cabins are all on this side of the lake. This one is mine and the resort office is in here.' He gestured towards the building next to them. 'How about we go in and get the paperwork out of the way?' Fee didn't move. She stood by her car door, grasping the handle as if she planned to make a quick escape. 'Is that okay?' Finally she gave a brief nod and Tom caught her quick intake of breath. *What the hell was up with her?*

Tom leapt up the couple of steps to open the door and stood back to one side. After a few seconds' hesitation she stepped inside and he followed her in. Taking care to give her plenty of space, Tom walked around her and led the way into his office and sat down at the desk.

'If you wouldn't mind signing these and giving me your credit card details I'll show you to your cabin.' She didn't say a word but passed over her card before beginning to read the forms he put down on the desk in front of her with great care.

Tom launched into his standard spiel about how the resort came into being. Most people were interested to hear that the land had been in the Chambers family for nearly two hundred years but Fee showed no interest in asking any questions. He'd spent the last ten years restoring the cabins that had originally been built in the 1860s. Tom had saved the buildings from collapse and they'd done the same for him, but he omitted that part because no one needed his sob story.

'Feel free to come by if you need anything or have any problems with the cabin. I'm usually around but if I'm not just leave me a note and I'll get around to it soon as I can. Otherwise I leave guests to themselves.' A brief flash of gratitude brightened her sharp blue eyes leaving him strangely pleased to have said *something* right at last.

Tom pointed across the hall. 'I've recently fitted out a communal room for guests to use. There's a TV and DVD player set up with a selection of movies, books and a few board games. If people want company they'll sometimes come over and hang out here. I've even done a couple of barbecues and we've all eaten together. But no pressure, ever.'

Fee nodded and cleared her throat. 'Thank you.'

Wow, she'd granted him two more words – he'd hit pay dirt. 'There's no internet or cell phone service here, but you knew that. You can drive back down into Pine Ridge for supplies. I'd say it's the nearest town but that's kind of an exaggeration.' He smiled, but her unrevealing expression didn't alter. 'There's Wi-Fi available in the Mockingbird Cafe along with the best biscuits this side of Knoxville. Of course my aunt makes them so again you'd call me biased.' Tom didn't miss the slight upturn in her mouth, giving the first hint of softness to her severe features. Everything about Fee Winter was pared down from her thin dark-framed glasses, short black hair, cheekbones sharp enough to hang clothes on and lean muscular legs. 'Your phone will work there too. I've got a radio here to use for emergencies.'

'Fine.'

Tom grabbed a set of keys from the board. 'Okay, let's get you settled. Yours is the second cabin along and is called Knox. I named them all after local counties here in East Tennessee. If you drive over and park outside I'll walk along to meet you there.'

'You could ride with me.' She stumbled over the words and the small amount of colour in her skin drained away.

'Thanks but I could do with stretching my legs.'

'Why, aren't they long enough?' she quipped.

Tom chuckled. 'Hey, you do have a sense of humour in there after all, even if it is a weird British one.' A rush of heat flamed her cheeks and he guessed she'd take back her words if she could. 'Sorry. That was rude. Mama would smack me if she heard me talking this way.'

She inclined her serious face in a nod and briskly walked back outside without saying another word.

Tom trailed after her and set off walking across the damp grass. It was a more direct route than the narrow road and he easily beat her to the cabin. He wasn't a boastful man but when he looked at Knox Cabin he felt a quiet sense of achievement. If he left nothing else behind preserving this small piece of his family history wasn't a bad legacy.

'It's beautiful.'

Fee's surprisingly gentle voice next to his shoulder took him by surprise and he turned to meet her appreciative gaze head-on.

'Yeah, it is.' He risked carrying on, afraid to break the thin thread of communication strung between them. 'They sure knew how to build. No modern tools. No decent plans. Hell of a leap of faith.'

'It must've taken a lot of time and work on your part to get it back to this.'

'The best things always do.'

Fee's eyes shone, the way women's do when they are about to cry. Too afraid to ask whether he'd said anything wrong Tom stayed silent and she glanced away. 'Right. I'll show you around and then leave you alone.'

'Good idea, Mr Chambers.'

Damn right. He'd make his escape as fast as possible and stay gone. Black Cherry was his refuge too.

Chapter Two

Fee couldn't believe she'd been stupid enough to make a joke about Tom's legs. It gave completely the wrong impression – one of friendliness and maybe more. Her sole purpose in coming here was to begin the long, slow path back to a level of balance in her life. But something about the genuine warmth in Tom Chambers' deep brown eyes and his frank, open smile had thrown her off kilter.

She picked up her two small bags and headed down the narrow hall to the bedroom. Fee stood in the doorway and admired the polished wood floor, unadorned windows and stone-clad fireplace. Neat, clean and practical, it fitted her sensibilities down to the ground. The simple wood-framed double bed wasn't piled with unnecessary pillows and the green and white cross-stitch quilt screamed warmth and comfort. Maybe giving up her sleeping pills would be possible here.

Five minutes later she'd hung her few clothes in the small wardrobe and stowed her underwear and odds and ends away in the solid oak chest of drawers. Years of nomadic living meant she travelled light, moving in and out of her latest abode in far less time than most women took to apply their make-up in the morning.

Fee wandered into the bathroom next door and happily checked out the perfect combination of a modern shower and antique bathtub. She'd gone without proper facilities for weeks on end but it'd only given her a deep appreciation for good plumbing when it was on offer. As she spread her paltry array of toiletries out on the narrow glass shelf a piercing memory slammed back and Fee gasped for breath.

On the last morning with Pierre she'd teased him about being the only man to wear designer cologne in a war zone.

He'd laughed and blown her a kiss as he stepped out of the front door of the press hotel in Kabul. Fee lifted her camera to capture the moment but seconds later he stepped on one of the notorious IEDs and blew up in front of her eyes. She'd carried on taking photos through the tears streaming down her face and when she discovered his betrayal later it'd only made his death more painful.

Sinking to her knees on the cold tiled floor she let the tears flow.

'Hey, honey, are you okay?'

Strong arms lifted her up to her feet and a masculine scent of plain soap and heat sneaked into her awareness. Fee's eyes flew open and she registered the fact she was plastered against Tom Chambers' broad chest. He stubbornly held onto her as she tried to jerk away.

'I'll let go when I'm sure you're not going to fall down again.' His deep, soft drawl eased her fear. 'I'm not going to hurt you. There you go.' Tom assured her as he dropped his hands away.

'What are *you* doing here?'

'I came with your towels. When I set up this morning they were still in the dryer. I knocked but you didn't reply and I heard you crying through the open window. I couldn't ignore it.'

'I wish you had.'

'Yeah, I bet you do.'

'Uh, the towels?'

'I dropped them in the other room when I came looking for you. I'll go and fetch them.' Tom hurried away and she rested her hands against the edge of the washbasin.

Fee refused to look at her reflection, knowing it'd be the pale, tight, strained visage that had become her new normal. She ran the cold tap and scooped up the freezing water to splash over her face and neck.

'There you go.'

She snatched the soft white towel he thrust into her hand and rubbed at her skin until it burned.

'Better?'

She managed to nod and turned back to face him. 'Thank you.'

'You're welcome. I'll leave you alone, unless …' Tom shook his head. 'Forget it.'

'What? It isn't easy to forget something you didn't hear in the first place.'

'Forgot my golden rule.' He shrugged. 'Leave the guests alone.'

Fee couldn't resist a tiny smile. 'What were you going to suggest?'

'Only coffee,' he protested. For some reason she found his obvious embarrassment endearing. 'You looked so damn miserable,' Tom mumbled and stared at the floor, toeing the edge of the small patchwork rug with his worn boots.

'I was,' she murmured. 'What do you Americans say about waiting for the rain another day?'

Tom frowned before a shy smile crept across his face intensifying the attractive creases fanning out around his eyes. 'You mean you want to take a rain check?'

'Yes, please. Now's not a good time.'

'Sure.' Tom crammed his hat back on and walked away.

She took several long, slow breaths and remembered her therapist's instructions when she left. *Take baby steps. Remember you took a long time to get sick and you'll take a long time to find your way back*.

'Thanks again. I mean it,' Fee called out as he reached the front door and Tom turned with his hand on the latch.

'No problem.'

Fee dropped down into the nearest chair as the door closed behind him. The silence was deafening. There was no escaping herself now and she was supposed to find that a good thing.

If his foot could reach his ass he'd give himself a hard kick. Mr Saviour. It'd been Gina's pet name for him. She always said he was on a mission to save the world but it hadn't done him a damn bit of good when he couldn't save his own wife. They'd been drinking coffee on their front porch, the first time in weeks that they'd spent any appreciable amount of time together without arguing. Out of nowhere Gary Higgins had appeared and aimed a gun at Gina. She hadn't stood a chance and the image of his beautiful wife crying out his name with her dying breath still haunted him. Tom had been instrumental in getting Higgins sent to prison and within days of his release the man tracked them down to get his revenge in the worst possible way. As soon as he heard Fee's distress today he'd rushed in like Superman.

Tom strode off back towards his own cabin, kicking gravel and cursing under his breath all the way there. He pushed the cabin door open and headed straight for the office, checking out the clock on the wall to discover it was almost lunchtime. Tuesday was chicken and dumplings day at the Mockingbird Cafe and Aunt Ina's good home cooking would do more than comfort his growling stomach. She'd fuss over him and right now he could do with a touch of family love.

He ran outside and hopped into his truck, firing it up and gunning the engine as he shoved it into gear and roared off down the gravel road. By the time he took the third hairpin curve at speed his temper abated and he eased back on the gas. If he arrived in town mad his mother would hear about it and he'd get one of her famous lectures. Over the last seventeen years he'd suffered more than his fair share of *those*.

Tom pulled into a parking space outside the cafe and got out. He couldn't help grinning as he ran his gaze over the outside of the building. Mary-Jo must have been busy because Halloween decorations completely covered the bright yellow paint. His fun-loving cousin was studying graphic design at UT Knoxville and enjoyed practising her skills on her long-suffering mother's business. If there was an inch of the small building not covered with fake spider webs, gory skeletons and ghosts it escaped Tom's attention. He headed towards the door and lowered his head to avoid becoming tangled up in the decor.

'Uncle T, Uncle T!'

A red-haired bombshell raced across the room and threw herself at his knees. Tom scooped up his adorable toddler cousin and turned her upside down. He held onto her plump little legs while he swung her around, setting off a crescendo of happy high-pitched screams and giggles.

'Thomas Michael Chambers, put that child down right now or she'll lose her lunch all over you and it'll serve you right.' Aunt Ina threw him a fierce glare as she ran out from the kitchen to rescue her youngest granddaughter. 'As if I don't have enough goin' on without you turnin' up.' Her laughing eyes belied her stern words. 'I might've guessed you'd drag your sorry self in today to be fed.'

'You know I never miss your chicken and dumplings if I can help it.'

'We might be sold out,' she protested.

'C'mon we both know you always set a plate aside for your favourite nephew. Admit it, you wonderful woman.' He squeezed her in a quick hug.

Ina snorted and tried to hold on to a wriggling Lulu with one hand. 'You think you're a charmer like your father.'

'And you can't resist it,' he teased. Tom let go of his aunt and snatched Lulu back. He swung her up into his arms and the little girl wrapped her little hands around his neck. She gave her grandmother a triumphant smile.

'Fine, have her. She can pester you instead of gettin' under my feet. Mary-Jo won't be back until four so we've a long day to get through yet.'

Tom's smile tightened as he thought about Lulu's absent father. Luke Durham, the tough football quarterback hadn't been so sure of himself when faced with the prospect of fatherhood in his senior year of high school. Durham Senior, his slimy attorney father, shoved a bunch of money at Mary-Jo and dragged his son off to play for a big college out west. Every time Tom saw the jerk playing on national TV it made him want to puke.

'Mary-Jo's doin' fine, don't fret over her. You know we wouldn't be without this little sweetheart,' Ina murmured, ruffling Lulu's soft curls.

'Yeah, I know. I'm sorry.'

'Life's not always easy. You know that better than most.' Her eyes softened. Tom hated sympathy more than anything and bit back a smart reply.

'Uncle T. Me want ice cream,' Lulu yelled in his ear.

'Tell you what, pumpkin, if you help me eat some of Mommy Ina's chicken and dumplin's we'll get us a dab of ice cream after.'

'Good luck.' Ina laughed. 'The little madam only ate two bites of the hot dog I fixed her before you came.'

'Fetch us a bowl and two spoons and we'll do fine,' Tom declared and swung his lunch partner back down on her feet. 'Come on, sweetie, where we gonna sit?'

Lulu studied the room before pointing at a table over by the window and dragged on his hand, tugging him along behind her. Five minutes later with Lulu on his lap and digging into a bowl of hot, savoury chicken and dumplings Tom's world settled back down.

'Has she been a good girl?' Ina came to see how they were doing.

'Of course.' Tom kissed the top of Lulu's head. She beamed up at him and her innocent smile sucked the breath from his body. He'd expected to have a brood of kids of his own by now but things hadn't worked out that way. 'How about I take her up to mine for a couple of hours?'

'Haven't you got work to do?'

'No more than you have. I wouldn't get much more done today anyway.' He didn't explain and she didn't ask.

'It's fine by me if she'll go with you. If you're lucky she might take a nap.' Ina frowned. 'Remember to ask if she needs to go potty. We're doin' well but she forgets sometimes.'

'No problem. Remember I pretty much raised the twins.' He'd spent half his teenage years with his younger sisters Rayna and Chloe attached to him like limpets so one three-year-old wasn't a big deal. Tom tweaked Lulu's ponytail. 'Hey, pumpkin, you want to come and feed my ducks?'

'Yep, but you promised we'd eat ice cream.' She pouted.

He bent down to whisper in the little girl's ear and caught his aunt's eye over Lulu's head. 'Don't tell Mommy Ina but I've got three flavours in my freezer.' Her big, brown eyes widened and she planted a sticky kiss on his nose.

'You're stuck with her now,' Aunt Ina declared with a throaty laugh.

That was fine with him. One woman could help take his mind off another.

Chapter Three

Fee finished writing her journal entry and closed the book before hiding it away in the dresser drawer. Initially it'd been part of her therapy but now she found she missed it if she got too busy to write. She ought to eat lunch but instead Fee slipped on her shoes and grabbed a small red apple from the dish before stepping out onto the front porch. Maybe later she'd sit in one of the rocking chairs on her tiny front porch and start one of the books she'd brought with her.

Until you get antsy. This relaxed mode of life was so alien. Surely a Martian would experience the same misgivings if dropped on planet earth and told to fit in. Without the camera she'd been ordered not to bring with her, and which she hadn't been without in over twenty years, Fee felt she was learning to live without one of her limbs.

It's time to face life with no lens in the way.

The doctors didn't understand. Few people did. Apart from her free-spirited mother she didn't have much in the way of family, and friends tended to drop off the radar because she was rarely around. Relationships with men were hopeless because no one wanted a woman who would cancel a date and disappear for four months on an assignment without bothering to send an apologetic email.

Fee dragged herself down the couple of steps, determined to take one of the walks she'd been assured would do her good and headed for the two-mile trail around Black Cherry Lake. For a woman who'd trekked for days on end in harsh terrain this should be nothing more than a gentle stroll but with her low-energy light on full blast she wasn't sure she'd make it all the way.

Small steps, Fee. Small steps.

Turning her face into the mild autumn sun she set off slowly at first and gradually increased the length of her strides as the blood pumped through her body. Fee ignored the twinge in her knee and hoped it'd work itself out if she didn't push too hard. She passed the other cabins quickly in the hope she wouldn't be spotted and forced into conversation by any of the other guests.

After a few minutes she relaxed and began to enjoy herself. A family of ducks swam close to the shoreline making her wish she had something to feed them. Fee shaded her eyes from the sun and followed the progress of a large bird flying low across the lake until it disappeared into the shade of the trees. She wondered if it was some sort of eagle but couldn't be sure. Tom probably knew every inch of his land and what lived on and around it. He'd happily tell her if she asked which she wouldn't. Fee's senses sharpened, honed by years of developing an acute awareness of her surroundings for her own safety. She glanced over her shoulder to see a small, brown and white spotted deer watching her from a few metres away. The urge to take its picture and capture the intriguing mix of vulnerability and composure swept through Fee and she cursed her doctor. How would he care to have his medical license snatched away? Hardly daring to breathe she held the deer's wide-eyed gaze until it blinked and leapt back into the shelter of the trees.

Shoving her hands in her pockets she walked on again and found herself back where she'd started sooner than expected. Fee studied the cabins, spaced a decent distance apart when they were built so the owners would have had neighbours for protection but not close enough to lose their privacy. People's longings for a home and community were the same all over around the world and in a small way she always hoped her pictures would increase that understanding. She was smart enough to get the irony of a photographer with no settled home celebrating such things. Whenever her therapist probed too deeply into her background she avoided his questions, but he would bide his time and come back to the subject when she least expected.

Fee strode in front of Tom's cabin and stopped dead at the sound of childish laughter ringing out from his front porch. Tom rocked in one of the chairs with a tiny red-headed girl perched on his knee.

'Faster, horsey, faster.' The child giggled and shouted, banging on his legs. Fee couldn't drag her eyes away as Tom whinnied and made loud horse noises. Why had she been so sure he was a loner like herself? Usually she did a good job of recognising fellow outcasts but her radar must have failed her this time. The afternoon sun picked up burnished highlights in Tom's hair she hadn't noticed earlier making it obvious where the girl's bright curls came from.

'Miss Winter, are you enjoying the lovely day?'

She started and met his knowing smile, aware she'd been caught staring. 'Yes, I've walked all around the lake. It's very beautiful.'

The girl tugged at Tom's arm. 'Hurry up we've got to win the race.'

'This horsey's tired, sweetheart. He sure could do with some ice cream.'

'Ice cream. Ice cream.' She bounced harder and Tom eased the child off and stood up, his movements graceful and economic for such a big man. 'Lulu, this is Miss Winter. Say good afternoon, ma'am.'

The girl parroted him and Fee blinked back tears. Children weren't her thing so why did this particular scrap of a girl get to her? She tried to rationalise it by telling herself it'd happened before in other times and places. It was part of being human, nothing more.

'Does *she* like ice cream?'

Tom's eyes crinkled at the corners. 'I don't know. You wanna ask her, pumpkin?'

Lulu raced down the steps. 'Do you want to eat ice cream with us? We've got three kinds.'

Fee caught a hint of challenge in Tom's expression. He

thought she'd find an excuse and run off but the man didn't know her at all. She'd never backed down from anything even if it was life-threatening. Ice cream was something she could do.

'Do you have any strawberry?' she asked and Lulu glanced back up at Tom.

'Yeah,' he declared, 'plus vanilla for unadventurous people or to put on pie, and of course chocolate marshmallow—'

'For big boys who never grew up?' Fee teased.

'I've been known to share if I'm asked nicely,' he protested, hooking his thumbs in his pockets and staring her down.

'No problem. I'm a strawberry girl myself.' One of her few good childhood memories was of eating strawberry ice cream with her mother every time they were in Cornwall. They'd go there sometimes to stay with Will Sawyer, the most consistent of her mother's numerous boyfriends. He was the only one to show her any kindness instead of merely tolerating her presence and his rambling old house, only a stone's throw from the sea, became the closest thing she ever knew to a settled home.

'Thought so. Come and sit here with us. I'll go fix the ice cream.'

Tom hurried indoors letting the screen door close behind him and stood still for a moment to gather his senses. He couldn't rationalise why Fee Winter rattled him. She was no raving beauty and the imaginary barbed wire fence circling her should be enough to warn him off, so why did she still intrigue him?

You gotta let go of Gina one day, bro. He'd fought with his oldest brother last Thanksgiving until his father dragged him off. They'd both had a few too many beers when Sandy told him what he thought of Tom's self-imposed punishment. He didn't understand a lifetime would never be long enough to assuage the guilt that gnawed at him day and night. The fact that Gina died because of him was brutal enough but almost worse was the painful knowledge that their marriage had been pulling apart at the seams with no apparent hope of repair. His biggest regret came from not having been the husband Gina needed and deserved.

He opened the freezer and tossed the tubs of ice cream on the table. Eating ice cream with his young cousin and a guest meant nothing. *Yeah, right*. Tom took out bowls and spoons then started to dish up, gathering everything on a tray to head back outside.

'Here we go, ladies.' Tom set the bowls down on the white oak table carved in the shape of Tennessee that he'd made over the winter. Opening one of its drawers he pulled out a stack of paper napkins and set them out for everyone to use. Tom fetched a small child-sized stool and set it down near his chair. 'Here's a special spot for you, Lulu.' He put her strawberry ice cream in front of her and touched her hand to get her attention. 'Try not to get it on your pretty dress or Mommy Ina will scalp us both.'

'Yes, Uncle T.'

Lulu nodded so seriously he had a hard job stopping himself from laughing. Tom pushed a bowl towards Fee and caught her looking at him with unabashed curiosity.

'Uncle T?'

In an instant Tom realised what Fee meant by her question. She'd assumed Lulu was his daughter. 'I should've introduced my special lady. This is Miss Lulu Chambers, my beautiful cousin. Her Mama is in school today so we get to play, don't we, pumpkin?'

'Yep.' Lulu grinned at Fee. 'Uncle T's my favourite uncle. He's got ducks, books and ice cream.'

Fee's face softened and Tom got a hint of how she'd look when a man was loving her. 'That's all a girl needs. You're very lucky.'

He sensed a deeper meaning behind her words but this wasn't the time or place, and if he was sensible it never would be.

Instantly she glanced away and scooped up a spoonful of ice cream. 'This is delicious.'

'It's homemade by my cousin, Suzy-Beth. She's got a store called Sweet Scoops in Pine Ridge.'

'Goodness, does your family run the whole town?'

Tom shrugged. 'There are a lot of us because we've been here for generations. Aunt Ina, my Dad's sister, owns the Mockingbird Cafe. Ina's oldest daughter Suzy-Beth is married to John who is a local doctor. My Pop is the sheriff and my younger sister, Rayna, teaches at the elementary school. Rayna's married to Billy and they're expecting their first kid soon. Chloe, Rayna's twin, lives here too. She's married to Ken and is a stay-at-home mom to her four little ones. My older brothers are both police officers; Sandy in Oak Ridge and Mikey in Clinton, but they still live here with their families.' He stopped running his mouth and noticed Fee's bright eyes dancing with amusement. 'There are more cousins and everything but your ice cream's melting,' he muttered. A trickle of pink dripped down Fee's chin and Tom itched to reach over and brush it away. He noticed Lulu wriggling. 'Do you need to go potty, Lulu-Belle?' Her eyes, the regular Chambers family deep brown specials, filled with tears and she pulled at the front of her pink flowery dress.

Tom jumped up and quickly swept her into his arms. 'It's okay, we'll go and get cleaned up.'

'But my ice cream ...'

'I'll fetch you more. I promise,' he whispered and she smiled against his cheek.

'Is there anything I can do to help?'

Fee's awkward smile said she wasn't at ease around children but wouldn't be seen as unwilling.

'Thanks, but we're good. I almost brought up my twin sisters when Mama worked at the cafe with my aunt. Seen it all. Done it. Not a problem. We won't be long.' He headed inside, glancing back at Fee. 'Don't you dare run off or I'll have an unhappy little girl on my hands.'

'But, I ...'

He strode off inside before she could argue. Tom raided his emergency clothes supply and pulled out a pair of white shorts and a blue cotton sweater which hopefully wouldn't be too big for Lulu. His family visited all the time so he'd raided the Goodwill store and stashed away a variety of sizes and genders of clothes because someone was always falling in the lake or splashing themselves with spaghetti sauce.

'There we go, Lulu. All clean and ready for more ice cream.' She peered at her reflection in the mirror then back at him. Tom guessed he'd scored a zero on the fashion front but plastered on a big smile and held out his hand. 'Come on, let's go show Miss Winter how cute you look.' Lulu didn't say a word. She didn't need to because a man always knew when he'd failed a woman.

Chapter Four

Fee glanced up as they stepped back onto the porch. The little girl clung onto Tom's hand and was wearing new, distinctly uncoordinated, baggy clothes. 'Well, aren't you looking prettier than ever?' Her attempt at cheering Lulu didn't alter the child's dubious expression. 'I love your cute blue jumper.'

'My what?' Lulu's nose wrinkled.

Tom cleared his throat and the edges of his mouth quivered. 'Miss Winter's talking about your sweater. Where she lives they call it a jumper.'

'That's silly, it can't jump,' Lulu declared.

Behind the child's back Tom gave Fee a long, slow wink and she fought against giggling, something she hadn't done in twenty years.

'How about more ice cream, ladies?' he asked.

Big tears welled in Lulu's huge eyes. 'I've had 'nuff, Uncle T. I want my mama.'

A slice of long suppressed pain cut through Fee's heart. She thought of the hundreds of times she'd begged for the exact same thing. Homeless children in Peru, abused women in Ethiopia, or downtrodden miners in the Congo – fighting for good causes was always higher on Maddy Winter's priority list than her only child. No doubt it was where she'd got her own single-mindedness where her job was concerned and why she'd never have a family of her own. She could never put a child through the loneliness she'd endured. Every child was precious and should be cherished – she'd seen enough families destroyed by war or famine but still holding on to the only things of real importance: the people they loved. Fee accepted there was something lacking in her make-up, the same as it'd been in her mother's. That was simply how it was.

Tom glanced at his watch. 'Sure thing, baby girl. We'll go

back to Mommy Ina's and your mama will be home real soon. I'll put our dishes in the kitchen and we'll be off.'

'I could do that,' Fee offered.

'No problem. Won't take me a minute.'

He probably didn't want her poking around in his home but was too polite to say so. Fee nodded. 'I'll be on my way and let you two get on.'

'Care to take a ride into Pine Ridge with us?'

Lulu tugged on Fee's hand. 'Please. Mommy Ina's apple pie is so good.'

'I couldn't eat another thing.' Fee mock-groaned. 'Your uncle stuffed me with too much yummy ice cream.' The little girl's face fell and she wished she'd thought before speaking.

'Nothing stoppin' you takin' a look around, is there?' Tom put her on the spot and Fee shook her head. 'I'll go in and grab my keys while you ladies get in the truck.'

Fee took hold of Lulu's small, warm hand and they walked down the cabin steps together. She lifted the little girl up and settled her in the car seat.

'Don't you know how it works?' Lulu whined when she struggled to buckle the seat belt, confused by the array of straps and where they were supposed to go.

'Here, let me.' Tom appeared by her right shoulder and she was instantly aware of his nearness and the clean fresh-air scent rising from his soft flannel shirt when he reached across her to snap Lulu's belt in place.

He popped a kiss on Lulu's forehead. 'Do you think I'll have to do Miss Fee's belt up too, pumpkin?'

The thought of his big, competent hands touching her again made her glance down at the ground, anything to avoid him recognising her embarrassment. 'Certainly not,' she retorted.

'Hop in the front and prove it, hotshot.'

Without another word Fee climbed into the passenger seat and fixed her seat belt. She stared straight ahead and folded her hands primly on her lap while wishing she could answer him back with a joke. For two pins she'd get out and race back to the safety of her cabin.

'Lulu will survive if you change your mind,' he murmured. 'I didn't mean to railroad you. I'm real sorry.'

Daring to look his way, the worry lurking in his warm eyes gave her the courage to shake her head.

'Hurry up, Uncle T. I want my Mama right now,' Lulu yelled and kicked at the back of the seat.

'That's enough, Lulu. You need to be a good girl or Mommy Ina won't let you come play with me again.'

Tom's kind, firm tone quieted the little girl and Fee couldn't help thinking what a great father he'd make. Not that she had any personal experience because her father didn't even know of her existence. She was curious as to why such a warm, family-oriented man didn't appear to have his own kids.

As they started off back down the gravel road Fee smiled to herself imagining Doctor Michael's reaction if he could see her now. He'd be impressed to see her riding with a strange man and a child to meet people she didn't know with no sign of a panic attack.

'You can sit back and enjoy the drive instead of frettin' where to turn and watchin' out for our curvy roads,' Tom quipped.

'Thanks.' She managed a tentative smile. Fee was soon drawn in by the kaleidoscope of autumn colours shimmering in the late afternoon sun. She always appreciated timeless stretches of land and this was one, altered by man but still intrinsically the way it'd been created.

Although they didn't speak there was nothing awkward about the silence. Once Tom glanced in his rear view mirror and slid Fee a sideways smile, pointing back across his shoulder at the sleeping little girl. Maybe this was what parents felt like enjoying a smattering of quiet moments in the middle of a hectic day.

As they entered Pine Ridge she straightened and stared out

of the car window. When she drove through this morning she hadn't taken much notice of the small town. Most of the buildings were made of the local red bricks and all looked neat and well cared for. Several had colourful wooden signs indicating a shop or office and people strolled along the pavements going about their business. Fee couldn't imagine it'd changed much in decades.

'This is Main Street,' Tom announced with a touch of irony. 'I'm not sure why it's called that because it's the only business area we've got.'

'Perhaps to give it delusions of grandeur,' she teased. His instant warm laughter ran through her and she couldn't help smiling back. *Watch it*. 'Oh, goodness.' Fee startled as Tom pulled the truck to a stop in front of the one shop which stood out from all the others.

'This one has delusions all right courtesy of Mary-Jo, our sweet Lulu's Mama.'

Fee gaped, open-mouthed, at the array of Halloween decorations swamping the tiny building. 'Dare I ask what it looks like at Christmas?'

'When we've got through the trick or treatin' season in a couple of weeks, Mary-Jo will replace this little lot with pumpkins and scarecrows for Thanksgiving. After that's over it'll be the turn of Santa Claus, reindeer and candy canes. Maybe you'll hang around and find out what it all looks like. I, um ...' Tom paled and stumbled over his words. Luckily at that moment Lulu wailed from the back seat and Fee suppressed a smile as he leapt out of the car to rescue the tearful child.

Tom hung back by the cash register and left them to it. He'd intended to stay at Fee's side and protect her from his exuberant family but after her smirk when he'd stuck his size thirteen feet in a metaphorical pile of shit earlier she could manage on her own. He sipped a cup of coffee and wondered how soon he could suggest leaving.

'Your friend's an interesting woman.' Mary-Jo appeared by his elbow, balancing Lulu on her hip and nodding in Fee's direction.

'She's a guest, that's all.'

'Yeah, right.' His cousin sniggered. It must be his day for women finding him funny in the wrong sort of way. 'I wonder how she ended up here?'

He shrugged. 'She mentioned a friend telling her about Black Cherry Retreat but didn't give me any name so I'm not sure.'

'Are you as dumb as you look, Tom?'

What had he said now?

'When Fee told me her full name I knew who she was right away.'

Tom had noticed she wrote Freebird on her registration form but hadn't questioned it. 'She's got a weird name, so what?'

Mary-Jo rolled her eyes. 'I guess I picked up on it because of this semester's photography course I'm taking but you're always glued to the news so didn't you recognise it?'

'Get on with it, kid. I don't have a goddamn clue what you're on about.'

She wagged her finger in his face and her eyes danced with mischief. 'Language. If my mama hears you she'll bat you from one end of the cafe to the other. Don't you remember the story about six months ago of a French photojournalist being blown up in Kabul?'

'Maybe.'

'The photos ended up on the front of every newspaper in the world. And the woman who took them as it happened right in front of her?' Mary-Jo persisted. 'That was none other than Freebird Winter, winner of three Pulitzer Prizes and numerous other prestigious awards for her work in hotspots around the world. She's a legend in the photographic community.'

Tom cursed, well under his breath this time. 'Did you tell

Fee you'd recognised her name?' Mary-Jo shook her head. 'Good. Don't.'

'Why not? I bet if my media professor knew she was here he'd give anything to have her come talk to us.'

'I'm serious.' He grabbed Mary-Jo's elbow. 'Don't you dare say a word. If she wants to tell us that's one thing. Otherwise she's a guest and we respect her privacy.'

She jerked out of his grasp, rubbing at her arm. 'All right, don't be a bully. I can keep a secret if I have to.'

'Good. I ...'

Mary-Jo flashed him a warning smile and he shut up as Fee came over to stand next to them. 'Next time you come to town we'll get ice cream at Suzy-Beth's.'

'What is it with your family trying to stuff ice cream into me?' Fee joked. He struggled not to overreact as her cool blue eyes, the mesmerising colour of the sky on a cold December day, rested on him. 'Would you mind if we went back to the Retreat?'

'No problem,' he said. 'I'll say goodbye to everyone and we'll be off.'

Five minutes and they were back in his truck heading out of town complete with a chicken and rice casserole and apple pie his aunt foisted on him on the way out of the door.

'You're a lucky man.'

Fee's quiet, steady words touched him. At a wild guess he'd say she either didn't have family or wasn't close to them; neither of which he could imagine in his worst nightmares and he'd had plenty of those. 'Yeah, I know.'

They made the rest of the drive in silence and as he turned off the main road Tom's brain raced. Should he drop Fee off at her cabin or invite her in for coffee? When the resort came into sight he was no nearer to making a decision.

Chapter Five

Fee guessed the direction of Tom's thoughts and made the choice for him. 'I'm ready for a quiet evening. I'll get out at your cabin and walk on up.'

'You sure? I've all this food and only me to eat it.'

'Absolutely.' Fee needed to put a polite stop to whatever "this" was right now. She told herself she didn't need a friend and wasn't looking for another lover. 'I'll see you around.'

He parked but made no move to get out.

'Thanks very much for the ice cream and for showing me around town. It's kind of you to be so welcoming to your guests.'

Tom's eyes darkened and he turned away. Quickly opening his door he leapt out, striding around the truck to open hers before she could beat him to it. 'You're welcome.' He stepped back to let her out. 'Always happy to make guests feel at home. I'd better get on with the paperwork. It doesn't do itself.' Tom gave her a taut smile. He slammed her door and strode away, taking the couple of steps in one leap and disappearing inside his cabin without another word.

Fine. Be pissed off. I don't care. So much for his mantra of leaving guests alone. She should have said no to ice cream and the stupid Pine Ridge expedition in the first place. Fee slung her worn leather tote bag over her shoulder and headed along the path. Lights shone in the cabin next to hers so she hurried on by, anxious to reach the safety of her own porch. She didn't need any more well-meaning friendly people today.

Fee's hands shook and she struggled with the key before managing to unlock her door. Inside she rested her back against the smooth wood before taking several slow, deep breaths to steady herself back down. Before she left London her therapist helped her put together a timetable to structure her time here. So far she'd ignored it but now she snatched up the copy she'd abandoned on the coffee table earlier. Fee studied the instructions with a sinking heart.

Five o'clock. Half an hour of yoga practice followed by meditation.

Six o'clock. Prepare a light healthy supper.

Seven o'clock. Read from the approved list of books.

Eight o'clock. Take a warm bath with essential oils.

Nine o'clock. Go to bed and sleep without medication.

At this moment Fee wished herself anywhere on the face of the planet except stuck in this cabin with no one but herself for company.

Tom sat at his desk, kicked off his boots and slipped on his reading glasses before sorting through the mail. He put the bills to one side, tossed the junk mail in the recycling box and scanned over the one envelope left. An invitation to a police function in Knoxville. *Wonderful.* He wished they'd quit sending them. He'd no intention of sitting around with a bunch of fellow cops rehashing the old days because there wasn't much in the way of good memories where he was concerned. Sandy asked recently if he missed the job and Tom's cynical laughter made his brother wince.

Surely you're not happy babysitting a few dumb tourists?

When he assured Sandy he was perfectly content he'd got a disbelieving look in return. While he'd kept busy renovating the cabins his family stayed off his back but now the work was pretty much done they were getting on his nerves. Sure it was a quiet life but he found he didn't mind. There was time to fish, hike, dabble in a little guitar playing on long winter evenings and study up on the history about what had brought the Chambers family to the local area. If he wondered whether he'd soon be settled in the role of slightly eccentric uncle, Tom didn't let it consume him.

Forcing himself to get back to work he ploughed on and

in an hour had his desk clear. Tom glanced out at the fading light and realised he'd missed the chance to walk off his excess energy. He pushed back his chair and headed into the kitchen to reach for the bottle of Jack Daniels, then grabbed a glass and wandered back out onto the porch.

The warm, muted light drifting out from the cabin was soothing and Tom dropped down into his favourite rocking chair. The early evening air had morphed into the crisp October temperatures he relished. Tom poured a measured amount of whisky into the glass and sipped the deep golden liquid, allowing it to trickle down his throat so he could savour the long, slow burn. He'd never been much of a drinker apart from in the months after Gina's death. Falling apart hadn't suited him and after a hefty mental kick in the backside from his father he'd put a stop to his weakness as easily as if he'd never touched a drop. After a while he was able to allow himself the occasional glass but with self-imposed restrictions he never broke.

Mary-Jo's revelation rolled around his brain and he was glad there was no internet coverage up here or he'd be tempted to poke around and find out things it'd be better not to know. The small amount his cousin revealed was enough to make it clear why Fee was one messed-up lady. When he couldn't face staying around Pine Ridge another day after Gina died he'd spent two years doing security work in Iraq. Plenty long enough to be haunted at night and give him a hint of what Fee must've seen and been a part of. Afterwards it'd taken all his time to get somewhat back on even ground and maybe that's what she was striving for by coming to Black Cherry. Tom polished off the rest of his whisky and picked up the bottle, eyeing the level carefully before setting it back down.

A loud buzzing noise from indoors startled him and he realised it was the radio. Tom hurried in to hear his father's booming voice.

'I've got some news, son. Two prisoners escaped the Knox

County Jail this afternoon. One is the Kemp boy and the other was his cellmate. There's been a possible sighting of them in Chattanooga already and my guess is they're high-tailing it south. It's unlikely they'll head back our way but keep your eyes out and alert your guests just in case.'

'Will do, Pop. I'd recognise Pete but what've you got on the other one?'

'The name's Randy Watling. Age thirty-five. Heavy-set. Caucasian. Light brown hair. Blue eyes. Got a rattlesnake tattoo on his right arm and a jagged scar on his left cheek. He's dangerous and up for three murders.'

'Three murders? What the hell was he doing there in the county jail with all the two-bit criminals?'

'He was being moved to Riverbend maximum security tomorrow. I guess he persuaded Kemp to escape with him for his local knowledge. You know Pete will do anything anyone tells him. The boy's dumb as a bag of rocks.'

They both remembered the weak-willed youngster who'd caused more trouble in Pine Ridge than anyone in recent memory but always swore nothing was his fault.

'Thanks for the heads up. I'll have a wander around right now. I've only got two cabins occupied so I'll make sure the guests are warned.'

They said goodnight and Tom returned to clear up the porch before pulling his boots back on and grabbing a powerful flashlight from his desk.

First he went to the cabin next door and dragged Abel Burton away from sitting by the fire with his wife. The older couple were celebrating their golden wedding anniversary this week and Tom hated to spoil their peaceful evening.

'Don't worry, son. We'll lock up real good and won't do anything stupid.'

Tom smiled at the man's attempt to reassure *him* and took his leave. Now he had to tackle Miss Winter who'd probably slam the door in his face and send him away for pestering her again. *Tough.* He'd protect her whether she liked it or not. Outside her cabin he set his face in his best ex-cop "do not mess with me" expression before rapping on the door.

'Who is it?'

He heard the annoyance in her voice. 'Tom.'

The lock clicked back and the door opened a few inches. He could just about make out her pale features.

'Sorry to disturb you but I've had a police report all my guests need to know about.' Hopefully that made it clear he was only doing his job not singling her out.

'You'd better come in.'

'I can tell you from here. No problem.'

She sighed. 'I do have *some* manners plus it's cold. Get inside and don't be daft.'

Tom wasn't sure he'd ever been called daft before. He wouldn't call it cold but Fee didn't have a spare ounce of flesh on her so probably felt the chill in the air. He stepped in over the threshold as she opened back the door. *Hell.*

'Yes, I was in bed.'

Tom struggled not to stare at the soft pink pyjamas draping her slim frame and her slender bare feet. A soft lemon scent rose from her skin to fill the air between them. In one instant his traitorous body betrayed him and he prayed she wouldn't notice. He launched into a straightforward repetition of his father's story.

'I'm pretty sure they won't come here but I'll be on the alert. Check your locks and let me know if you see anything suspicious.'

'Of course.'

He caught a slight tremble in her voice and wished he could reassure her without stepping over the line she'd drawn between them. 'I've never lost a guest yet,' he joked.

'Let's hope the government never sends you on a diplomatic mission. You'd be a miserable failure.'

'I ...' Trying to stumble out an apology, Tom noticed the

edges of her mouth twitch into a half-smile and realised she was teasing him. 'You found me out.' He grinned.

'Oh, I found you out alright.'

Her cool, knowing words sent a shiver through his overheated blood.

'It's time I went back to bed. After I've locked the doors and windows of course,' Fee murmured.

'Good idea.' He'd better make his escape before he made even more of a fool of himself. 'I'll stop by in the morning when I check on the other guests.'

'I'm sure you will. You strike me as a man who'd do a thorough job.'

Tom mentally slapped himself at the unsuitable reply running through his head. 'I try.'

'Good night, Tom.'

The way she said his name in that crisp English way tortured him even more. He mumbled good night and hurried back out as fast as he could while sensing her eyes on him all the way. Tom strode off into the night, almost wishing a murderous escaped prisoner would finish him off and be done with it.

Chapter Six

Fee stared at the luminous red numbers on her alarm clock and sighed. Three a.m. The witching hour for insomniacs. Sleep wouldn't happen again this side of daylight.

Oh, I found you out alright.

Had she really flirted with Tom? In her defence she'd only responded to his blatant interest. When Doctor Michael mentioned a quiet place in Tennessee where a friend of his stayed the previous year she'd thought it sounded ideal but it was threatening to turn into a huge mistake. Fee shouldn't have allowed the recent bizarre phone call from her mother, after five years of silence, to influence her decision but she had.

I wanted to talk to you about your father.

A long time ago Fee had made it clear she wasn't interested when she saw a copy of her birth certificate with "Unknown" where her father's name should be.

Which man are we talking about today?

Allain Dupre the Third of course.

Her mother hadn't appreciated her sarcastic question about whether Dupre was the Southern gentleman from New Orleans who had wanted to turn Maddy into his own Scarlett O'Hara.

I got an email from Allain last week. He said that his wife died recently and he'd started thinking about me again. Allain looked me up online and found out about you. When he saw your birth date naturally he put two and two together.

To stop the conversation she'd agreed to let her mother send Dupre's contact details on the condition that it was totally up to Fee whether or not she decided to get in touch with him. Being on the same side of the Atlantic Ocean made the option more ... feasible if she chose to let this thing play out.

Swinging her legs out over the side of the bed Fee decided to get a drink. Last year in Afghanistan she'd relied on an unwise mixture of Percocet and whisky to get through the nights meaning both were off limits. Regular tap water would have to do. Fee padded across the room, surprised at how warm the smooth, uneven boards were under her feet and loving the idea they'd been walked on by generations of Tom's family. In the kitchen she ran the cold tap for a minute and filled a glass before wandering back into the living room. She eased one side of the red gingham curtains away from the window and stared out into the inky darkness.

A shiver ran through her blood. For all she knew two desperate men could be watching. She dragged the curtains closed and gripped onto the fabric for a few seconds before forcing herself to let go. Fee had no intention of being a victim. She returned to the bedroom and headed straight for the oak chest where she'd stored her clothes. Fee groped around in the top drawer beneath her neatly folded underwear until she found the lethal ivory handled knife she'd bought at the Kabul market.

Fee laid the knife on the nightstand and climbed back into her cold bed. She pulled the covers around her neck and prepared to wish the hours away.

A loud banging noise roused Fee and she struggled to open her eyes. She groped on the bedside table for her glasses and shoved them on before staring around the unfamiliar room. *Black Cherry Retreat. Okay*. Tom's warning flooded back and she tensed, reaching for her knife. *Escaped prisoners aren't going to knock on the door, stupid.*

She hopped out of bed and kept the knife sheathed and out of sight as she crept down the narrow hallway towards the front door.

'Fee, are you alright?'

Tom's deep, warm drawl registered and she flung open the door. 'Did you have to scare me half out of my skin again? Wasn't waking me up once enough?'

'Sorry,' he mumbled. 'I was just checkin' on everyone, that's all. Thought you'd be up by now.'

A blast of cold air hit her bare legs and Fee remembered she'd removed her pyjama trousers during the night when she got too hot. The shirt barely skimmed the top of her thighs and when she tugged at the pink flannel in a futile effort to make it longer the knife clattered to the floor.

'What on earth are you doing with that?'

'Uh, protecting myself?'

'That's what I'm here for,' he declared. Fee couldn't decide whether to laugh or cry. She'd love a thousand pounds for every time she'd been spun *that* line.

'What time is it anyway?' she asked.

'Ten.'

'In the morning?'

A faint smile tugged at his wide, well-shaped mouth. 'Yeah. The sun's out so I'm going with daytime on this one.'

The last time she slept this long was in the hospital when she collapsed after Pierre's death. That'd been an awful, drug-induced heaviness, but today she felt wonderful. 'Goodness, that's amazing.'

'Good Tennessee air does that for a person.'

Fee laughed at Tom's smug certainty and he joined in, the rich warm sound running like melted chocolate over her skin.

'I'll be on my way. Got things to do.' Tom dragged his admiring gaze away from her legs and hurried away before she could reply.

Thank goodness one of them had common sense. Fee wished it could be her for a change.

Tom didn't get it. Gina had been the town beauty, their high school homecoming queen and elected Miss Pine Ridge three years in a row to lead the Fourth of July parade. Petite enough to nestle under his shoulder, with enticing glossy brunette hair tumbling to her waist and the sort of curves to bring a man to his knees; he'd been the envy of all his friends. Since losing Gina he'd had plenty of offers from women and accepted the odd one or two but none had any real impact on him deep down. So why now, and why Fee? Her tall, angular body didn't fit his usual preference but still his fingers itched to explore every inch of the smooth, pale skin she'd unwittingly exposed a few minutes ago. Fee's ice-blue eyes were a mystery and the few times she'd allowed herself to smile it'd sent shards of desire straight to his core. He'd better not get started on her lips – wide, unpainted and so expressive it killed him not to kiss her and see what reaction he got. *Probably a knee right where it hurt.*

He'd planned to put a fresh coat of paint on his bathroom today but that wouldn't be sufficient to work off the excess of testosterone flooding his system. Instead he'd chop firewood to restock the piles he kept outside each cabin to use in their fireplaces.

Tom headed out of the back door and into the yard where he kept large logs ready to cut. The fresh, cool air allowed him to slip into an easy rhythm, swinging the axe in the steady way he'd learnt from his father. The morning's warm sunshine soon made the flannel shirt stick to his skin so he unbuttoned it and tossed it aside to work in his white undershirt. After a while he took a break to wipe the sweat from his face with the abandoned shirt.

'Oh, sorry. I didn't mean to ...' Fee hovered near the fence and her glowing face resembled a tomato dropped in boiling water ready for canning. It wasn't a comparison he intended to broadcast. He set the axe down on the chopping block.

'No problem.'

'The light bulb on my porch isn't working, and, um ...'

He should have felt sorry for her but like most men was vain at heart and flustering an attractive woman boosted his pathetic ego. 'It's what I'm here for. I'll wash up and be right over.'

'Please don't let me interrupt. Later will be fine.'

Tom shook his head. 'Nope, it won't. Your job will only take me five minutes.'

'Thanks.' She half-smiled, turned and fled back down the road.

Briefly he considered putting his flannel shirt back on but remembered the interesting flash of heat in her cool eyes and abandoned the idea. Tom whistled as he headed indoors – something he hadn't done in a long time. After cleaning his hands he took a minute to run a comb through his damp hair. As soon as he found the right bulb he set off and hoped he could avoid doing or saying something stupid.

'It's your friendly electricity guru,' he called out.

'That was quick.' Fee appeared in the doorway and kept her gaze fixed on his face.

'I'll pop this one in and leave you in peace.'

She nodded but didn't say a word so he carried on, sensing her watch his every move.

'All fixed.' He finished screwing the bulb in. 'You want to turn it on and make sure it's working?'

'Oh, yes, thanks.' She flicked the switch a couple of times.

'I'd better get back to work.'

'If you're not too busy would you care to join me for lunch?' The words tumbled out and she nibbled at her lip as if she'd bite them back if she could.

'You sure? Don't feel obliged.' Tom preferred to be straightforward and guessed this particular woman would appreciate honesty.

'I don't. I made the offer freely.' She folded her arms in front of her chest. 'Take it or leave it. Makes no difference to me.'

Why'd you ask then? 'I'll take it. What's on offer anyway?'

The tempting smile he received would be flirtatious on any other woman but he wouldn't dare make the same assumption about Fee.

'I don't cook unless I'm forced to so it'll only be a sandwich.'

He pretended to consider the offer in an effort not to appear too keen.

'Oh, for goodness sake. I'm only talking about a simple lunch.'

'A sandwich would be great. We could eat out here on the porch.'

'Okay. Why don't you make yourself comfortable and I'll bring the food out in a few minutes.' Fee disappeared inside.

Tom sat down and kicked the chair off to a steady rocking motion with the toe of his boot. The day was certainly improving.

Chapter Seven

Fee's hands shook as she buttered the bread. Anyone would think she hadn't seen a fit man engaged in physical activity before – men have muscles, they sweat, they look hot – so what? She was nearly forty and hadn't exactly been in a convent for the last twenty years so why was she behaving like a fifteen-year-old girl with her first crush?

She had no clue what combination of lettuce, tomato, pickle, mustard, butter or mayonnaise Tom preferred and it hadn't occurred to her to ask.

She covered all bases and put a little of everything on the sandwich before adding a handful of crisps to the side of the plate. If she didn't make one for herself too he'd conclude she was even more peculiar. Unwilling to get into a discussion about the dietary restrictions she was supposed to follow with her stress-induced ulcer she used the same wholegrain bread but only added a scrape of low-fat margarine and lean turkey.

She rubbed at the low-grade headache pulsing in her forehead. This was all so damn complicated.

'Is everything alright?' Tom popped his head in around the door and she plastered on a smile.

'I'm sorry I've been so long,' she apologised. 'I'm not good at the whole kitchen thing but it's ready now.'

'You want me to take the plates out for you?'

'Thanks. Will lemonade be okay to drink?'

'Sure, it's my favourite. Can you manage?'

'Of course.' She bristled, hating how she always seemed incompetent around him.

Tom rested his hand on her arm. 'Fee, that's me bein' polite. Don't take everythin' to heart.'

His kindness broke through her thin veneer of control. She could deal with the violence of war, face up to seeing people with terrible injuries without flinching, stay calm as homes were reduced to rubble and objectively take pictures of it all. But let a starving child offer to share his meagre meal, or a woman insist on washing Fee's dusty feet in a shallow bowl of precious water and she crumbled. In the end it'd stopped her functioning and drove her to the excesses which had almost killed her.

'Are you okay?'

Fee bit back a sob, but a fat, hot tear rolled down her cheek and soon she was crying so hard she couldn't catch her breath.

'Steady. I've got you.' Tom wrapped his arms around her and pulled her up against his solid chest – the rhythm of his steady heartbeat pushing back the panic.

She stared up into his warm, compassionate eyes and he loosened his grasp and allowed his hands to drop away.

'You're not in a good place right now, honey. I've been there myself and got through it, but it leaves you different, I know.'

The sorrow lacing through his words broke through her self-absorption. It hadn't occurred to her that she wasn't the only screwed-up one here and finding out people's stories was what she did for a living. It wouldn't be long before Tom told her his, although revealing her own was quite another thing.

'How about we go back to where we were and eat lunch?' he suggested and Fee managed to nod, her throat too tight with emotion to speak. 'You get our drinks and I'll carry the food out.'

After he left she poured lemonade into two tall glasses and went to join him.

Tom rocked in the chair and waited.

'Here we go.'

He'd caught a drift of Fee's fresh, lemony scent before she spoke, but tried to glance up as if he hadn't realised she was there. 'Thanks.' Tom took the glass from her outstretched hand and gulped down half in one long swallow.

'I'm sorry for ... you know ... in there.'

'No problem. Sit down and eat. Forget it.'

'Forget it?' Her voice rose. 'Do you think I go around weeping over strange men every day?'

Tom set his glass down on the table. Why did women always pull everything apart? 'Fee. Don't do this to yourself. Please.' He chose his words with care. She wasn't aware that he knew anything about her past and it might be wiser if she didn't for the time being. 'You're human.' He tried for a smile. 'Don't blab this to the rest of the world but I've cried a few times since I was a little kid.' In fact more than a few since he lost Gina but he wasn't going there with the conversation.

'Thanks for trying to make me feel better.' Her tight smile was even more forced than his own. 'Let's eat our sandwiches and talk about the weather.'

'I can do that.'

He didn't say another word and picked up his sandwich to take a large bite. Tom almost choked on the strange combination of flavours but forced himself to swallow.

'I wasn't sure what to put in yours so I went with everything.' A tiny smile pulled at her mouth. 'Did I overdo it?'

He cautiously peeled back one corner. 'Can't say I've ever had butter, mayonnaise and mustard on a sandwich at the same time but it's interesting.' Bravely he kept eating and waded his way through the whole thing, all the time sensing her watching him. Tom drank the last of the lemonade. 'Thanks for lunch. I'd better get back to work because the logs won't cut themselves.' He noticed she'd barely touched her own sandwich. 'Weren't you hungry?'

Fee shrugged. 'Not really. I'll put it in the fridge and eat it later.'

'You gonna be okay?' He stood and rested his hand on her shoulder, the tension radiating through his fingers.

'Why wouldn't I be?'

'No clue.' Tom prepared to make a swift retreat. 'You know

where I am if you need anything.' He left, striding off back to his own cabin without a backward glance.

Fee clasped her hands over her face and sank back into the rocking chair.

If she didn't do something constructive she'd be tempted to raid the emergency supply of sleeping pills she'd tucked into her bag before getting on the plane. Fee gathered their plates and glasses before hurrying back indoors. Before she could change her mind she put the dishes by the sink and went back outside. A brisk walk around the lake might take her mind off Tom plus get her some much needed exercise. Hopefully it'd also give her an appetite to face eating lunch on her return.

Half way around she pushed her worries aside and started to enjoy herself. Fee slowed her pace and a tiny grey squirrel scurried in front of her toes. The dappled sun trickled in through the trees to brighten the fiery autumn leaves and she made a snap decision. To hell with Doctor Michael. Tomorrow she'd go into Pine Ridge and buy a camera. It didn't matter if it was the cheapest on the market – anything would do rather than missing capturing the photos she framed in her head everywhere she went.

When she made it back to Tom's cabin she hurried on by. Fee searched in her pocket for her keys but remembered she'd been too agitated when she left to think about locking up. *Idiot.*

'Good afternoon, my dear. Isn't it a beautiful day?'

She jerked around, coming face to face with a white-haired older man. He gave her a kindly smile and gestured towards her cabin.

'Lovely places, aren't they?' He held out his hand. 'Abel Burton. My wife, Emily, and I are in Sevier cabin next door.'

Fee managed to introduce herself and make polite conversation for a couple of minutes.

'I'd better be going or my better half will wonder where I've got to. If she sees me chatting up a pretty young woman she might get jealous.' His cheerful grin made it clear there was only one woman for him and a pang of envy shot through Fee.

She didn't have any clue how people did the loving-for-life thing. All she'd seen growing up was a constant rotation of men through her mother's life, most not staying long enough for Fee to remember their names. Maddy Winter's philosophy was that being tied to one man was unnatural.

'It was very nice to meet you.' She smiled and hurried away before her neighbour could decide to invite her for dinner or something equally sociable. From now on she'd keep to herself as she'd intended to in the first place.

Chapter Eight

Tom purposely left Fee's cabin until last. He'd made neat stacks of wood behind all the other cabins during the afternoon and there was only hers left to do. He was wary of going to the door again but if he sneaked into the backyard she might freak out and come after him with the knife. Tom tried to imagine how he'd explain to his father that he'd been stabbed by one of the guests. Hank would roar with laughter and call him every name under the sun.

A couple of minutes later he stood at Fee's door but before he could knock she flung it open.

'Are you psychic?'

What was the woman talking about now?

'I couldn't decide whether to tell you or not.' She frowned. 'I'm probably making something out of nothing.'

Tom removed his hat and scratched his head. 'Okay. Let's start again. *I'll* tell *you* why I'm here then *you* tell *me* what the heck you're jabbering on about.' As he explained about the wood delivery a shy smile illuminated her serious features.

'Oh, God, now you must be officially convinced I'm mad,' she groaned. 'Thanks for bringing the wood. The evenings are cooling off and I might be tempted to light a fire soon.'

'No problem. Now what were you talkin' about?' Tom asked but she only nibbled her lip. 'Is something wrong with the cabin?'

'No, not exactly.' She conceded. 'I went for a walk earlier and forgot to lock up.' Fee held up her hands. 'I know you told us to and I'm sorry.'

'Hey, I'm not going to throw you in jail. I only mentioned it for your own safety.'

Fee idly kicked the mat. 'I came back into the kitchen planning to finish my sandwich, but ... it wasn't there.'

He wouldn't dare to suggest she might've thrown it in the trash, or misplaced it. The normally even-tempered Gina was furious at him once when he asked if her missing car keys might still be in the ignition. The fact that's where they turned out to be didn't help.

'And yes, I'm *sure* I put it in the fridge. I'm *not* an idiot and I'm *not* hormonal.'

'I didn't ...'

'Yes, you did,' she retorted. 'I've worked with enough bloody men to know the signs. I'm pretty sure Tennessee squirrels aren't smart enough to open refrigerator doors either.'

'What's your theory?' he sighed.

'Somebody came in here while I was out and ate it?'

It took all Tom's waning self-control not to laugh. 'Right. Like who? One of my starving guests?'

'Don't mock me. Maybe your escaped prisoners?'

It suddenly clicked that she was scared stiff, but would die rather than admit it to him. 'Hey, I'm real sorry. Sometimes I'm a dumbass.'

'Only sometimes?' A hint of a smile pulled at her mouth and he didn't mind appearing to be a moron if it lightened her worry.

'Maybe.' Tom grinned. 'Did you notice anything else out of place?'

'I don't think so, but I haven't really ...' Fee's voice trailed away.

'Do you want me to take a look around?'

'Would you mind?'

Tom felt even worse. He'd no right to make her feel a nuisance.

'Of course not. Do you want to stay out here or walk through with me?'

'Um, come with you, I think,' she mumbled but didn't move out of the way.

'It might help if you let me inside,' Tom suggested and she

awkwardly stepped back out of the way. He walked in past her and quickly checked out the living room. The only unusual thing to strike him was the lack of any personal possessions lying around. His next stop was the bathroom which held none of the usual feminine clutter. Tom stepped back out and headed for the bedroom where everything was equally pristine. Fee's yoga mat, neatly rolled up in one corner, and a small stack of books on the dresser were the only signs of occupation. At a guess he'd say Fee had spent so long living in temporary, confined spaces she didn't know what to do with a whole house to herself. Without a word he headed back towards the kitchen and she followed along behind.

'Everything looks good to me.'

She nodded. 'I thought it would. Maybe I really am going a little crazy.'

Tom stopped in front of her and settled his hands on her shoulders. 'You're not crazy. I believe you when you said the sandwich was there and now it's not. I don't have an explanation, but that doesn't mean you're loopy.'

'If you say so.' The smile didn't reach her worried eyes.

'When I questioned witnesses I made a point of believing them unless proved otherwise. It tended to work better than assuming they were mistaken or lying.'

'Witnesses?'

Shit. You should've kept your mouth shut. 'Yeah, I was a cop for a while,' Tom admitted.

'Doing this job must be quite a change. I wouldn't think it was as challenging?'

Getting through each day is challenge enough for me sometimes.

'Sorry. That's none of my business. Anyway thanks for checking and I'll be extra careful about locking the cabin from now on. I'll let you get on with your wood delivery.'

He'd politely been given his marching orders. 'No problem, and don't hesitate to call if you're concerned about anything else.'

Fee nodded and quietly closed the door in his face.

Get on with your work, and stay well away from tempting Englishwomen with broken souls. You don't do fixing jobs on people any more.

Fee covered her face with her hands and allowed the wave of embarrassment to roll through her.

If Tom hadn't turned up with the wood she'd have kept her mouth shut about the disappearing sandwich. She made a pledge not to speak to Tom Chambers again for at least twenty-four hours. That should cure her ridiculous curiosity about the good-looking loner with more hidden levels than a complicated video game. A police officer? His revelation made complete sense considering his controlled, ultra-aware manner. In the same way as most military veterans the job never completely left them. She'd love to discover what made Tom quit his job and retreat here in the woods. Odds were that there was more to it than upholding the Chambers' family legacy.

You're not interested, remember?

Fee dug around in her pocket and pulled out Doctor Michael's timetable. *Wonderful.* It was nearly mind-numbing yoga time again to be followed by a healthy supper and more "improving" reading. The only thing this would achieve was boring her to death which she supposed would be some sort of result.

In her head she heard Pierre's mocking laughter. They'd shared the same world-weary, ironic sense of humour and an awful lot more over the years. If he were here now he'd toss her yoga mat out of the window and pull out a bottle of whisky. But their dangerous lifestyle led her to this lonely place, struggling to find out who and what she wanted to be for the rest of her life. Fee had no nonsensical fantasies about marriage and children. If the sights she'd seen in her travels around the world hadn't already cured her of such thoughts

Pierre's betrayal had slammed the door and thrown away the key.

She came close to believing him when he claimed to love her but after his sudden death the lie was tossed back in her face. Fee somehow managed to shake Helene Marchande's hand at the elaborate Parisian funeral and utter polite commiserations to the widow she hadn't known existed. When Helene showed off pictures of one-year-old Ethan, the spitting image of Pierre, she'd fainted on the spot and her collapse was put down to sorrow over the death of the man she'd worked with for many years. Fee was never sure if Helene knew about their affair but by that point it'd hardly mattered.

Tonight she couldn't face yoga and healthy food could take a running jump but that didn't mean she was stupid enough to eat the pizza she craved. She would risk her favourite childhood supper of cheese on toast, made with low-fat cheese and wholegrain bread and compared to the bad old days her stomach should feel well-treated.

Fee wondered why she didn't feel better about sending Tom away. Doing the right thing often sucked.

'Uncle T, up, now.' Lulu giggled and tugged at Tom's leg. He swung her through the air to sit on his shoulders, being careful to crouch so her head didn't bump the ceiling.

'That child has you wrapped around her little finger,' Aunt Ina scoffed as she bustled out from the kitchen carrying several plates of food.

'Hey, it's what beautiful girls do.' Tom laughed.

She stopped in her tracks and gave him a searching stare. 'What about if they're over the age of three?'

Tom kissed the top of his aunt's head. 'It works when they're any age far as I'm concerned,' he joked, not stupid enough to fall for her obvious probing.

He'd done his usual chores around the cabins this morning and had a quick word with Abel Burton but managed to avoid his nemesis. There was a new family arriving from Florida later so he'd checked everything was clean and ready for them. When he returned to Black Cherry he'd take back some grocery essentials to leave in the new guests' cabin – all part of the service he provided. Tom had made sure to finish in time for lunch at the cafe to get his fill of Friday's special fried catfish.

'Mama! Down, Uncle T, down.'

Lulu's piercing yell deafened Tom and he lowered the little girl carefully to the floor. He watched with unabashed envy as she raced to the door and flung herself at a smiling Mary-Jo. Tom's throat tightened. No child would ever run to him that way.

If you'd been the one to die would you have wanted Gina to be alone the rest of her life, and abandon her dream of becoming a mother? His grandmother's sharp comment the last time he visited slammed back into him. He'd dutifully replied the way she expected but hadn't fooled her.

'You alright, son?'

His father's gruff voice startled Tom and he jerked around to face the man who'd always seen right through all his kids.

'Yeah, fine. Why wouldn't I be?'

Hank Chambers' thick, dark grey eyebrows rose up to the ceiling and he snorted. 'Maybe because you look as sorry as when I walloped you for eating half the cake your mama made for the church sale.'

Tom hadn't forgotten because it'd been the last time he cried until Gina died. 'Cut it out, Pop. I'm good. Any news of Kemp and Watling?'

'Nope, the trail's gone cold. We're keeping an eye on Kemp's family home but the men could be anywhere by now. Won't hurt to tell your people to keep watching out though.'

He kept the story of Fee's missing sandwich to himself because his father would laugh that one out of the hills. They chatted about this and that and caught up on all the family news. Rayna was getting impatient for the arrival of her first baby and both his brothers were expecting new additions in the spring.

'I guess there'll be no shortage of Chambers around Pine Ridge for a few more generations,' Tom joked.

'No thanks to you,' Hank teased. 'You ever goin' to pull your head out your ass, boy? Your mama frets over you somethin' awful.'

'Broadcast my private business in front of everyone, why don't you?'

Hank rolled his eyes. 'Everyone in here knows us. Most of them are wondering why I don't give you a swift kick up the—'

'That's enough,' Tom snarled.

'But we—'

'I know you love me.' He glowered. 'I get it. Now leave me alone goddammit,' he shouted and stormed off towards the door. He flung it open and pushed past a woman trying to enter, briefly registering Fee's shocked face, but not stopping. They could all go to hell.

Chapter Nine

'Are you alright, ma'am?'

A uniformed policeman grabbed hold of Fee's elbow to steady her. He didn't need to introduce himself because this was Tom Chambers in another twenty years or so.

'I'm fine, thank you.'

'I apologise on behalf of my son. Don't know what gets into the boy sometimes.'

'Please don't worry. I'm sure he had his reasons.' She'd been curious to find out more about Tom and now was being offered the opportunity on a plate. Fee stuck out her hand and turned on the warm, open smile she'd used so many times to persuade an unwilling subject to be photographed. 'I'm Fee Winter and I'm staying at Black Cherry Retreat for a few weeks. It's absolutely beautiful there.'

'Thought you were a stranger 'round these parts, ma'am. Sheriff Hank Chambers at your service.' He stuck out his hand and shook hers so hard Fee was afraid it might drop off. The sheriff retained the strength and vigour of a much younger man, almost convincing her living a healthy, contented life might have its benefits. 'How about joinin' me for a spot of lunch?'

Yesterday's added stress had done a number on her ulcer last night meaning she needed to be extra careful today. 'Thanks, but I only came in for a cold drink. I'm happy to sit with you though.'

He grinned, and his eyes warmed to the identical shade of good quality hot chocolate as his son's. 'Deal.'

Half an hour later, Fee had to concede she'd been grilled by an expert. The man's charming smile, slow deep drawl and easy manner disguised a sharp mind. Hank Chambers had found out more about her in thirty minutes than Tom had in days. She'd told him all sorts of things from where she grew up, to her present job and a ton of stuff in between. While they spoke Hank managed to shovel down an enormous amount of food, spoke to everyone going in and out of the cafe and still made her feel she'd been completely focused on.

'It's the ice cream lady.' A high-pitched squeal rang out and next thing Fee was smashed back in her seat as Lulu flung herself at her, arms and legs flying in every direction.

'I see you've met the family star,' Hank joked, his indulgence matching Tom's where the tiny girl was concerned.

Lulu wriggled around in Fee's lap and pouted. 'Uncle T didn't stay to play, it's not fair.'

'I expect he had work to do.'

'Uncle T said a *really* bad word and my mom told me he'd gone away to put soap in his mouth. Soap's nasty. Why'd he want to eat soap?'

Fee caught Hank's eye and struggled not to laugh. She'd leave explaining Tom's behaviour to his father.

'Come here, Lulubelle.' Hank held out his arms and she instantly switched allegiance, hopping over onto his lap instead. 'You know you get mad at your mama when she tells you off?' The child nodded and shoved her thumb in her mouth. 'And you sometimes sass her, don't you?'

'Maybe.'

The slow, dragged out admission made Fee smile.

'Well, pumpkin. I told Uncle T off and he didn't like it so he sassed me.'

'Did he make you cry?' Lulu asked, her big eyes wide. 'I make Mama cry sometimes.'

Hank swallowed hard and forced out a smile. 'No, Lulu, but I sure was mad at him.' A sad rasp tightened his voice and Fee wished Tom could hear his father's pain. 'But we'll be okay again, just like you and your mama. I promise.'

'I always give Mama a big kiss and then she loves me again.'

'Oh, honey, she always loves you.' Hank ruffled Lulu's bright red curls.

'I know that.'

Lulu's certainty hit Fee in the gut. She'd never experienced the same level of assurance with her own mother, always convinced she came way down Maddy's priority list.

'I ought to be going.' Fee needed to get out of there and do some thinking. 'Thanks for the lemonade.'

Hank shifted the little girl into his arms and stood up with her. 'Come in anytime, ma'am.'

'Bye, nice ice cream lady.' Lulu leaned down and gave Fee a sloppy kiss on her cheek, leaving behind a sticky trail.

Back outside Fee sat in her rental car for a moment and watched the scene around her. She picked up the brown paper bag on the passenger seat and peeked inside, unable to keep from smiling. The cheap digital camera was something she'd give a child to learn on but maybe that was what she needed. To look at things though the eyes of a novice photographer might reignite the simple love of creating a picture that she'd discovered with her first camera. Will Sawyer gave her an inexpensive one on her tenth birthday after she showed an interest when he was taking photographs. He'd taken her on many expeditions around the Cornish coast, giving her encouraging hints and teaching her the basics of composition.

Her mind's eye captured Tom, dark-eyed and furious as he'd stormed past her earlier. The perfect shot would have horrified him because there'd been nothing mild-mannered about him as he almost shoved her to the ground in his haste. Tom must have been pushed past his limit and snapped. It was plain her surface impression of the Chambers as one big, happy family wasn't completely accurate but in her experience few things were. Pulitzer Prizes weren't awarded for sweet, cuddly stories but to those with the courage to search for the dark side. Everything and everyone had one.

An ex-boyfriend criticised her for not personally caring about anything. *You see everything through a damn lens. It filters all you do. You'll never truly love another person because you're too busy framing the next perfect shot.*

Pierre, and her fellow photographers understood if you didn't maintain a slight distance it consumed you and spat you back out. But if you weren't lucky in the end it sucked you dry. After everything that'd happened with Pierre she had nothing left to give which was what had brought her here. Fee shoved the camera back into the bag with a heavy sigh. She'd go back to Black Cherry Retreat and hope it worked the magic she needed. Right now she had nothing to offer Tom or anyone else.

Tom watched the level decrease in the whisky bottle without caring. Fee's shocked expression wouldn't leave him and neither would the hurt he'd put in his father's eyes. He pushed the toe of his boot into the floor to set the chair rocking and closed his eyes as he drank.

'Mr Chambers?'

'Who's askin'?' He opened one eye. A prissy young man with tortoiseshell glasses and a superior expression stared at him from the bottom step. Tom noticed a couple of kids and a sour-faced blonde woman peering out of the gleaming red Volvo parked on the road.

'Quentin Waters. We've got a cabin booked.'

Shit. He'd forgotten all about the new guests and left their groceries behind in the cafe. Luckily his own pantry was well stocked so he'd be okay. 'Sure thing. Come on inside and we'll get the paperwork out of the way.' He dragged himself up to standing.

'Have you been drinking?'

'Against the law in Florida, is it?' he challenged.

'Well no, but—'

'Fine, don't worry about it none then.' Tom strode away, flinging open the door and taking it for granted the man would follow. Dropping down into his desk chair he fumbled with the computer for a moment and brought up the right screen. While he took the man's credit card and printed out a receipt he ran through the usual spiel about the resort. 'Right, we're done.'

'Aren't you're going to show us to our cabin?'

Tom retained enough brain cells to realise he was being an ass. Running this place gave him a huge measure of freedom but everything had its down side and thankfully annoying guests were a rarity. 'Of course. Come back out and I'll direct you where to drive then walk up to meet you.'

Tom got through the next half hour by the skin of his teeth. He'd never known a guest ask so many questions. Where are the spare towels? Maybe in the closet marked towels and bed linens. What kind of bug spray do the children need? Perhaps one that stopped them screaming. When he dared to give the children a sharp look their mother promptly informed him they believed in encouraging freedom of expression. Hank would say they needed a good swat on the backside and to be taught some manners. After his own bad behaviour today he was damn lucky not to have got the same thing himself – nearly forty-one or not.

'I'll leave you to settle in. You know where I am if there's anything else you need.' He tipped his hat and made a quick escape. This could be a long week. Tom had a sinking feeling Quentin Waters would be bugging him every five minutes.

On his porch he sat back down and reached for the glass again but the sour smell of the whisky turned his stomach. Tom stared into the dusk and wished the long, lousy day was over. Off in the woods an owl started its night-time call and a tingle ran down his spine as a vague shape moved down the path towards him.

'Is it safe to come closer or are you going to knock me over again?' Fee's lilting voice took him by surprise.

'I never knocked you over,' he protested.

'You came bloody close. I'd have been on the ground if your sweet father hadn't rescued me.' Without waiting for an invitation she strolled up the steps and sat down next to him.

'I thought I'd come and see if you'd rejoined the human race or if you were still off in your angry place?'

He glared, but she only gave him a compassionate smile. Whatever macho trick a man needed to silence women with a single look he'd well and truly missed out on.

'Whisky's always a bad idea.' She pointed to the half-empty bottle.

'Says who?'

'Me. Been there. Done that. '

Tom wasn't in the mood to swap sob stories with a pretty woman he'd much rather kiss. 'You'd better go, honey,' he grouched.

'Why?'

'I've had a shitty day. Don't want to talk about it either.'

'I wasn't offering to listen. You're sorry enough for yourself without me joining in the pity party.' She folded her long legs underneath her and rocked alongside him.

'Why *did* you come?' He wished she'd leave before he made even more of a fool of himself for one day.

'Not sure really,' Fee said with a shrug. 'Tired of my own company?'

He scoffed. 'And you thought mine would be better?'

'There's not much choice around here.'

'You could spend time with the Burtons and learn the secrets of a long happy marriage or go visit your new neighbours and they'll put you off the idea of marriage and kids for good. Take your pick.'

Fee's eyes gleamed with curiosity. 'Which camp do you fall in?'

He guessed she was asking something important and the real question was whether or not to give her an honest answer.

Chapter Ten

The faint light trickling out from his cabin highlighted the planes and shadows of Tom's face making Fee yearn to fetch her camera. He wouldn't share anything if she was stupid enough to put a lens between them.

'Oh, I'm a believer, honey. I've seen too many great examples not to be. I shouldn't criticise the new guests either just because I find them annoying.' He rubbed at his stubbly jaw line. 'I also know it's possible because I came close to having it once.' A strained rasp roughened the edges of his voice. 'For two short years.' Tom slumped in the chair, staring down at the floor.

'What happened?'

Tom wearily straightened his shoulders and she couldn't avoid meeting his sad eyes. 'She died. Gina died because of me.' He exhaled a long, deep sigh. 'And my family think I should forget and move on.'

She guessed his loving, close-knit family hated to see him lonely and blaming himself for his wife's death. 'Is that what they say?'

He shrugged. 'Not exactly.'

'Could there be a nugget of truth in their advice?'

A palpable silence filled the air between them and he shifted in the chair.

'Maybe?' she probed.

Tom sprung out of the chair and planted himself right in front of her. Fee's heart thumped but she'd perfected the art of disguising her fear a long time ago. Staring down one angry man was nothing.

'Yeah. There probably is. Are you satisfied now?' he growled.

'You brought up the subject.'

'I bet you're good at your job. You don't take no for an answer do you?' It didn't come across as a compliment.

What would happen if she shared her secrets with him? The idea disappeared before it could take root. Tom rested his trembling hand against the side of her cheek and Fee unconsciously leaned into his touch.

'Go now, while I can still send you away,' he pleaded.

'Is that what you want?'

His rough burst of laughter tore through her. 'Course I don't, but it's what's goin' to happen, sweetheart. I haven't lost all my common sense despite my behaviour earlier.' Tom jerked away and shoved his hands deep in his jeans pockets.

Fee unravelled her legs and slid up to standing. She rested her head against Tom's broad chest and his deep, heaving breaths rumbled through her. He didn't move away so she tipped her head slightly and their mouths almost touched. His searing gaze bored into her and her skin tingled.

'I daren't kiss you,' he sighed.

'I know, but that doesn't have to stop me.'

'It should.'

She'd always been a rule breaker and today was no exception. Heat. Whisky. Clean pine soap. The beguiling scent of clothes dried in the fresh air. Her senses exploded as she pressed her lips into his and slid her hands around his thick, solid neck to pull him closer. Fee flicked her tongue around the edges of his mouth, nipping and teasing.

'Oh, God, Fee.'

'Excuse me, Mr Chambers. I hope I'm not interrupting anything ... important?'

They sprang apart and Fee would've toppled over if Tom hadn't grasped her hands.

'Thank goodness I didn't send my children over to witness this disgraceful display.'

Fee stifled a laugh and Tom's mouth similarly twitched at the edges.

'I don't know what sort of establishment you're running here. When we arrived you were drinking and now you're … you know, out in public. Have you no consideration for your guests?'

'I certainly do, and I didn't mean to offend you but having a glass of whisky and kissing a woman aren't flogging offences in Tennessee.'

'Hmm.' The man grunted in obvious disapproval. 'I came over to ask what you're going to do about our cell phones.'

Tom frowned. 'Your cell phones?'

'They're not working.'

Fee bit her tongue as Tom patiently explained the situation regarding the phones and internet coverage and the fact he made this clear in the resort's brochures. The man complained a while longer but left when it was clear there was nothing Tom could do.

'Fee, I …'

'He saved us,' she quickly interrupted. 'Maybe we should thank him.' *Liar.*

'Tomorrow?'

'Maybe.' Fee couldn't manage to smile and hurried away down the steps. Tom didn't try to stop her and she knew she should be grateful.

Tom was surprised his mother waited so long. She must be getting more restrained in her old age although if he dared use her name and those last two words in the same sentence she'd put him on a spit and turn him 'til he was crispy around the edges.

Standing on his doorstep at barely eight o'clock in the morning she held out a cardboard box and warm, cinnamon-scented aromas wafted in his direction. His mother's kind smile didn't fool him for a second. Sarah Chambers was a stellar detective and the fact she'd never been a police officer was irrelevant because no one bested her when it came to in-depth investigations. No doubt she'd gathered evidence from his father and anyone else who'd witnessed his outburst in the cafe. Probably even Lulu got the third degree after being bribed with ice cream.

'Mama, you're a sight for sore eyes. I swear you get prettier every time I see you.' Tom bent to kiss her cheek.

'You can stop your flannel right now. I got up at six this morning to make these cinnamon rolls so let's eat. You'd better have a pot of coffee ready. After we've eaten you'll *listen* to me for a change.'

He opened the door wider and his mother pushed in past, making a beeline for the kitchen. Tom trailed in after her and rubbed at his temple as the nagging hangover he'd woken up with intensified.

'Serves you right. You and drink don't do well. I thought you'd at least learnt *that* lesson.'

'I ...'

'Don't lie. Your eyes are dull and your jaw-line's puffy. Can't get away with it at forty like you could at seventeen. I haven't forgotten when your delinquent brothers helped you celebrate your birthday by sneaking Daddy's whisky bottle out of the cupboard and replacing the contents with cold tea afterwards.'

He didn't waste time arguing and slumped in the chair while his mother bustled around the kitchen. For a good ten minutes she tidied up, complaining under her breath at the dirty dishes strewn all over the place. Once the dishwasher was loaded and the countertops wiped down to her satisfaction she found clean plates and forks and opened up the box she'd brought with her. His mother dumped a massive warm, fragrant roll on each plate and passed one to him before pouring two large mugs of coffee.

'Eat,' she ordered. 'We're not spoiling my rolls by talking about your bad behaviour.'

Ouch. Knowing how to turn the guilt screw on their kids must be a specialty of mothers everywhere. Food was the last thing his queasy stomach needed but he'd shove the roll down if it killed him. If he showed anything less than rampant enthusiasm it'd be another black mark against him and he'd already racked up enough to win an Olympic gold medal.

'You haven't lost your knack, Mama.' Thankfully he didn't need to lie because as he swallowed the first bite his appetite started to creep back. Even Aunt Ina who could bake the heck out of most people couldn't make a cinnamon roll to touch his mother's. He received one of *those* looks making it clear she'd let him sweet talk her for now but when she chose the right moment he'd better watch out.

It took four minutes and thirty-five seconds.

'So, Thomas Michael, when're you going to apologise to your daddy?'

Full name. Always bad. 'Uh, lunchtime?'

'Good answer.'

Tom took another swig of coffee. 'And of course to Aunt Ina, Lulu and anyone else I offended.'

'Sometimes you're not as dumb as you look.'

He'd take the back-handed compliment as the best he'd get.

'Your grandmother called me.'

'Who told her?'

His mother snickered. 'Who didn't is more to the point? The story was all over town before supper time.'

What would it be like to live somewhere no one knew or cared who you were? Tom reminded himself he'd been there, done that and hated it. From the little he'd picked up it was how Fee had spent most of her life so no wonder she was prickly as a cactus if anyone got too close. He hadn't seen her this morning and guessed the incredible kiss they'd shared freaked her out. Maybe if she knew it'd done the same to him that might help.

'Look, I'm sorry. Alright?'

'I know you are.' She squeezed his hand. 'When're you going to quit being a hermit?'

Tom pulled away. 'I wish y'all would stay out of my private life. Why's it so hard for everyone to accept I don't intend replacing my wife? I was a terrible husband in more ways than I care to admit and because of that Gina's dead. I've got a decent life now. Much better than most. I'm good.'

'You don't get it, do you?' His mother shook her head. 'No one's asking you to forget Gina but it doesn't mean you're condemned to be lonely the rest of your life. It's time you forgave yourself. We're all human. We make mistakes.' Deep hurt was etched into every line of her face.

'Mom. I've nothing left to love anyone else with.'

'Oh, Tom, you're wrong. There's a ton of kindness in you and it wouldn't take much to turn it into love with the right woman. It might be a different kind of loving but no worse for that. I wish you'd give it a chance.'

He'd never been good at lying to his mother but if he didn't pull it off now she'd hound him forever. 'I'll think about it, okay? But you've got to tell the rest of them to back off. I don't tell them how to run their lives. Maybe one day I'll be lucky enough to meet someone special who'll change my mind.' Tom pushed away the vivid image of Fee, so sweet and responsive in his arms last night.

'You promise?'

Tom nodded. 'And you'll do what *I* asked?'

'I will. I'll make it clear.'

That's all it would take because everyone paid attention to his mother. Now he'd be left alone to live on his own terms.

'I'd better be going, son.'

'I'll pop down at lunchtime.'

She stood up and gathered her coat and purse. 'You'd better see your daddy on his own first.'

'I'll stop by the office.' Tom pushed his chair back and joined her to walk back out to the porch.

'Look after yourself.' She pulled him into a tight hug before letting go and fixing him with her fiercest stare. 'Just so we're clear if I don't hear about an improvement in your non-existent social life in the next couple of months *I'll* break *my* promise too.'

He should have known better than to think he could pull one over on his mother.

'I don't want to hear you've slept with any tramp either.'

Tom was struck dumb.

'You might try being friendly to the pretty girl your Daddy told me about – the photographer lady. She sounds perfect to practice your rusty charms on.'

Before he could protest she hopped into her car and with a blast of her horn left him alone to stew.

Chapter Eleven

Fee pushed away the plate of uneaten fruit and wholegrain toast. She was supposed to have small, frequent meals but her stomach churned at the idea of eating.

What would have happened last night if the new guest hadn't appeared? The question wasn't really a question because it was obvious. Their first kiss lit her up from head to toe and going by Tom's response it'd had the same effect on him. His late wife hadn't been on his mind then which would annoy him no end today.

Honourable, loyal men were a mystery. None of her mother's transient boyfriends fitted the bill and the men she'd worked with were usually loners like her, or serial cheaters who believed what happened on the road stayed there. Tom had made a promise to one woman and was determined not to break it for the rest of his life.

She popped a grape into her mouth and thought some more. From the moment she set eyes on Tom she'd been drawn to his quiet, laidback strength but the more layers she unpeeled the more fascinated she became. He was the opposite of urbane, sophisticated Pierre with his flexible morals and world-weary manner. Doctor Michael's theory was that she'd been searching for lasting love all her life and when smooth-tongued Pierre told her what she wanted to hear she'd refused to listen when other people warned her off him. No one ever mentioned a wife and child either because they genuinely didn't know or perhaps didn't consider it their business to tell her.

Absentmindedly, Fee spread low-sugar strawberry jam on her toast and took a big bite. Tracking down Mary-Jo was first on her to-do list for the day. The chatty girl could be a goldmine of information about Gina, and she needed to find out more about the woman Tom had loved.

* * *

There was no need to cut more wood but Tom didn't know any more satisfying way of burning off the mixture of anger, frustration and flat-out resentment surging through his body. With the first swing of the axe he demolished his mother's argument. He should have asked her whether she'd jump into bed with the first man who asked if his father suddenly died. The fact he'd be smacked from one end of the house to the other as soon as the words left his mouth was irrelevant. She was still wrong. So what if he was lonely? Lonely was better than dishonest.

Dishonest? Who's the dishonest one? You wanted Fee last night and don't deny it.

Honesty was both his strength and his failing because it left him nowhere to hide.

Tom swung the axe again and hit the sweet spot on the log, the perfect place for it to split right down the middle. He refused to think any more until he was dripping with sweat and a massive pile of wood was stacked up neatly against the side of the shed.

From now on he'd treat Fee Winter the same way as every other guest. He might give his brothers a call and see if they were up for a few beers later to get him out of temptation's way for a few hours. He collected the shirt he'd abandoned and trailed back into the house. Tom opened the fridge and reached for his aluminium water bottle but it wasn't there. He checked the other shelves and on the door in case he'd set it in the wrong place. Slamming the door shut he grabbed a glass from the cabinet and filled it with cold water from the tap. Tom gulped it down before getting a refill and then opened the cinnamon rolls his mother had left behind. He blinked at the empty box. She'd brought four and they'd eaten one each which even with his debatable math skills left two. Fee's disappearing sandwich ran through his mind before he remembered the Waters' children. Quentin came by earlier to complain about the poor quality of the kitchen utensils and the kids raced off through his house before their father corralled them. He could hardly accuse guests of stealing his food especially when they were already dissatisfied. Waters would no doubt insist on calling the police and Tom's father was mad enough with him already without adding fuel to the fire.

He'd save his appetite for lunch. Today's special was meatloaf and could be his reward after he'd grovelled to his father.

The joy came back, one shot at a time, and Fee's stomach loosened and relaxed. Back in the cabin she popped the photo card out of her camera and into her laptop to watch a slideshow of the pictures she'd taken around the lake over the last couple of hours.

There were several gorgeous shots of the sun filtering in through the trees. Close-ups of plants she couldn't recognise but would research later. Best of all was a whole series of the same deer who'd returned to see her. Maybe that was a fanciful idea but for once she wanted to believe the unlikely. Its coy almost flirtatious expression as it met her gaze without blinking was priceless.

She checked her watch and realised it was well into lunchtime at the Mockingbird Cafe. She'd wait and go down later for a drink because the last thing she needed was to bump into Tom. Around two o'clock should work and while she was there she'd ask Ina when Mary-Jo would be back from Knoxville. If she had time to spare she could check out the ice cream shop as well and meet Ina's other daughter.

She lost herself in editing her new photos and the time flew by. Fee backed up her files to her USB drive and closed down her computer, but instead of leaving the laptop out she took it into her bedroom and hid it under the folded jumpers in her drawer.

Now she was ready for her fishing expedition.

Fee had skipped lunch so her idea of compromise was to order a slice of cake but only drink water. At the first forkful of soft white sponge topped with whipped cream and fresh coconut she tumbled head over heels in love.

'Are you enjoying that?' Ina asked.

'It's wonderful. Absolutely divine.' There was no need to lie to gain the other woman's approval. 'I was hoping to see Mary-Jo again. Will she be in soon?'

Ina glanced up at the clock. 'She hoped to be back in time to get Lulu from day-care at four. If she's early I'm sure she'll pop in here first for something to eat.'

'Do you mind if I check my emails while I wait for her?'

'Go ahead, honey. Let me know if you need anything else.' Ina smiled and bustled away to see to a couple of new customers.

'Hey, Aunt Ina. Did I leave my ...'

Fee saw Tom, his face pale and strained, filling the doorway. After several long, dragged out seconds he blinked and focused his attention back on his aunt.

'My phone. I think I left it here earlier. Did you find it?'

'Sure did.' Ina fumbled in the pocket of her red gingham apron and held it out to him. 'I was goin' to give it to Ms Winter here if you didn't come back.'

A slow, heated blush crept up his neck colouring the thin strip of pale skin exposed by a brutally short, fresh haircut. Fee missed the gentle waves usually brushing the collar of his shirt. 'That would've been fine,' she interrupted, forcing him to speak to her. Tom grunted something she guessed might be "thanks" and in return she flashed him one of her sweetest smiles.

'Better be going, I've got work to do.' He kissed Ina, gave a vague nod in her direction and strode out of the cafe, slamming the door behind him.

'I thought his mama sorted him out this morning but seems to me he's as antsy as ever,' Ina declared with a loud sniff.

'Mr Chambers appears to be a little distracted.'

'Hmm. That's one way to put it.'

Fee didn't press and at that moment Mary-Jo hurried in.

'I'm starving, Mama. Fix me something quick before I go pick up the monster, please. Pretty please.' She flung her arms around her mother's neck and kissed her. 'Oh, Fee, there you are. Great. We can have a chat. I'll come and sit with you while my sweet mama gets me a plate of food before I pass out.'

Anyone less likely to faint from a lack of nourishment Fee hadn't seen recently. Everything about the girl sparkled, from her glossy reddish gold curls to her 50s style yellow and white polka dot dress and shiny yellow kitten heels. Fee longed to take out her camera but restrained herself. She gestured towards the nearest chair and smiled. 'I could do with some company.'

Ina set down a plate in front of Mary-Jo. 'Chicken salad, grapes and chips, okay?'

'Yep, perfect. I promised Lulu we'd get ice cream from Suzy-Beth's today.' She looked back at Fee. 'I bet you haven't been to Sweet Scoops yet, have you?'

She shook her head, deciding not to mention the fact she wasn't supposed to eat too many sweet, high-fat foods. Finding out more about Tom should be worth a little minor discomfort.

'I apologise for my daughter's bad manners.'

'What's wrong?'

'You didn't *ask* the poor girl. She might have other plans. She's on vacation,' Ina declared, folding her arms across her ample chest.

Vacation? Not exactly. 'I'd love to join you and thanks for the offer.'

'See.' Mary-Jo gave a satisfied grin and dug into her delayed lunch. 'Excuse me pigging out but I haven't eaten since breakfast and Lulu will throw a tantrum if I'm late. Typical redhead!'

Her laughter was infectious and Fee couldn't help joining in until they both received despairing head shakes from Ina.

'Thanks, Mama. We're goin' to get off now.'

'Have you got something to feed the poor child later?'

Mary-Jo rolled her eyes. 'Yeah, we've still got half of the beef stew you gave me yesterday plus leftover chicken pot pie from the day before. We won't starve. I'll see you in the morning. Come on, Fee. We need to hurry.'

She closed down her laptop and packed it away. 'Where is the day-care?'

'One block over. We'll walk.'

Being dragged along in Mary-Jo's wake was a new experience for Fee. Everyone they passed greeted the young woman with a smile and asked how Lulu was doing. Somehow she managed to smile and answer them all while walking.

'Do you know *everyone* in town?' Fee asked.

'Pretty much. Between Sheriff Hank, Mama, Suzy-Beth, her husband Joe, Tom and his brothers, we've got the place covered. Then there's Lulu's Daddy's family – they're big shots around here. I guess it's the same where you come from?'

She shrugged, not sure how to answer.

'Is that a yes or no?' Mary-Jo persisted.

'I'm not really from anywhere in particular.' Mary-Jo stared at Fee as if she'd grown a second head. 'I was born in London but we moved around a lot when I was growing up and since then I've travelled non-stop with my job.' She plastered on a bright smile. 'I'm a free spirit with no desire to be tied down.'

'Sounds lonely to me, but everyone to their own I guess. I'd like to travel some but can't imagine not having Pine Ridge to come back to.'

Fee's throat tightened around the tears she refused to shed. Pierre had dangled the promise of a regular life in front of her before snatching it away again. A sudden trickle of panic seeped through her. Was she using her undeniable attraction to Tom to create something which wasn't there and never would be where she was concerned? Everyone wasn't suited to a so-called "normal" life. Wasn't it better she accepted it now rather than screw him up alongside her?

'Hey, we're here. Are you okay?'

Fee dragged out a smile. Thank goodness she'd seen sense before she made even more of a fool of herself. If Tom wanted to mourn Gina the rest of his life it was nobody's business but his. She'd stay well clear of him and concentrate on herself and getting better. In a few weeks she'd leave and her Tennessee idyll would be over. 'I'm fine.' Impulsively she gave the girl a hug. 'Thanks.'

'What for?' Mary-Jo frowned.

'Helping.' She didn't explain and her companion didn't ask but Fee wasn't stupid enough to think it'd be the last time she'd hear about this.

Chapter Twelve

Burrowed into an easy chair at the back of the small library, Tom lost himself in researching the Chambers' family history. If he needed to take his mind off everything else going on in his life this always worked and was one of the few reasons he regretted not having internet coverage at Black Cherry.

Fee's swift, cool appraisal of him at the cafe and the tiny, knowing smile lingering around her lush mouth had shaken him. The damn woman could have made a polite, friendly comment to put him at ease but instead held her tongue and let him imagine what was going through her mind.

He only had ten minutes left before the library closed at five o'clock but the florist next door didn't shut for another half hour so he had plenty of time. His brothers wouldn't be free from jobs, wives and children until at least eight so he had several hours to himself. Tom packed his laptop in the bag and went to buy a bunch of flowers. Outside the cemetery he parked and fetched the cleaning supplies he kept in the bed of his truck then tramped across the damp grass. Because he came so often Gina's grave never got dirty, but he tried to keep it perfect. He'd failed her enough in life without neglecting her now too. Tom brushed off a small amount of lichen before working at the last stubborn piece with the rounded edge of a popsicle stick. Pouring water from a gallon container into a small bucket he carefully scrubbed from the bottom of the stone upwards, rinsing his brush frequently and changing the water when it got dirty.

'There, that's better, sweetheart,' he murmured. Tom dried the surface gently with a soft cloth and ran his fingers over the simple inscription – her name, the too-short dates of her life and the simple, guilt-laden words he'd chosen "Beloved Wife of Tom". Kneeling in the dirt he leaned back on his heels and reached for the large bunch of chrysanthemums he'd set down while he worked. Gina loved all the rich fall colours and she'd insisted they marry in October. The red and gold shades set off her dark hair and creamy skin to perfection and she'd been a beautiful bride. Eighteen years ago today.

Tom struggled to arrange the large, floppy blooms in the container sure Gina was watching him from somewhere and smiling. 'It's the best I can do. I'm sorry.' There was so much he was sorry for, not least of which were his new and unwelcome feelings for Fee. He stood back up and stretched his aching knees. When he'd cleared everything away he pulled his phone out of his pocket and texted his brothers to cancel their evening together. Why he'd suggested they got together today of all days was downright crazy and only proved Fee had jumbled up his brain. Tom turned the phone back off so he wouldn't see their replies.

Company was the last thing he needed tonight.

An hour later he was settled out on his porch with the wedding album Gina had spent many long winter evenings putting together open on his lap and a mug of coffee on the table next to his right arm. The sound of vehicles crunching along the gravel road startled him and Sandy's black truck came to a stop in front of the cabin followed close behind by Mikey's blue minivan.

'Hey, little brother.' Sandy leapt out and stepped onto the porch, his heavy leather boots clunking on the bare boards. He set down the cooler in his hand and opened the lid. 'Get this down you.' He popped the top on a can of beer and thrust it at Tom.

'I don't—'

'Drink, or we'll pour it down you.' Mikey brandished a couple of pizza boxes and made a grab for the beer. 'We brought food and we're staying the night with full permission of the ladies.'

Tom reluctantly closed the album and laid it back on the table. He took the beer from Sandy's outstretched hand.

'We told Mama about your message and she remembered the date. We knew you'd be—'

'Grieving?' Tom snapped. 'What's damn well wrong with that? Gina was my wife.' Tears pressed at his eyes and he blinked to push them away.

Sandy rested a comforting hand on his shoulder. 'It's not wrong, bro. We didn't want you to be alone, that's all.'

Tom jerked away and walked across the porch to lean against one of the wood posts. 'I appreciate it, okay, but when you go home to your families I'll still be here.' A glance flitted between his brothers. 'Mama sent you to turn the screws, didn't she? Could her timing be any worse?'

'Hey, sit down, and take it easy.' Mikey stuck his oar in. 'I'm goin' to throw the pizzas in the oven to warm.'

'Fine,' Tom grouched. 'I guess I'm not gettin' rid of you both anytime soon.' He sat down as Mikey reappeared.

'Smart, isn't he?' Sandy jibed and they both tossed him the annoying older brother smiles he'd suffered all his life.

Deep down Tom was glad to see them. His own company was lousy at the best of times and this was the absolute worst day of the year to get through. 'What've you been up to?' he asked Sandy. He rested one foot up on his other leg and half-listened to his brother complain about work.

In the middle of a long, convoluted tale about a bank robbery that went wrong and the man they suspected of being responsible but couldn't get enough evidence to charge, Sandy stopped and gave him a piercing stare. 'You're a sneaky devil.'

'I'm not a complete moron.' Tom grinned. 'Mama sent you to find out how I'm doin', man-to-man, right?'

'Maybe.'

He took a long, cold swallow of beer and scrutinised his brother. Not many people could put one over on Sandy, a twenty-year veteran detective, and it'd be foolish of him to try.

'It's up to you, bro. I'm simply following instructions,' Sandy declared. 'You wanna tell me to piss off it's no skin off my nose. I'll report your answer back minus the cuss words.' His easy laugh loosened something in Tom's gut.

'I don't want to get you in trouble too.'

Sandy rubbed at the condensation on the beer can and wiped his damp thumb on his jeans. 'It doesn't bother me none. Why's she so bent on hassling you now anyway?'

'Not sure. Maybe because I turned forty last year? Who knows with our sweet mother?' Tom ventured. Nothing more was said. The comfortable silence was only punctuated by the sound of slow, steady drinking and the scraping of the chairs on the porch floor. Mikey hauled himself to his feet and disappeared inside the cabin.

'There we go. Gourmet pizza courtesy of our favourite aunt.' Mikey set a couple of oversized pizzas down on the table along with three plates.

Immediately they all dove in and munched away without bothering with any conversation.

'You got many guests in?' Mikey asked, reaching for another slice.

'Three cabins are full. A decent older couple from South Carolina who leave tomorrow. A family of four from Florida – the father's obnoxious, mother's a pain and the kids are all out brats. They're here for the week.' He hesitated a second before mentioning Fee. 'There's an English woman booked in for a month. She's some sort of photographer.' Tom caught the knowing glance ricocheting between his brothers. He'd been set up.

'We hear she's a smart lady. She sure won over Pops.'

Mikey's casual comment didn't fool Tom for a second.

'Good looker is she?' Sandy chimed in, and Tom swallowed the last of his beer before pulling out another can from the cooler at his brother's feet. He popped the top open and took a long deep swallow.

'Not particularly.' He flat out lied. 'Pleasant enough, I guess.'

'Doesn't float your boat then?' Mikey's blunt question

meant he'd been stuck with the bad cop role tonight, leaving Sandy to play the nice guy.

Tom glowered. 'I'm not interested. Thought you'd all have got that by now. Worst thing to ask today, don't you think?' Attack was often the best defence.

'Fair enough.' Mikey backed off with a conciliatory smile. Tom recognised it as nothing more than a temporary reprieve. He'd better stop drinking and keep his wits about him.

Soft, yellow lights glimmered on Tom's porch and Fee, sitting outside her own cabin, strained to pick out the voices drifting up the road. She couldn't decide if it was all men or maybe included a woman with a low, sexy voice. *Pull yourself together. You're not getting involved, remember?*

She'd spent a lot of time thinking since her latest visit to Pine Ridge. Whilst bonding with Mary-Jo over a kid's size serving of pear and pecan ice cream it'd been a cinch to extract the story she'd sworn not to ask anything about, finding out more about Gina Chambers than she really wanted to. It only took the minimum of encouragement to get Suzy-Beth to join in and gossip about her cousin.

It was a simple, sad story. Tom and Gina were childhood sweethearts from two long settled Pine Ridge families who got married as soon as Tom became a police officer. Fee hated the flash of envy when the women spoke about the beautiful, charming Gina whom everyone loved.

She worshipped him and everyone assumed they'd grow old together but Tom worked a murder case and when the man he charged got out of prison he was set on revenge. Gary Higgins shot Gina while she and Tom were sitting on their front porch. Tom's never been himself since. He went away for a while and worked as a security consultant in Iraq but couldn't stay gone. There was no way he could return to police work so he made the cabins his project and they saved him.

No wonder he'd recoiled at being drawn to her the other

night. An unbearable sadness filled Fee at the idea that such a loving man would close himself down. This wasn't simply about his clear desire for her but also the longing in his eyes when he played with Lulu. It didn't take a genius to guess he'd been picturing the children he'd hoped to have. After Pierre's death she swore never to get close to anyone again because it'd hurt too much when things fell apart. If she was foolish enough to let Tom into her heart he'd let her down too because that's what happened. She couldn't take the chance.

Fee pulled her cold, bare feet up on the chair and tucked the soft red blanket in around her to ward off the chill in the air. Rocking back and forth she allowed herself to dream.

Chapter Thirteen

'Higgins gets out next week.' Sandy's blunt statement hit Tom straight in the gut.

'You're fuckin' kiddin' me!'

Sandy shook his head. He wore the same blank, serious expression he used to cover up his feelings in front of criminals and defence attorneys. 'You knew he was goin' in front of the parole board again. They sent an invitation for you to go and speak but you refused and never asked how it went.'

Tom grasped the arms of the chair. 'I couldn't face seeing him again and didn't think they'd be dumb enough to listen to his whining excuses.' He leapt to his feet. 'I'm goin' to walk. Leave me alone, alright?' The pity written across his brothers' faces made him give the table leg a swift kick, sending the remains of the pizza and a couple of beer bottles skittering across the porch.

Tom leapt down the porch steps and strode out towards the lake. There was enough moonlight to stop him falling flat on his face on the rough path. He'd prefer to run and pound his feet into the gravel while pretending it was Gary Higgins' pale, fleshy face but that wasn't an option. He turned left to walk clockwise around the trail so he wouldn't pass the other cabins until he could manage a polite greeting if necessary. He launched into a brisk pace and twenty minutes later emerged from the trees and gradually slowed down until his breathing returned to normal. Tom hovered near the shed where he stored the boating equipment. He couldn't face his brothers again yet but didn't know what else to do.

The glowing light on Fee's porch lured him closer to her cabin. There was no reason to think she was sitting outside this late at night so he guessed she'd left it on for security. No way could he go and knock on her door.

'Tom, is that you?'

Her tremulous voice cut through the crisp night air and he cursed under his breath. The last thing she needed was him sneaking around and scaring her half to death. 'Yeah, sorry, didn't mean to freak you out.' Tom walked over and hesitated by her bottom step.

'Then don't creep up on me another time,' she teased, smiling at him from one of the rocking chairs. She leaned forward and frowned. 'Is something wrong?'

Tom swallowed hard and stared down at his feet. Her light, clean perfume drifted in the crisp night air and when he glanced again she'd made her way down the steps to stand in front of him.

'What it is, Tom?'

He could still walk away. Go back to his own place and talk to his brothers. Tom froze as she took hold of his right hand.

'Do you want to join me in a mug of chamomile tea?'

He'd received some unusual offers from women in his time but this beat them all. Tom managed to nod and gave her a tight smile.

Fee tugged on Tom's hand to encourage him. As soon as they stepped onto the porch he wrapped his arms around her waist and clutched her against his broad chest.

'Tea?' Her voice wobbled.

'In a minute. Just let me hold you. Please.' His deep voice, smooth as honey and dark as the night settling in around them, trickled over her senses and she snuggled further into his gentle, caressing hands. 'You're an extremely peaceful woman. That's a rare thing.'

Fee took it as a compliment and decided to take a huge chance. 'I've never told you why I came here.' Tom was smart enough to guess she was giving him a break by offering something of herself. 'How about we sit and talk a while.'

Tom tightened his hold. 'But, I need ...'

She silenced him with a light kiss, brushing against his warm lips while aching for so much more. 'I know, but I don't intend to be someone you regret.' Fee pulled away.

'I'll be a good boy and sit here while you fix whatever weird drink you offered.' He walked over to grab one of her chairs, shifting it closer to the other one and lowering himself into the seat with a quiet sigh.

Fee hurried away inside and headed for the kitchen. She boiled the kettle and made a fresh pot of tea. While it steeped she rested against the counter and wondered if she'd manage to send him away later or whether she even wanted to. Without coming to any decision she poured out two mugs and made her way back to the porch. For a moment she stopped by the open doorway to watch Tom, his face etched with worry. Doctor Michael would tell her to run as fast as she could in the opposite direction because she wasn't strong enough to take on Tom's problems as well as her own. He'd encouraged her to come here largely because she didn't know anyone and could hold herself apart. But he hadn't bargained on Tom's kind eyes and gentle voice luring her in.

'It's safe to come out. I promise I'll behave.' He flashed one of his endearing smiles.

Fee managed a bright smile. 'Here's your tea. It'll soothe you and help you sleep.'

'We'll see. Thanks.' He nodded and took the cup she was holding out, sliding his fingers around hers so she couldn't move or she'd spill hot tea over them both. After several lingering seconds Tom loosened his grasp and Fee pulled away. She sat down and wrapped her hands around her drink to steady her shaking fingers.

'You know how to be quiet too,' she commented after several companionable minutes slipped by without a word between them. 'A police habit or simply you?'

Tom shrugged. 'Bit of both I guess. I've always been an observer.'

‘So what’re you seeing now?’

‘A starkly beautiful woman, highly intelligent and well-travelled but who doesn’t know her destination anymore.’

His spot-on observation shook her. ‘Wow. You don’t mince words, do you?’

‘Do you want me to?’

Fee shook her head. ‘I’m guessing you know what I do for a living?’

‘Yeah. Mary-Jo shared it with me and then your name registered. You do great work.’

She swallowed hard, taken aback at the unexpected compliment. ‘I suppose you Googled me and now there’s nothing of my life left hidden?’

‘Nope. I figured you’d tell me if you wanted to.’

This man with his huge, loving family could never understand her nomadic upbringing and solitary mentality. Maybe it was better to get it out in the open now. ‘My mother could never settle so we moved around all over the place. She always had a cause to follow and dragged me along in her wake.’ Fee tried to hide her bitterness. ‘Will Sawyer was the only one of Mum’s boyfriends who ever gave a damn about me and he gave me a cheap camera for my tenth birthday. I soon found out it’d never let me down.’ She could hardly bear the wave of sympathy flooding from Tom. Making him sorry for her was the last thing she’d intended. ‘As soon as possible I left home and never went back. I haven’t seen my mother in almost twenty years and we rarely speak on the phone.’ She briefly considered mentioning Maddy’s recent phone call but that could wait for another day. A flare of shock tinged his warm eyes but he didn’t say a word. ‘Photo-journalism felt a natural fit for me and there’s very little I haven’t seen and documented over the years.’

‘I’d imagine it gets to you in the end, doesn’t it?’ Tom murmured.

‘Rather like police work.’

‘Yeah. It sure makes relationships tricky.’

She clasped her hands together and looked straight at Tom. 'That's why I didn't do them long-term until ... Pierre. I'd learnt from my mother never to trust men's promises—' Fee held up her hand to him. '—please don't try to tell me otherwise. It's the way she was and it rubbed off on me. I've never craved stability and family and all that entails.' Her protests sounded hollow.

'Pierre hurt you.'

The blunt statement sliced right through her. 'I let Pierre into the one place I'd always kept private, my heart, and he ripped it in two and tossed it out with the rubbish.' Fee fiercely wiped away the tears trickling down her face.

'Do you want to sit with me?' Tom whispered. Without speaking she moved over and lowered herself onto his lap. He settled her into the curve of his body and began to rock the chair again.

'I'm sure Mary-Jo told you Pierre died in front of me.'

'Yeah, she did, sweetheart.' His voice thickened. 'I wish like hell we didn't have this in common.' Tom's eyes glistened. 'Gina was shot while we sat on our porch drinking coffee.' He worked his jaw, as if he wanted to say more but couldn't force the words to emerge. 'It never goes away.'

'At least *you* know she loved you.' He didn't respond straight away and his hesitation made her wonder.

'Why do you doubt Pierre loved you?'

'Perhaps because the wife he'd never mentioned arrived at his memorial service showing everyone pictures of their beautiful baby son and their gorgeous house in Paris.' She blinked back tears. In her head she saw the blonde, elegant Helene in her black Chanel dress giving Fee a sympathetic pat on the back and thanking her for being Pierre's friend.

'Shit.'

'That about sums it up.'

'You didn't have to share all this to make me feel better you know.'

'Did it work?' She struggled for a touch of humour.

'Maybe.' Tom toyed with the ends of her hair. 'I ought to go.'

'Why?'

'My brothers are visiting and I kind of stormed out on them.' Tom's bashful expression touched her heart. 'Can I see you tomorrow when they're gone?'

'You know where I am.' She stood up. 'Good night.' Fee turned away and walked back into her cabin, quickly closing the door behind her. She didn't move again until his footsteps faded into the distance and she could trust herself not to run after him.

Chapter Fourteen

Tom ambled into the kitchen rubbing at his tired eyes and needing an infusion of hot, strong coffee more than oxygen.

'Glad to see you've dragged your sorry ass out at last.' Mikey grinned over his shoulder before turning back to concentrate on the eggs he was scrambling. 'The bacon's ready and I've popped the bread in the toaster. Get your caffeine fix and sit down. I'll feed you.'

'Turned into Mom, have you?' Tom complained half-heartedly. They hadn't talked much after he got back from Fee's last night – correction – he'd kept silent and his brothers let him get away with it. 'Where's Sandy?'

'Work.' Mikey shared the eggs out between two plates then piled on a mound of bacon and toast. He set one in front of Tom before sitting down himself. 'Sandy met your English lady when he went for his usual run. Said you were blowin' smoke when you claimed she wasn't anything special.'

Tom laid down his fork. 'For a start she's not *my* English anything, and I didn't say …'

'Lighten up, bro, I'm havin' a bit of fun, that's all.' Mikey shovelled in a mouthful of eggs then bit into a strip of bacon, blackened to a crisp the way everyone in their family preferred.

'Yeah, I know. It's me. Sorry.'

'No worries.' Mikey went back to eating.

'I'll tell you somethin', but if you breathe a word outside these four walls you're dead meat.'

Mikey froze, his fork halfway to his mouth. 'What the hell have you done?'

'I haven't done anythin', well not really, I mean …'

'Get on with it, idiot, or I'll beat it out of you.'

Tom sighed, wishing he'd kept quiet. 'I kissed Fee the other day.'

'Okay.' Mikey dragged out the word as though unsure where to take the conversation next. They normally joked about anything under the sun except for the subject of Tom and women. 'You wanted to do more, right?'

'Yeah. What does that make me?'

'Um, normal?'

'What about Gina?'

Mikey took a swig of coffee and stared at Tom. 'You really want the truth?'

Did he? 'I guess.'

'Gina would call you an idiot. If it'd been the other way around I damn well hope you wouldn't have expected her to lock herself away for the rest of her life.'

'She died because I screwed up. There's a big difference,' Tom snapped.

'No, she didn't, you moron. She died because Gary Higgins is a vicious thug.' Mikey rested a hand on Tom's shoulder and the unexpected contact made his throat tighten. 'No one's telling you to forget Gina but you're still alive so live for Christ's sake. It's got to be better than this half-assed thing you're doin' now.'

Tom's jaw gaped open. His taciturn, quiet brother was never this blunt.

'You'll catch flies in a minute,' Mikey teased. 'Finish your breakfast. I didn't waste my time cookin' so you could let breakfast go cold and greasy.'

He dutifully picked up his knife and fork and followed orders because it was easier than replying. Even if he chose to risk dipping a toe back in the dating pond it didn't change the fact Fee was in a bad place emotionally. Their timing was lousy.

'You're thinkin' too much.'

'How would you know? Not something you ever do, is it?' Tom tossed right back. 'Fee's … complicated.'

Mikey's coarse laughter filled the room. 'Show me a damn woman who isn't. They're all a goddamn mystery, you idiot.'

'But I might be the worst person for her.'

'Am I suggesting you marry the woman tomorrow?' Mikey jibed. 'Have you ever heard of dating and getting to know someone? It's what normal people do. Try it and see what happens.'

Tom took a large bite of toast. After eighteen years alone he wasn't sure he had the guts to put himself out there again. He'd never done casual where women were concerned and was pretty sure he couldn't start now. He respected Fee too much and knew enough of her past to be aware it wouldn't take much to hurt her.

'Next time I'm gonna let Mom do her own screw turning,' Mikey announced with the faintest hint of a smile. 'You do what you want.' He pushed his dirty plate away and stood up. 'I gotta head out of here. I'm working this afternoon and Janet's got more things on her honey-do list than I'll get around to in a million years.'

'I'll clear up,' Tom said. 'Tell your sweet wife thanks from me.' He stumbled over how to express his gratitude.

'Shut it. That's enough soppy crap. Just get your act together. Bring your little woman over to Mama's on Sunday if you think she won't be scared off by the gang.'

Little woman? Fee would tear Mikey limb from limb if he dared call her that to her face. Tom wasn't sure throwing her in the deep end with his noisy family was a good idea, although she'd had no problem with a modified version of them in the cafe the other day.

'Maybe. I'll let you know.'

'Fine. I'm off.' Mikey walked back out to the other room and grabbed his overnight bag off the sofa. 'I won't be blabbing to Mom either. You can tell her what you want.'

'Thanks.'

'Hey, we've got to stick together. The Three Amigos, right?' Mikey chuckled, reviving their old childhood nickname. It'd always been the three boys against the two girls who'd tagged themselves the Deadly Duo.

'Yeah, always.' Tom forced out a smile.

They made their way outside and the crisp morning air helped to clear his head. Tom changed the subject back to sports, their usual favourite topic. After a few minutes discussing how the UT football team might fare against the much-hated Alabama side on Saturday his brother left.

Tom didn't rush to go inside until Mikey was out of sight and by the time he finished washing all the breakfast dishes by hand he'd talked himself in and out of asking Fee on a date at least a hundred times. Using the dishwasher wouldn't have had the same effect. The best he could come up with was to stop by her cabin, gauge her mood and go from there. Not exactly Mr Decisive but it'd have to do.

Fee snapped out of her meditative pose as the alarm clock buzzed. The idea was to gradually come back to full awareness but she didn't have the patience. This morning she'd cooked herself a healthy egg-white omelette for breakfast followed by a leisurely bath and her yoga practice. Unfortunately her emotions were still as jangled as they'd been when Tom left last night.

This was ridiculous. She'd change clothes and take her camera out somewhere away from Tom Chambers. Fee began to roll up her mat but a sudden series of loud knocks made her drop it back down on the floor. 'Who is it?'

'Tom. Are you decent?'

Fee suppressed a laugh and hurried to open the door. The sight of Tom, his gleaming auburn hair still damp, clutching at his black cowboy hat and shifting awkwardly from one foot to the other endeared her to him all over again.

'Come on in. I won't eat you,' she said with what she hoped was an encouraging smile. He sidled in past her and stood by the table, not quite meeting her gaze.

'I wondered if you'd care to go out tomorrow and see some of the fall colours? The Cumberland Gap area is about an hour drive from here and real pretty right now.' The words tumbled out. 'There's an old settlement on top of Brush Mountain that was home to the Hensley family back in the first half of the twentieth century. It fell into ruins but it's been renovated as a living history museum. There's one tour a day going from the visitor centre in a minibus and it lasts about four hours. I could call and see if there's room if you're interested?' He raced on before she could reply. 'It only runs for another week or so before they close for the winter. We could get a bite of lunch somewhere nearby when we're done.' Finally he stopped and gazed hopefully at her.

'Are you asking me on a date, Mr Chambers?'

Tom's skin became red above his shirt collar. He straightened to his full height and fixed her with his deep, chocolate-brown eyes. 'Yep, I do believe I am. How about it?'

Fee had thought her days of being shy around men were long behind her but she felt sixteen again. 'Yes, please.' The feathered smile lines around his eyes deepened and she reached out and took hold of his hands. Neither of them said a word as she ran her fingers over the marks of his outdoor life; the calluses and multitude of tiny scars hinting at his story. Fee lifted her gaze to meet his gleaming eyes and softly pressed her lips against his, aware of the faint scent of bacon and coffee overlaid by a layer of mint toothpaste.

'Honey, I won't get out the door if you keep doin' that.' His raspy voice sent a shiver of desire trickling down her spine.

'Of course you will although maybe not quite as soon as you intended.' Fee murmured, unable to resist wrapping her arms around his neck. 'You wouldn't deny a lady a kiss to greet the day would you?'

Tom sighed. 'Not sure I can deny you anything and believe me I've tried.'

'Me too. It works both ways.'

'Good.' He circled her slim waist with his broad hands and pressed her against him. Fee loved the fact there was nothing weak and insubstantial about this man. Tom lowered his mouth to hers and kissed her with no hint of the diffidence he'd shown a few minutes earlier. 'You're this way all over aren't you? Sweet and so soft,' he murmured. He stopped kissing her and frowned. 'Does it frighten you too?'

Tom's honesty rendered her speechless. 'Yes,' she whispered and a relieved smile crept over his rugged face.

'Good. Do you want to take a chance on gettin' frightened together?' Tom asked.

Fee kept her reply to a simple nod. Sometimes less was more.

Chapter Fifteen

Tom watched indulgently as Fee took yet another photo of the weathered, old barn. They'd been lucky to get the last two seats available for today's tour. His intrepid companion grasped his hand more than once on the hour long drive most of which was along a steep, winding one-track road. The park ranger escorting them was a descendent of the original owners of the land who had sold it to the Hensley family and everyone was enjoying his interesting stories.

'How many people lived here?' Fee asked their guide.

'About 150 at its height and nearly all of them were related to the Hensley family by either blood or marriage. They never had electricity or indoor plumbing and were pretty much self-sufficient.' The man grinned. 'It's been said there was more than a little moonshine made here but you didn't hear that from me. I'd take a guess they needed something to barter with the folks down the mountain for the things they couldn't make themselves.'

As the rest of the group walked on to see inside the next restored cabin Fee lingered by the long split-rail fence built to keep out deer and bears. She framed a shot out over the rolling fields.

'The fog's lifting. Look how the colours are starting to glow.' She tossed him a satisfied smile. Fee's enthusiasm was infectious and he loved seeing the familiar place through her fresh, observant eyes. 'Next time I'll bring a decent camera. This thing frustrates me.' Fee glared at the offending object but carried on taking more pictures.

'I'm surprised you didn't bring your regular one along with you.' Her smile disappeared and Tom wished he could rip out his tongue, unsure what he'd said to upset her. 'Forget it. None of my business.'

She lowered the camera and touched his arm. 'It's okay. My therapist persuaded me not to bring a camera on this trip. He says I've been hiding behind a lens for too long and need to face people and life without it.' Her monotone voice made it clear she didn't agree.

'Sounds crazy to me. It's what you do.'

'I almost asked him how he'd like having his medical license taken away, but I didn't.' A hint of a smile twitched at the corners of her mouth. 'I disobeyed and bought this a few days after I arrived. I'm going to buy a better camera tomorrow before this one makes me scream.'

'Good idea.' Tom noticed the guide waving at them. He was beckoning for them to come and rejoin the group. 'Let's go.'

They finished the tour by seeing the tiny one-room schoolhouse with its plain wood and cast iron desks and wood-burning stove and ended at the family cemetery with its poignant, worn headstones. The last person buried here was Sherman Hensley, the original founder, who'd been forced off the mountain in 1951 because none of his family wanted to stay there and he couldn't manage on his own. Tom admired the fact he'd stubbornly insisted on being brought back up the mountain to be buried by his late wife in 1979 and chosen his own epitaph "When we all get to Heaven". He was pretty sure Sherman had cordoned off a separate corner for his family.

'Time to stop dreaming. Are you ready for another hair-raising drive?' Fee spoke nearby and Tom was startled back to awareness.

'I should be asking you that question,' he said with a laugh. 'I didn't grip onto you as if my life depended on it.'

'I wasn't that bad,' she protested. 'Anyway it's better than going by horse or walking. No wonder the women rarely left the mountain.'

'It'll be getting cold soon.' Tom slipped his arm around her shoulder. 'You goin' to do a Nancy Gibbons and knit some thick wool socks to see me through the winter?' He'd seen her horrified face when their guide told them about the poor woman who knitted two pairs for everyone in her immediate family each winter. A total of fifty-six socks.

'Knit your own or go to Wal-Mart.' Her pithy remark, accompanied by a sharp poke to the ribs made Tom chuckle.

'Yes, ma'am.' He sneaked a quick kiss. 'Come on. Get on the bus and think about the good lunch I'll reward you with when we survive the journey.'

'I'm sure you've planned out where we're going. Food is usually a priority with you.'

'I might've done,' Tom admitted. 'If you don't mind us driving about twenty minutes or so we can refuel at Boone's Country Store. They've got good Southern cooking and free Wi-Fi. I could do with checking my emails because I'll miss goin' into town today.'

'Of course. I probably ought to catch up too.'

'No problem.' He nodded. 'They won't be overrun because it'll be well past most people's lunchtime by the time we get there.' Tom helped Fee onto the bus and they settled into their same seats at the back of the bus. They chatted to the other tourists and the drive down seemed to go quickly.

As soon as they parked in front of the restaurant Fee pulled her camera out. 'It's gorgeous. Is the building original?'

'Yeah, mostly. It was used as a store when the pioneers were going through this area heading west. For a long time it fell out of use and then was rebuilt using as much of the original materials as possible. The wood is mainly eastern hemlock.'

She gave him a shrewd look. 'That means a lot to you doesn't it?'

Tom tried to explain the lure of preserving the past in a good way and the strong links he felt with his own courageous ancestors who'd made their way over the Appalachian Mountains from North Carolina in the early nineteenth century. 'The more I discover about them I find out an equal amount about myself.' She didn't look convinced. 'I'm guessin' you don't feel the same way?'

Fee shrugged. 'Not really. Partly because I don't have anywhere I really "come from" plus I've seen people the world over fighting and losing their lives over small areas of land. I can never quite understand why. If I'm not content in one place I move somewhere else.'

For a few seconds he wasn't sure how to reply. Tom hesitated to put into words his theory that part of Fee's problems stemmed from not belonging anywhere and having no family to keep her solid and grounded. 'We're all different I guess.' Tom left it at that although it felt dishonest. 'You ready to go in for lunch?'

'I certainly am. Lead on.' It was clear she knew what he was doing but wasn't ready to have the conversation either.

They were fortunate enough to get a table by the window looking out over the beautiful countryside saturated in the vibrant colours of fall. Tom always thought it was a toss-up between this and spring for his favourite seasons. If pushed he'd have to plump for fall because there was something brave about the defiant splash of colour before the onset of winter.

Tom read the menu and was immediately a happy man. 'Today's special is fried pork chops, mashed potatoes, creamed corn and turnip greens. Don't tell Aunt Ina but the chops are better than hers,' he confided.

'Do they have anything else, only...'

'Only what?'

'I'm not supposed to eat a lot of fatty foods,' she apologised. 'Over the last few years I developed a stomach ulcer mainly down to stress and need to be sensible about my diet.'

'Is it painful?'

'It can be if I ignore it.'

'So pepperoni pizza with extra cheese is out then?' Tom teased.

'Unless I want to wind up at the nearest hospital I'd have to go with a yes.'

He glanced back at the menu. 'They've got a hearty vegetable soup or a choice of sandwiches.'

'The soup will be perfect and maybe a wholegrain roll. You order what you want, it doesn't bother me.'

Tom didn't argue. The pull of excellent pork chops was too strong. 'Okay.'

Half an hour later Tom pushed his chair back so he could stretch out his over-stuffed body. He'd succumbed to the lure of the cook's famous apple cake with homemade vanilla ice cream for dessert and was pretty sure he wouldn't be able to move for a week.

'Will that keep starvation at bay for a few hours?' Fee teased.

'Maybe.' He poured a generous measure of cream into his coffee before pulling out his phone. 'You sure you don't mind?'

'I told you it was fine. I'm going to do the same.' Fee assured him and retrieved hers from the battered tan leather tote she told him had done more miles than most airplanes. He took her at her word and started to check through his accumulated messages.

She deleted the mountains of spam and narrowed the rest down to half a dozen she might actually want to read. Fee sighed as one name leapt out.

'Is something wrong?'

She glanced up to meet Tom's worried eyes. 'Not really but I've got a message from my mother.' Was Maddy really not going to abandon the idea of playing happy families with Allain Dupre after all these years?

'Do you want me to read it for you?' he asked.

'I'm not helpless.' Tom flinched and she regretted her sharp reply. 'Sorry.'

'It's alright.'

Fee glanced down at her phone.

'Just because it's called a smartphone I don't think it'll read itself, sweetheart. Can you imagine what the folks at the Hensley settlement would've thought of all this modern technology? Sometimes I wonder who's better off.'

'You are. Trust me.' Her vehemence poured out. 'I've seen enough people living in primitive conditions, women dying in childbirth, kids not making it past their first birthdays and people scrubbing their clothes in a dirty river to know it sucks. Don't let anyone tell you they're happy and content with their lot in life because it's rubbish. If you offered them a washing machine, decent health care and electricity they wouldn't give a crap about sticking with the traditional ways.' Fee's frustration demolished the filter she usually kept firmly in place. She became aware of the other diners openly staring at her.

'I know, honey. I didn't mean it literally.'

'Sorry. I've forgotten how to behave.'

'You've got nothing to apologise for.' Tom squeezed her hands. 'You still feel deeply for people and after all you've been through I'd say that's huge.'

Tears blurred her vision and Tom passed over a fresh white linen handkerchief. He didn't say a word while she removed her glasses and wiped her eyes.

'Do you want to get out of here? We could sit on the porch.'

She nodded and Tom caught the waitress's eye to get the bill. After he paid they gathered their things and went to sit together on an old wood swing. For several minutes they swung idly without talking and the gentle silence finally loosened her tongue.

'I felt so deeply for the people I photographed it was slowly killing me and Pierre's death was the final straw. I still feel guilty for giving up but I wasn't doing any good.'

'Sometimes we have to know when to quit,' Tom said firmly. 'You'll find another way to be useful. I couldn't be a cop any more after Gina died because I felt the system let me down.'

'How did we get to this from me checking my phone?'

'Hey, don't fret. I appreciate your honesty. I've never been one to pussyfoot around.'

She planted a kiss on his generous mouth and Tom's face lit up. She'd never met such an easy-going man before with no agenda or expectations. Fee warned herself not to be reckless. She mustn't dive in headfirst again no matter how tempted she was.

'Phone.' Tom reminded her and she remembered why they'd come out here in the first place. Fee opened her mother's email.

Call me, Freebird. I need to talk to you.

She couldn't hide all this from Tom. 'There's another reason I came to America.' Before she lost her nerve Fee told him about her mother's recent phone call. 'Apparently she had a brief thing with this Allain Dupre in London while he was on holiday from his American university. After he left she discovered she was pregnant but didn't tell him.' Fee shrugged. 'He returned to London again later that year to find she was pregnant and wanted to marry her.'

'Why didn't she?'

'She claims she lied to him about her due date and insisted it wasn't his baby.'

Tom frowned. 'Why? I don't get it.'

'According to her, Allain was engaged to a girl called Ellen when they first met and my mum didn't want to spoil his life.' *So she spoiled mine instead.* 'She convinced Allain that Will Sawyer was my father.'

'Are you going to ring her?'

'I suppose so.' Reluctantly she found her mother's number and crossed her fingers that it'd go to voicemail and she could get away with leaving a message.

'Freebird?'

Her mother's distinctive low, gravelly voice hummed down the line.

Chapter Sixteen

'Hello, Mum,' Fee murmured.

'Allain rang me today.' Maddy sighed. 'I'm not sure he believed me when I swore I'd passed on his phone number and email to you.'

'Please say you didn't tell him how to get in touch with me?'

'Of course not. What do you take me for?'

You don't want to know.

'The last thing he wants is to upset you but he really wanted me to pass on how much it would please him to be ... in your life in some way. I promise I won't bother you again and you don't have to tell me if you decide to contact him or not. How much more transparent can I be?' she pleaded and briefly Fee felt sorry for her mother.

'I'll think about it some more and that's all I'm agreeing to. I've got to go.' She said a quick goodbye and turned the phone off, shoving it back in her bag.

'It's time we went.' Tom's quiet words reminded her where they were. 'We'll talk later.'

A few minutes later Fee discovered herself sitting in Tom's truck with her seat belt fastened but with no recollection of getting there because her mind was elsewhere.

'Lie back and close your eyes. I'll wake you up when we're home.'

She didn't have the energy to argue.

Tom approached the entrance to Black Cherry and glanced down at Fee who was still fast asleep. Her fresh perfume and the heavy warmth of her head pressing against his shoulder had disturbed him all the way and made him think. This complex woman was sneaking into a place he'd long ago closed for business. Wasn't one broken heart enough for anyone's lifetime?

Gina had deserved better than him in a myriad of ways. She should have married Phil Donaldson instead with his steady nine to five accounting job. Phil wouldn't have forgotten his wedding anniversary because he was consumed with nailing a suspected murderer or neglected to call his lovely wife when he couldn't make it home for dinner for the third night in a row. One evening, Tom remembered dumping his frustration all over her when she expected him to admire the new kitchen curtains she'd made after he'd spent his day working a particularly nasty child abuse case and couldn't erase the images from his mind. Life in the law enforcement community wasn't for everyone and it wasn't Gina's fault she had expected more from him than Tom was able to give. He stopped the truck outside Fee's cabin and rested his hands on the steering wheel.

'Are we here already?' She blinked and opened her eyes. 'Have I been asleep?'

'Yeah, you could say that,' he agreed. 'If you don't mind I'll leave you here for now and catch up on some work.'

'Oh, right. I'd hoped we might talk?'

'Can I take a rain-check?' His reaction appeared to confuse her and Tom came close to admitting the truth.

'Of course. Don't worry I've plenty to occupy my thoughts for the rest of the day.' She agreed with a smile although he sensed a deeper meaning behind her words. Fee retrieved her bag and denim jacket from the floorboard under her feet. 'Thanks for an interesting day out.' She opened the door and jumped out before he could remember his manners. Tom watched her fumble with the door key before disappearing inside her cabin out of sight.

He fired up the engine again, turned the truck around and drove down to his own cabin. Fee had come close to begging for his help and he'd blown her off because he was scared of risking everything all over again. *Good one*. Without letting himself think any more, he hurried inside and headed for the office. Maybe later he could ... *Don't go there, idiot. Stay away.*

The next time he glanced at the clock he'd got through the best part of two hours' work with only sore shoulders and a growing headache to show for his trouble. Tom logged off his computer and closed down for the night. He grabbed a can of beer from the fridge and tugged on his faded dark green sweatshirt before heading out on to the porch. Lights were on in all the occupied cabins meaning his little community were settled in for the night. The Burtons had probably eaten an early supper and were now sitting together in front of a log fire. No doubt the Waters clan were doing an educational family activity but they weren't bugging him so it was all good.

And Fee? For a second he could've sworn he smelt lemons in the air. Tom decided she'd made him more than a little crazy.

'Are you drinking alone?' Fee spoke from the bottom of the steps and he stumbled to his feet.

'Where did you spring from?' Through the shadows he made out the slight curve of her smile.

'I came to give you another chance.'

The woman must be mad. He'd rejected her earlier so what made her so sure he wouldn't do it again? Was she simply braver than he was? Fee joined him on the porch and wound her arms around his neck before kissing him softly on the mouth.

'Do I get any say in this?' he murmured. 'You're making a big mistake, sweetheart. I've nothing to offer you.'

'All I'm offering is me, now, tonight.'

Tom stroked his thumbs over her cheeks and trailed his hands down to rest on her backside.

'Is that a yes?' she whispered and a heart-stopping smile crept across her beautiful face.

'What do you think?' Fee was probably used to men who communicated for a living but Tom hoped his straightforward desire for her would be enough. 'Shall we go inside?'

Without any hesitation she nodded and Tom swept her into

his arms and carried her into his cabin hoping against hope neither of them would regret this in the morning.

Later he'd go over this in his head minute by minute but right now Tom refused to think too much. Instead he fixed his gaze on Fee's beguiling smile.

'It's been a long time for me,' he explained. 'A very long time.'

'I can't say the same. Does it matter?'

He shook his head and cupped her face in his large hands so he could kiss her properly. Taking his time, Tom was hyper-aware of everything from Fee's short, rapid breaths to the soft scent rising from her warm body and his own pounding heartbeat. He slipped his right hand down to the hem of her sweater and teased his fingers underneath, making her gasp as he stroked her bare, smooth skin.

Tom made himself ask her again before he went any further. He focused on her sparkling blue eyes, flared wide with desire for him and prayed she wouldn't change her mind. 'Are you still sure?'

A smile tugged at her wide mouth. 'Yes, Tom. I'm absolutely sure. I could send you a written invitation if you prefer?'

'Send it Next Minute Delivery, or it'll be way too late,' he joked.

Fee rubbed her fingers over the end-of-day stubble roughening his face and shivers of pleasure raced through him.

Without another word he began to undress her and made short work of getting rid of her shoes, jeans and sweater. Tom stopped for a moment and feasted his eyes on her simple nude coloured bra and panties before removing them too, pushing her hands away when she attempted to cover herself. 'You're beautiful.'

'I wish I had more curves. I know men like ...'

'Don't assume. We all have our preferences the same as you do.' Tom trailed his hands in a lingering sweep down over her lean, strong body until she shuddered. 'And right now my preference is for you.' He let go of her and stripped off, tossing his clothes to the floor.

Fee pressed her hand over his racing heart and a wicked smile crept over her face. 'That's perfect because mine is very definitely for you.'

He walked over to the bed and pulled back the covers. Tom tossed her a challenging grin, patting the clean white sheets. 'Are you coming to join me?'

'Oh, yes.'

Tom grabbed her hands and pulled her down on top of him. 'Right answer, sweetheart.'

They laughed together and the touch of fun did the trick, freeing him to go ahead and love her exactly as she'd asked him to.

Chapter Seventeen

Tom surfaced from sleep enough to zero in on the fact his limbs were entwined with Fee's in a wonderful tangle. He snuggled closer and pushed her short, silky hair out of the way to kiss the back of her neck and she wriggled back against him with a happy sigh.

Loud knocking sounds penetrated his half-comatose state and he realised they were coming from his front door. He reluctantly shifted to glance at the bedside clock. 'Seven o'clock. Who the hell's botherin' us at this ungodly hour?'

'I suppose you'd better go and see.' She sighed. 'One of your other guests might need you more than I do.' Fee pulled the covers up around her shoulders and smiled. 'You'd better put on some clothes first.'

'Open up, Tom you lazy devil.'

'Wonderful,' he groaned. 'It's Sandy, my oldest brother. You met him the other day when he was out for a run around the lake. You might want to stay in here unless you want all of Pine Ridge to know how we spent the night.' Tom leapt out of bed and scrabbled around on the floor for his clothes. 'Comin' bro, hold on,' he yelled out. Tom dragged on his jeans and sweatshirt. 'If I don't hurry he'll pick the lock.' Fee raised her dark, straight eyebrows at him. 'Remember he's a cop.' He hurried from the bedroom and slammed the door shut behind him.

Fee had a multitude of faults but being a coward wasn't one of them. She was a free agent and so was Tom which meant they had nothing to hide. Taking a shower would only be a delaying tactic so she skipped the idea and got dressed. Fee glanced in the mirror and cringed at the sight of the pink blotches left on her face and neck by Tom's rough stubble.

She crept out into the narrow hall and listened for a few moments. The two men were talking and by their deep, gruff tones she guessed all wasn't well. Fee took a few steadying breaths and plastered on a bright smile. Tom glanced around as she approached and his face was dark with anger. She hoped he wasn't mad with her but took a chance and walked over to stand by him. Fee linked her arm through his and was relieved when he didn't push her away.

'Fee, you remember Sandy.'

His attempt to smile didn't reach his serious eyes. He gave her a silent nod and crushed her fingers in a rock-hard handshake.

'Would you prefer it if I left?' She directed her question at Tom and was pleased when he shook his head.

'Let's all sit down.' Tom led her towards the sofa.

'Are you sure?' Sandy asked, fixing his hard stare on Tom. *Private matter. She's not family*. It didn't take a genius to work out his thoughts.

'Yeah. Fee knows about Gina. I'm good with sharing,' he declared.

Sandy shrugged and turned to face her. 'I don't know how much Tom's told you but Gina's murderer, Gary Higgins, was paroled the other day.' Tom's stony face told Fee he'd plunged back into his deepest, darkest place. 'Our father found out this morning that Higgins skipped out on his last meeting with his parole officer and no one knows where he is.'

'Could he be headed here?' Fee asked.

'Possibly,' Sandy admitted. 'I wanted to warn Tom because we don't want him doin' anything stupid.'

Tom snorted. 'You mean like paying him back for killin' my wife?'

'Yeah, exactly, you dumbass. Do you want to break Mama's heart all over again?' Sandy's brusque reply helped Fee to readjust her impression of him. They were a tight family and she was the outsider.

'Nope,' Tom said with a heavy sigh. 'I'm not a moron.'

Fee caught the first hint of a smile in the depths of Sandy's standard-issue Chambers family chocolate-brown eyes. 'Do you have a recent photo?' she asked. 'I'd feel safer knowing what this man looks like.'

He reached into his jacket pocket to pull one out and passed it over. 'He's a dangerous bastard.'

'One assumes a murderer would be.' Her dry comment made both men smile. Fee studied Higgins' pale, angular features and took note of his bright green eyes and distinctive shoulder-length white-blond hair.

'I don't see any need to show that around to the other guests,' Tom declared. 'They'll think they're staying in a hotbed of dangerous criminals instead of a peaceful retreat.'

'Peaceful? I've decided that's rather a misnomer,' she teased.

Sandy glanced between the two of them. 'I'd better be getting off. Some of us have work to go to.' He lumbered to his feet and headed towards the door.

'Stay safe, big brother,' Tom said and the serious edge to his voice clutched at Fee's heart. She couldn't imagine how hard it was for their mother every single day. At one time her husband and all three sons were in the police force. When she sent them off to work Sarah Chambers must always wonder if they'd come home safe.

'Will do. Promise you'll call me or Pop if you see Higgins?'

'Yeah,' Tom murmured. Fee knew he wouldn't break his word. The core of decency and honesty running through him was the main reason she'd been drawn to him in the first place although she couldn't have articulated it then.

'Good to meet you again, ma'am.' Sandy nodded and opened the door. Fee stayed behind as Tom followed his brother outside. She heard more conversation going on before car tyres crunched on the rough gravel.

'Now we're well and truly up how about I fix us some breakfast?' Tom's cheery smile didn't fool her for a minute. She considered forcing him to tell her what had been said but kissed him instead. Later would be soon enough to find out what he was holding back.

* * *

Tom would be buying Sandy's beers for a damn long time but it'd be worth it. Out of Fee's hearing he'd asked his brother not to gossip about them, hopefully buying them some time. Fee showed more guts than him this morning and Sandy's parting comment was that Tom had found him a good one and he better not screw up. The casual observation stopped him short and made Tom wonder what Fee might expect of him now. After breakfast he'd made the excuse of needing to finish painting the canoe shed but Fee only gave him a sweet smile and invited him to join her for dinner later. Tom came within a hair's breadth of offering to go with her when she mentioned her plan to drive into Knoxville and buy a new camera but managed to resist.

He took advantage of the pale sunshine and worked through lunch to get the last coat of white paint on the shed door. A sudden movement in the trees caught his eye and Tom glimpsed a large, dark shape moving through the shadows. Pretty sure it wasn't an animal he laid down his brush on top of the open paint tin. He inched along the path before veering off through the long grass moving in the quiet deliberate way his father taught him when they first went hunting. An empty cigarette packet lay in the grass and he bent down to pick it up. Officially, smoking wasn't allowed in the resort but he had to trust his guests to comply. Walking further along he spotted a crumpled crisp bag and an empty soup tin before a glint of metal caught his eye. Tom frowned as he retrieved his aluminium water bottle from the dense grass He pushed away the niggling idea of any connection between this and the two escapees, reassured by his father's update last night on another unconfirmed sighting of the pair in Jacksonville. He kicked at a large stone and exposed a small ring of blackened ground, the remnants of a recent fire. Kids with nothing better to do messing around that was all.

'Long time no see, Mr Chambers.'

Damn. 'Hello, Pete.' Life in prison hadn't filled out the young man's scrawny body but his deep-set eyes were dark with weariness. 'I thought you'd have headed for sunnier parts by now.'

'Who've we got here then, boy?' A deep, gravelly voice boomed out and a man with a massive build stepped out from the trees.

Randy Watling. 35 years old. Heavyset. Light brown hair. Blue eyes. A rattlesnake tattoo on his right arm and a jagged scar on his left cheek.

'Tom Chambers. He owns this place.' Kemp's voice wobbled. 'He's an ex-cop. His daddy's the local sheriff.'

'You dickhead.' Watling snarled. 'You didn't fuckin' tell me that when you brought us here.'

'But your pal from Florida wasn't around to pick us up and we didn't have no money. We couldn't pester my folks because the cops would be checkin' up on them so I thought—'

'Thought? You haven't got a damn brain to think with, you moron. I should've known better than to trust some dumb yokel.'

'What're you goin' to do, Randy?' Kemp asked and Tom was pretty sure he wouldn't care for the answer.

Watling swung his right hand out from behind his back and waved a gleaming knife in the air with a harsh laugh. 'I'm thinkin' I might cut up his pretty face.'

'That wouldn't be a smart move,' Tom ventured.

'How'd you work that one out, smartass?'

He forced his legs to relax because if he decided to make a run for it he needed them to function. 'It won't be hard for the authorities to put things together.'

'Oh yeah, and what fuckin' difference is it going to make to me?' Watling jeered. 'I'm headed for Death Row anyway. I might as well go down for you too. One more don't matter.'

Tom swallowed hard as the cold logic settled in the air between them.

'I'm not gettin' involved in no murder.' Kemp turned chalk white. 'That wasn't our deal. I said I'd get us to the meetin' point and you'd give me a ride to Florida then we'd split up.'

Watling swung his other arm in a wide arc and swatted Pete to his knees. The young man flung out his hand in an effort to stop himself falling but his wrist hit the ground and buckled. The loud crack of bone breaking ricocheted around them along with Pete's agonised screams. Instinctively, Tom moved to help the boy.

'Leave him,' Watling yelled. He gave his accomplice's arm a swift kick, setting off another round of pitiful cries. 'Shut up or I'll slice you.'

On his own he could outrun Watling but Tom's conscience wouldn't let him abandon Pete. The boy might be dumb but didn't deserve to be murdered in cold blood. He forced himself to ignore Pete's whimpers and faced the other man. 'I'll do you a deal.'

'*You'll* give *me* a deal?'

'You escape from here on your own and I'll take care of Pete,' Tom offered. 'Why did you bother with this useless kid in the first place?'

'He knows the area.'

Tom snorted. 'Have you any idea how many times this dipshit got caught doing stuff around here growing up? He's a goddamn liability. Got the brains of a peanut.'

'You'll set the cops on me.' Watling's eyes turned to ice.

'There's no cell phone coverage here. I'd have to drive into Pine Ridge and that'll give you a forty-five minute head start before anyone can get back here.' Out of the corner of his eye Tom saw Pete move. The kid grabbed his partner's ankle with his good arm and Watling stumbled, lashing out with the knife and barely missing Pete's neck. Tom hurled himself forward but the man suddenly crumpled to his knees with a loud yell.

'Don't move,' Fee hissed. With one knee pressed into Watling's back she reached her right hand around his neck to rest a curved knife against the man's throat.

Tom stared at her in shock. 'What the hell do you think you're doing?'

Chapter Eighteen

'I don't like sandwich thieves,' Fee declared and Tom's raised eyebrows said she was one crazy woman.

'Where the devil did you spring from?' He crouched down to check on the younger man who was clutching his injured hand and throwing wild-eyed stares at them both.

'Do you mind if we discuss this later?' Fee asked. The man wedged underneath her foot wriggled and she pressed her knee harder into his back. She exerted enough force on the knife to scratch the surface of his skin. 'Don't mess with me. I've sliced a man to pieces with this before today.' He didn't need to know she'd never even used it to peel an apple. The sight of a thin line of blood trickling down his neck made her stomach churn. 'Can you please find something to tie this idiot up with?'

'Will you be okay if I go back down to the canoe shed for some rope?'

Hopefully the disparaging glance she tossed his way made her answer clear.

'Right. I won't be long.' He smiled for the first time since she'd turned all Warrior Princess on him. 'You're quite a woman,' Tom said with a shake of his head before he hurried away.

Fee inwardly sagged with relief when Tom reappeared with an armful of stout ropes. He made a swift job of tying the struggling man's arms and legs together before wrapping another rope around a nearby tree and linking the two. After a few fruitless attempts to stand Watling admitted defeat and slumped to the ground. Tom took a roll of bandages from a first aid kit and began to tend to Pete Kemp's wrist. A sudden wave of nausea swept through Fee as she realised she'd come close to losing him.

'You'll be okay. I'll take care of you later.' Tom's voice thickened with emotion.

'I know,' Fee whispered.

'You'll have to walk, Pete.' He helped the boy up. 'Fee, my truck's down by the canoe shed so I'll take Pete with me and we'll drive back to my cabin. Once I get on the radio, Pop will send backup. This one won't give you any trouble. Between my Boy Scout knots and your ... knife skills he's not goin' anywhere.' Watling threw them both a filthy look.

The next hour disappeared in a fog as Tom's father and several local deputies arrived ready to take away the two prisoners. Hank collected the basic details of what had gone on and told Tom to bring Fee down to his office in the morning for them to make an official statement. The instant they were alone Fee wrapped her arms around Tom and clung on tight.

'It's alright, honey.' He eased her down to sit with him on the porch and tucked her into his lap. Tom's gentleness freed her tears and Fee sobbed into his warm, solid chest. 'So, woman, have you got dinner fixed yet? It's seven o'clock and I'm starving.'

Fee lifted her head and met his beautiful, laughing eyes. She leaned in and kissed him.

'That'll do for an appetiser,' Tom joked. 'I guess we'd better go inside and I'll get us fed.'

Tom stirred the soup pot as if his life depended on it, knowing it'd be a damn sight easier talking to Fee if he didn't look directly at her.

'Do you want me to start?'

Her straight-to-the-point question cut through his indecision and he glanced back over his shoulder. 'I'm being a wimp, aren't I?'

'No. You're a normal man. Most males would rather be forced into a silk dress and high heels than talk about their feelings.' Tom hated being lumped in with the rest of the male sex but she was completely justified. 'Why don't you dish up our soup before you stir it to death?' Fee suggested. 'I'm starving.'

'Get two spoons out of the drawer and let's eat.' Tom gestured towards the nearby cupboard. He carefully shared out the soup between a couple of pretty blue and white pottery bowls. 'How about some bread or crackers?'

'No, thanks, but don't let me stop you.'

'You won't,' he joked. Tom carried the brimming bowls over to the table. 'There you go. Home-made chicken noodle soup. The cure for every known ill.'

'Home-made? Another of your many talents?'

'I can't lie, honey, it's my mother's specialty. She doles out gallons for us all to keep in our freezers for sickness and emergencies. I reckoned today counted.'

'Can't imagine why.'

'Me neither. Pretty run of the mill I'd say.' Tom broke off a hunk of crusty bread and slathered it with butter. 'I assume you make a habit of threatening convicted murderers with lethal knives?'

'Certainly not,' Fee insisted. 'It was the first time ... and the last, I hope.'

'You scared Watling shitless.'

She laid down her spoon. 'And you?'

'I was terrified he'd turn on you and I wouldn't be able to ...' Tom's voice cracked. 'You about killed me,' he whispered. 'I failed to protect Gina and I was damn sure I'd screwed up again today.'

'Oh, Tom.' Fee sighed and leaned closer to rest her head on his shoulder.

'Remember, I didn't know you were Superwoman reincarnated.' He struggled to crack a joke.

She must put this to rest before he tore himself to pieces. 'I took an extensive self-defence course before I went to Afghanistan the first time. I'm an expert marksman and my defensive driving skills are up there with James Bond.' A little exaggeration wouldn't hurt. He needed to know she could take care of herself. 'Another time no fretting.'

'Another time? You promised ...'

She stopped him with another kiss. 'I'm joking, okay?'

'Sorry if I don't have much of a sense of humour when people I love are in danger,' Tom muttered. 'Aw hell, probably shouldn't have said that, should I?'

'Did you mean it?' Fee could have kicked herself for asking. 'I mean, um ...'

'Hey, don't panic.' A quiet smile crept across his face. 'There are many kinds of love. I'm thinkin' we got one figured out last night. Maybe we'll be lucky enough to find a different kind one day.' Tom cradled her hands. 'Are you willing to give it a chance?'

Was she?

'Think about it,' he said. 'I'm not sure how I'm doin' with the idea either if that's any consolation?'

'It helps.'

'Fair enough. Now, eat your soup before you fade away,' he insisted.

'You like bossing people around, don't you?'

'And you enjoy arguing.'

'I'll eat if it'll shut you up.' Fee picked up her spoon again and shovelled a big spoonful into her mouth. 'That's wonderful.'

'Yep, my mama sure knows how to cook.' Tom chuckled. 'I expect she could even teach you.'

Fee pinched his arm. 'Don't push your luck.'

'This'll make you smile. Poor Mary-Jo is tearing her hair out because she sewed an awesome butterfly costume for Lulu but the little minx has changed her mind. Two days until Halloween and she's insisting on being Little Red Riding Hood instead.'

'And being a good mother she'll make it happen.' Fee hoped

she didn't sound bitter. Every time she thought she'd made it past her resentment over her mother's indifference she was pulled up short.

'Yep I expect so. Anyway how did you get on in Knoxville?'

Fee happily launched into every detail of the new camera she'd been tempted to buy.

'I hung around Market Square for a while to try it out and got some great shots of the older buildings. I stopped and listened to a fiddle player and he let me take his picture. His whole life was written in his face and that set me off thinking about a new project.' A level of enthusiasm she hadn't experienced in a very long time took hold of Fee and she tripped over her words. 'I took a few candid shots in the cafe the other day. Everything about your Aunt Ina's outward appearance says what a capable, strong woman she is and yet she had tears in her eyes because Lulu wrote her own name for the first time.'

'Some of the best work I've seen of yours is close-ups of people.' Tom's quiet praise touched her.

'The problem is how to find a new angle – pun intended.' She chuckled. 'Seeing a community or a country through people's faces isn't a unique idea. I'll have to give it some thought.' Fee picked up her bowl. 'Let's get all this cleared up.'

'How about you take a long, hot bath while I do the dishes? Isn't it what all women crave after a tough day?'

She struggled not to laugh at his desperate efforts to please her. 'I'm not *all women,* Tom. I hate baths. I'm a brisk shower sort of girl which comes from the distinct lack of hot water in most of the places I've lived. I never wear make-up, have manicures or fuss over what to wear. I'd break my neck if I tried to walk in high heels and if you're looking for a girly sort of woman I'm not your type.'

His intense, sweeping gaze heated every inch of her skin. 'I'm a plain man, Fee Winter. I've never been one for fuss of any sort.'

'What about Gina? I get the impression she was ...' Her

voice trailed away and she wished she'd never mentioned the other woman's name.

He stroked her cheek and rested his fingers on her lips. 'You're two very different women that's for sure. But I'm not the same man either, Fee.'

'Fair enough.' She'd leave it there for now. One day she suspected she'd want to know more, but not today. 'Do you know what I think?' Fee kissed him and sighed with pleasure as he pulled her to him. 'The dishes can wait.'

The instant flare of desire in Tom's eyes told her all she needed to know. With a huge contented smile she led him back to the bedroom.

This was all he needed from life. Tom drank in the sight of Fee, in sleep as warm and soft as she was cool and controlled when awake. Before drifting off in his arms she'd admitted that before coming to Black Cherry she relied on sleeping tablets to get through the night but didn't need them any more. He'd agreed with her theory about the improvement being caused by the fresh, clean air and relaxed lifestyle here while silently hoping he had more than a little to do with her recovery.

An unwanted memory of yesterday's horror slammed through him and Tom struggled to keep breathing. He could have so easily lost her. From experience he knew it didn't take long.

'I'm fine,' Fee whispered. 'You're worrying again, aren't you?'

Maybe one day he'd be able to put into words the awful sense of helplessness he'd experienced when he lost Gina. He'd never wanted to feel that way again but came close to it yesterday.

'Sorry,' Tom apologised. He tucked the duvet in around them and rested his head next to hers on the pillow.

'What time are we supposed to meet your father?'

He glanced over at the clock and groaned. 'He said around

ten and it's nine-thirty already. I'll give him a heads-up on the radio to let him know we'll be late.'

'I'd better go back to my cabin to shower and change. I'll be as fast as I can.' Fee got up and pulled on her abandoned clothes.

'We'll grab something to eat at the cafe on our way. Pop won't mind.'

'See you soon.' She laughed and ran off out of the bedroom.

For a few seconds he didn't move. He'd always been a man to plan things out but since the day Fee breezed into his life she'd turned everything upside down. Not having a clue where they were headed disturbed him. Her contrasting philosophy, honed by an unsettled childhood and years of having to be adaptable in her job, was to take things as they came. Tom sighed and hoped he could work out a way to keep Fee around for a very long time. *Like forever*. How she'd take that idea he didn't know but he guessed he'd find out.

Chapter Nineteen

Fee exhaled a long, deep breath as they emerged from the sheriff's office. He'd asked them every possible question, filled in enough paperwork to destroy a forest of trees and warned them they'd be needed as witnesses when Kemp and Watling were brought to court.

'Your father doesn't stand any nonsense,' she observed with a wry smile.

'Never has done. Imagine being one of his children.'

Tom's laconic comment made her smile but underneath she was envious. She couldn't imagine how different her life might have turned out if she'd had a real father instead of whatever figment of imagination her mother dreamed up that particular week. *Or if she'd accepted Allain Dupre's proposal?*

'You've no idea how lucky you are,' she blurted out. Tom stopped walking and turned to face her.

'Oh, trust me, I know,' he murmured and cradled her face with his large hands, leaning in to rest his forehead against hers. 'I might not be alive today if it wasn't for Pop.'

This was hardly the place for serious conversation but if Tom was willing to open up she would seize the moment. 'What do you mean?'

He pulled away and shifted from one foot to the other, kicking at a stray stone with the toe of his boot. 'After Gina died I fell apart.' Tom held up two fingers an inch away from each other. 'Came this close to ending it all. I couldn't see the point in anything.'

Fee couldn't wrap her head around the idea of this strong man considering such a terrible solution to his problems.

'It's the truth.'

'I never said it wasn't,' she protested.

'Pop knew the memories around here wouldn't leave

me alone so he got me a job with a security firm in Iraq. I managed to hack it for a couple of years and by the time I came back ...' He hesitated and Fee wished she could make this easier on him. 'He knew I couldn't be a cop anymore and gave me the idea of renovating the derelict cabins on our old family land. They'd fallen into disrepair and we only ever went there to fish in the lake and have the occasional picnic.'

'He's a smart man.'

'Yeah. I wish I could be half as shrewd.'

You are. Fee held the thought in her head. 'How about we get some breakfast? Or is it lunchtime by now?' They'd wanted to get the interview over with so hadn't bothered to eat when they arrived.

'Who cares? Aunt Ina will feed us anyway.' Tom laughed. 'Have you thought anymore about contacting *your* father?'

The sudden question took her by surprise and for a moment Fee held back. She'd never discussed her absent father with anyone before.

'Plenty.'

Tom slipped his arms around her waist and pulled her to him. Glancing over his shoulder she saw Mary-Jo staring at them from across the street with her mouth gaped open in shock. 'Oops, we've been outed.'

'What're you talkin' about?'

'Don't look now but your dear cousin is watching us with her eyes out on stalks. Any second now she'll go into the cafe and tell your Aunt Ina and anyone else who's in earshot. I'm guessing your mother will get a phone call in the next five minutes.'

A slow, sexy grin spread across Tom's face. He lowered his mouth to hers and drew them into a long, knee-buckling kiss and when he pulled away his smile held a distinct tinge of satisfaction. 'Might as well give her something exciting to report.'

Fee tried to pull away but he clutched her tighter.

'Do you honestly care?'

Put on the spot she refused to lie. That was no basis for any honest relationship. 'No, I don't.'

'Good, neither do I. We're both over the age of consent unless you've been lying to me.'

Tom's cheeky comment gave her the nerve to kiss him back. 'There. That should establish the fact it's mutual.' She smoothed back a rogue strand of auburn hair from his forehead. 'I do believe we're both in need of food. Let's eat.'

'You didn't answer my question about your father.'

'Later. When we're on our own.' Tom never let her get away with anything. 'I wish I could put off deciding forever.' Fee gave in to a heavy sigh.

'Always better to face things head on.'

'Rather like your cousin?'

'Exactly.' Tom popped another kiss on her mouth. 'Come on, into the frying pan.' Taking Fee's hand he steered them across the street.

'This is so not funny,' Mary-Jo protested as they reached her. 'Why am I the last to know you two have something going on?'

'Hold your horses, kid, you're not,' Tom insisted. 'You're almost the first.'

'I thought you were my friend?' She turned on Fee who didn't know what to say.

'Don't pick on her.'

Mary-Jo burst out laughing. 'Oh, boy, you've got it bad. Sticking up for her already. How far have the mighty fallen.'

'Is it alright if we go and get somethin' to eat?' he asked sarcastically.

'Sure. On one condition.' Mary-Jo folded her arms and glared.

'Go on.'

'I intend on joining you so you can tell me all about this secret romance. Plus I want every detail of Fee's awesome warrior princess act. The whole town's talkin' about it.'

Fee's cheeks flamed. She hadn't bargained on that story getting out which was beyond stupid in this small, close-knit community.

'Okay, I guess,' Tom mumbled.

At least retreating inside would get them away from the other people standing around the street and watching them with unashamed curiosity. Tom yanked on Fee's hand and pushed past Mary-Jo to drag them both inside the cafe.

The second his foot crossed the threshold every pair of eyes in the place turned to stare at them.

'If it isn't my renegade son. This must be the lady I've been hearing so much about. Come and join me, both of you.'

His mother's blunt command silenced the buzz of conversation going on around them and Tom squeezed Fee's hand in an effort to reassure her.

'Mama, what a surprise to see you here.' He steered Fee in front of him towards his mother's favourite table over by the counter.

'Why? You know your Aunt Ina and I have coffee together most mornings.'

He wasn't about to admit his brain was too mixed up to know what time it was or even the day of the week. Mentally crossing his fingers he introduced the two women and caught a glimpse of the swift appraisal taking place on both sides. He and Gina grew up together so there were never any awkward "this is my girlfriend" moments to get through. *Girlfriend? Could a man have a girlfriend when he was almost forty-one?*

No sooner than they'd sat down, Aunt Ina emerged from the kitchen brandishing two cups of coffee. She set them on the table in front of Tom and Fee before pulling out a chair to join them. Mary-Jo dragged over another chair from the next table as well. At this rate he might as well make a public announcement.

Within twenty minutes Fee and his mother were chatting

and laughing like old friends but instead of being grateful, Tom had the distinct sensation of being ganged up on.

'Right, that's settled,' his mother declared. 'You're bringing Fee over to the house for supper tonight. Six o'clock. I'll call your brothers and see if I can round them up too.'

Tom opened his mouth to protest but Fee stamped on his foot under the table. 'Yes, Mama.'

'That's very sweet of you, Mrs Chambers,' Fee added with a smile.

'Oh, call me Sarah, honey. We don't stand on ceremony around here.' His mother patted Fee's hand.

'We'd be delighted to come, wouldn't we, Tom?' The mischievous glint in her eyes made him choke on his coffee.

'Of course.'

'I hope you'll excuse us but we need to head back to Black Cherry.' Fee pushed her chair back. 'Tom has work to do, don't you?' She tossed him a lifeline and he grabbed it with both hands.

'Yeah, a ton.'

'I'm sure you do.' His mother's dry response made him wince and before they could get into any more trouble Tom leaned across the table to kiss his mother and grabbed Fee's hand. Without another word he whisked her out of the cafe as fast as he could without engendering more pointed remarks from his nosy family.

'In a hurry, are we?' she joked. 'The day's not quite turning out as we expected, is it?'

'Understatement of the year, sweetheart.' Tom tossed his arm around her shoulder because there wasn't much point in pretending they were *just friends* now. 'I'm sorry you didn't get fed.'

'I'm sure you'll remedy that, Mr Gourmet Chef.'

Tom spotted his cousin, Suzy, striding towards them, her cheeks turning pinker in her obvious effort to hurry and not miss anything. The town grapevine had done its work. 'In the truck, now.' He hurried Fee across the street and had the engine running by the time she fastened her seat belt.

'Are we in a race?'

'Cousin alert.' He pointed down the street and waved at Suzy while he put the truck in gear. 'That's enough for one morning. I'm sure she'll find out every detail in about two minutes.' Tom pressed the accelerator to the floor and they shot off down the road. Hopefully his father wasn't around or he'd get a lecture on his driving later on top of everything else. He glanced at Fee and noticed the air of conspiracy lurking in her warm smile. The idea of having this woman on his side felt strange but good.

Chapter Twenty

'If you've got anything more urgent to do we can ...' Fee's voice trailed away as Tom shook his head.

'Nope. There's nothing can't wait around here. Thank goodness the Waters' family wrapped up their week here a couple of days ago and with them gone you're my only guest now and no one else is due until next weekend. Tell me more about your Mom.' Tom stretched out on the sofa and pulled her down between his legs to let her head rest back against his chest.

'My mother's a nomad. She gets itchy feet. She never stays in one place very long and growing up we moved so many times I lost count. It bewilders me how I got any kind of education because I never spent a whole year in one school. Maddy's a great one for causes and she's always protesting about something. Climate change, legalising marijuana, the plight of the polar bears, GM foods. Her latest interest was always more important than me.'

'I'm sorry. All kids need stability and the security of knowing they matter more than anything else. It doesn't have to be the same house or the same meal every Tuesday, but there's got to be an underlying knowledge of safety. You never had that, did you?'

She shook her head, struggling to swallow the tears filling her throat.

'You're one strong woman to have survived in one piece.'

Fee was used to getting praise for her work, but Tom's simple statement of pride touched her heart. 'I left home when I was sixteen and worked three or four jobs to put myself through a photography course. I could count on one hand the number of times I've spoken to my Mum since then. I know you can't imagine that.'

Tom's warm laughter rumbled through her back. 'Yeah, it's pretty difficult. My mama couldn't last ten days. When I was overseas she kept the US Postal Service in business and I'm taking a wild guess that I got more care packages than the whole damn Army put together. Everybody fought me for her homemade chocolate chip cookies.' He kissed the top of Fee's head. 'And yes, I know I'm lucky. I'm thankful for them every day even when they drive me half mad.'

For a second she couldn't speak. His mind reading was spot on which should have been scary but somehow was the opposite. Fee began to explain about her father including the fact his name and nationality changed at regular intervals until she'd given up knowing what to believe. 'Can you understand now why I'm reluctant to follow up on this man she swears is my actual father?'

'I sure can.'

'Come on. Spit it out.'

'Your mother didn't have to get in touch. Twice. Strikes me this means a lot to her. What've you got to lose?' He stroked his hand along her arm.

Fee twisted around to face him. 'Nothing much, I suppose.'

'Do you want my company or would you prefer to go into town alone to contact Dupre?'

Tom's openness gave her the freedom to admit she'd prefer to have him along. 'Maybe I'll phone him to get it over with.'

'I see where you're comin' from, honey.' A slight frown creased his brow.

'But?'

'An email will give him a chance to consider his reply. It gives you thinkin' time too.'

'I hate you being right,' she complained.

'Yeah, I know, women always do. If you want to avoid another run in with the Pine Ridge Mafia I suggest we go over to Norris instead. Nobody will hassle us there. It's only a thirty minute drive and we'll easily be back for interrogation time with my beloved family.'

'I suppose that'll work.' She managed a weak smile.

* * *

Tom turned the radio on low and hummed along with one of his favourite country songs as he negotiated the curvy mountain roads. Tension emanated from Fee in silent, rolling waves and her slim, pale hands clutched her phone as though it might run away. They pulled into Norris and he spied a parking space free outside the library.

'There's Wi-Fi in there or in a couple of the cafes. Your choice.'

The fine lines around Fee's eyes deepened. 'A cafe I think. That way we can get a drink and sit around a while in case ...'

'He replies? Good idea.' He took a guess at finishing her sentence and was rewarded with a grateful smile. Tom ran around the truck to open her door but Fee didn't attempt to move. He waved his hand in front of her face. 'You ready?'

'No, but I'm coming anyway.'

'Good.'

Fee stepped out and stopped for a second to glance around them. 'This is a pretty town. It's almost got an English look about it.'

'Yeah, it should do. I've read up on it some and they modelled Norris on the English garden towns Sir Ebenezer Howard tried to make popular at the end of the nineteenth century. You can pick them out by the common ground in the centre and the protected greenbelt running around the outside. The Tennessee Valley authority built this original part of the town to house the Norris Dam workers and they were some of the first all electric homes in the state. It's a recognised Historic District now.'

Fee stared hard at him. 'You're a surprising man, Tom Chambers. I never know what you're going to come out with next.'

He suspected continuing to be unpredictable in certain areas was good. 'You might like to come back and take photos sometime.'

'That'd be good.' She agreed but the light faded from her eyes. 'Pick a cafe and let's get this done.'

Tom ran through the alternatives in his head and dismissed a couple of the more popular places. 'Let's try the Magnolia

Tree. It's tucked away behind the Baptist Church and been here forever. They've got decent coffee and it's more popular with locals than visitors so they won't fuss if we sit a while.' For a brief moment he wished they could simply relax and enjoy themselves in the pale sunshine. 'Come on.' He held her hand as they walked along in silence.

He peered into the cafe and was relieved to see it was almost empty. Tom opened the door and rested his other hand at the base of Fee's spine to encourage her to step inside. 'You pick a spot and I'll get us a drink. What'll you have?'

'Sparkling water, or lemonade, either works,' she said with a touch of impatience, plainly not caring but trying to be polite.

While he placed their order Tom caught Fee frowning at the tablet she'd carried in and nibbling her bottom lip.

'What do you think of this?' She turned the screen to face him as he sat down. 'It's bad, isn't it?'

'Hey, hold your horses I haven't read it all yet.'

'Really?'

'Yeah, really. Us Southerners do things slow, but thorough, okay?' He grinned, relieved when she relaxed enough to smile back.

'You certainly do.'

He made himself concentrate on the task at hand and suggested a few minor alterations. After Fee made the changes and sent the email Tom covered her cold hand with his own. 'Let's talk about something else now. Alright?'

Fee nodded and picked up her glass of water. He hoped he wasn't being a bully but they couldn't sit here staring at the screen and waiting. Allain Dupre might only check his email once a week or could have changed his mind about connecting with his newly discovered daughter. Tom launched into stories about his family, hoping it'd take her mind off what they'd come here for plus prepare her for being thrown into the deep end of a Chambers' family dinner.

The tablet gave a short, loud beep and Fee's hand jerked

into the air sending a cascade of water down over her fingers and onto the table.

'A new email?' She didn't speak or move. Tom passed her a handful of paper napkins and she managed to take hold of them to dab at the wet mess 'Do you want me to see who it's from?' She nodded and he leaned across to pick up the tablet. 'It's from Dupre.' Tom laid the tablet back down and fished out a clean handkerchief from his pocket to dry off her hands before setting it back in front of her.

She scanned the message at least twice before glancing back at him, her pretty eyes shimmering with tears. 'He wants to meet me. He's offered to come here or for me to visit him in New Orleans.'

'That's good, isn't it?' Tom was bewildered by her lack of enthusiasm.

'I suppose so. I hadn't actually gone any further in my mind than exchanging a few emails.'

'Wouldn't you like to see him?'

'I'm not sure. I've done without a father for nearly forty years and I'm not sure what to do with a possible one now.' Her attempt at humour fell flat. 'I should send a reply.'

'Hang on a minute, sweetheart. He doesn't know you've seen the message yet. Take some time to think.' Relief flooded her pale features and Tom mentally patted himself on the back for saying the right thing. 'Send him a reply tomorrow.'

'Do you think that'd be alright?'

'It'll be fine. If the man's got an ounce of common sense he'll be unsure too.' Tom wrapped his hands around hers. 'Why don't you close down for now and we'll go and have a wander around the town. I'll buy you a pretty little trinket then drive you back to Black Cherry. What do you say?'

Fee leaned against him. 'I'd say you're a wonderful man, Tom Chambers.'

Wonderful worked fine for him. He hadn't been any woman's "wonderful" for a very long time.

Chapter Twenty-One

Amid the cacophony of seven adults and five children competing to be heard Fee mentally retreated. This was when she needed her camera to hide behind because right now she'd rather face a hail of bullets than the loud, happy Chambers family.

'Supper's ready, come and get it.' Sarah popped her head in around the door and yelled. 'Fee, you're sitting by me. I've been too busy cooking to have my turn with you.'

Fee's pleading glance at Tom only got her an apologetic smile and a shrug.

'Mama's orders, honey. It's more than my life's worth to argue.'

'Are you a man or a mouse?' she hissed.

He shuffled from one foot to the other. 'Mouse when it comes to my mother. Sorry.'

He didn't *look* terribly sorry but she could hardly start an argument here. She'd already endured an hour of being examined by his brothers, their wives and assorted children – her only reprieve came from his father who'd been delayed at work. Fee hoped a mini crime wave swept through Pine Ridge and kept the sheriff away as long as possible.

'Fine, lead me to my execution,' she murmured.

'Don't fret. She's a sweet lady and loves you already.'

Fee didn't fall for Tom's effort at reassurance. Sarah was a shrewd lady who ruled her family with a rod of velvet-covered steel. In theory his mother might want Tom to meet another woman but Fee wasn't convinced a frayed-around-the-edges, nomadic English war photographer was what she had in mind.

The spread of food covering the massive oak dining table was enough to feed an army but she suspected there wouldn't be much left when they were all done. She'd try to make careful choices and hope no one noticed.

'Meat loaf, fried chicken, sweet potatoes, green bean casserole, fried apples, turnip greens and cornbread,' Tom recited, pointing to everything in turn with a massive grin on his face. Plainly nothing made the man happier than sitting down to a tableful of his mother's cooking. The fact she could barely manage to heat up a tin of soup was another black mark against her. 'Hey, Mama, I just realised Mee Maw's not here. Is she all right?'

'She said she was tired and goin' to have an early night. Your daddy checked on her this afternoon and found out the doctor changed her heart tablets and it's thrown her a bit that's all.'

'Everything looks wonderful, Sarah.' Fee was in awe of all the work Tom's mother had done.

'Thank you, hon it's nothing fancy but it'll fill up the boys.'

Fee glanced over at "the boys" – three hulking good-looking men who were shovelling food into their mouths as if they might not see another meal for months. With a pang she remembered multiple times in her own childhood when her stomach ached with hunger. If she asked her mother when they'd be eating Fee usually received a blank stare. Maddy would tell her to find herself something in the kitchen and not to bother her.

Under the table Tom squeezed her knee and she managed a tiny smile. He knew this was hard for her. Fee plunged right in and asked his mother a myriad of questions about what Tom was like as a boy. This served the dual purpose of finding out more about him and slowing down her own interrogation. Sarah was happy to launch into a long story about her youngest son involving a dead snake and his least favourite teacher. Suddenly she stopped and frowned at Fee's untouched plate.

'I suppose this isn't your sort of food?'

If she wanted to win over Tom's mother, and she wasn't convinced on that score yet, not appreciating her food wasn't going the right way about it. Fee recognised another plain-spoken woman when she met one and came to the instant decision not to be foolish. Without any fuss she explained about her ulcer and the restrictions it placed on her diet.

Sarah glared at Tom. 'Why didn't you tell me? I'd have been more considerate about what I fixed.'

Everyone stopped to listen and Fee wished she could slink under the table.

'It wasn't my story to share. Fee prefers to deal with it her own way.' Tom's firm tone made his mother's face colour up and for a moment the room was silent.

'You'd better have saved me some food, you scavengers.' Hank Chambers breezed in, tugged off his uniform jacket and hung it on the back of the empty chair next to his wife. 'What's up?'

'Nothing, Pop. If you're lucky you might find a chicken bone left,' Tom joked. Fee didn't miss the quick silent exchange between the two men and envied their easy communication.

'Huh. It's a bad thing when a man's got to fight his own kids for a bite to eat.' He sat down and grabbed the nearest bowl of food to start piling green beans on his plate.

The normal loud level of conversation resumed and Tom gave her a quick, sly wink.

For the first time that day Fee relaxed and wondered if she could do this after all.

Tom worked on seeing his family from Fee's point of view. He'd grown up with their brash noisiness so it all went in one ear and out the other, but she was an only child with almost no family so it must be overwhelming. She'd spent her career observing people from the outside and the sense of separateness wrapped around her had intrigued Tom from the beginning. He'd itched to find out what made her tick underneath the remote exterior and got a kick out of discovering the passionate woman she kept well hidden.

'Are you doing okay?' He kept his voice low and reached for

her wrist to play with the simple silver bracelet she'd chosen in one of the small gift shops in Norris.

'Maybe.' She glanced down at her new jewellery. 'It's pretty isn't it? I don't do pretty.'

Her wistful explanation tugged at something deep in Tom. 'I don't know why.'

Fee's eyes darkened. 'It's nothing earth-shattering.'

Getting you to open up is worse than hacking an oyster shell with a blunt knife. His mother clapped her hands and everyone paid attention.

'Kids, off you go to play. The ladies are going to sit down in the other room while the men do the dishes. I'll serve dessert afterwards. Any questions?'

We wouldn't dare. Tom noticed Fee frown. 'Don't worry. They won't bite. I'll get through as quick as I can and come join you.' She gave him the same determined stare he'd received yesterday when he implied brandishing a knife at a murderer's neck might not be smart.

'I'll be perfectly fine. Go and do your cleaning duties.'

'Yes, ma'am.' Underestimating Fee wasn't a wise move. He should have realised that by now. Tom headed for the kitchen before he could drop himself in any more trouble.

'Feisty one, isn't she?' His father chuckled and gave him a hard slap on the back. 'Good move to go for someone completely different.'

'What are you gettin' at?' Tom glanced around to make sure Fee was nowhere in sight.

'Hey, don't take me the wrong way, son. She's a good one and your mother's plainly taken to her.'

Tom struggled to keep his temper. 'I'm nearly forty-one and don't need anyone's approval for whatever private life I choose to have, or not as the case may be. Fee's only here for a few weeks. You don't seriously think she's going to give up a top-notch career to bury herself in the backwoods of Tennessee? Or that I'd ever consider marrying again?'

Hank rested a hand on Tom's shoulder. 'Hey, calm down, son. We're happy to see you smile again and if a woman did the trick then good on you. I don't know her well but Fee strikes me as quite a gal.'

She is. Tom wondered if bringing Fee here tonight might have been a big mistake on several levels. Apart from anything else it implied a level of attachment he'd no right to assume, or even want. 'Sorry, Pop.' He turned away to start loading the dishwasher. Tom was certain Mikey and Sandy, who were ferrying dirty plates in from the dining room, hadn't missed a single word. After he left, Tom would be the sole topic of conversation and he'd get interfering, brotherly phone calls tomorrow.

'Don't even think of skipping out on dessert or your mother will make you regret it.' His father used his best sheriff's voice, the one he used to keep both criminals and his own sons in line. 'Crack on and get finished up, boys, or the Dragon Queen will be on our case.'

'She certainly will.' Sarah swept into the room, her gaze quickly checking around her domain. 'I can't believe four grown men take so long clearing up a few dishes. If I find you've been drinking beer and watching football on my TV you're in trouble.' They'd clubbed together the Christmas before to buy her a small television for the kitchen so she could keep up with her favourite soaps while she cooked. 'I'm putting the coffee on and then I'll find out what everyone wants. When I come back in to fix the desserts you'd better be finished.'

Tom kept his head down and finished wiping down the countertops before turning on the dishwasher. Making his escape he joined Fee but she threw him an icy stare before turning away and carrying on her conversation with Sandy's wife. Something was bugging her but asking about it now wouldn't be smart with too many big ears listening.

After he'd put away a large slice of his mother's world-famous coconut cake plus a piece of chocolate pie Tom asked Fee if she was ready to leave.

'Yes.'

The single brief word was her only response so he gave up and made his way around the room to say goodbye to everyone. They headed back outside loaded down with Tupperware boxes full of leftovers amid promises to return for Sunday supper. In the truck Fee stared resolutely out of the window, the rigid set of her body warning him off talking to her. Tom had a sulking woman on his hands and no idea what he'd done wrong.

Chapter Twenty-Two

Fee quietly seethed. How dare his family see her as nothing more than a convenient female to bring their miserable son back to life. She'd been walking towards the bathroom when she heard her name mentioned. The old adage about listeners hearing no good of themselves was true. In Fee's mind the worst part was the fact Tom hadn't said anything to defend her.

She sensed him sneak glances at her at regular intervals but he wasn't dumb enough to start an argument on these treacherous roads.

'I don't know about you but I'm ready for an early night.' Tom's casual air riled her but she refused to let on.

'Me too. I enjoyed meeting your family but I've had enough company for one day.'

Without a word he slowed the truck down to take the last turn into Black Cherry. Fee held her tongue as he drove past his own cabin and brought the truck to an abrupt stop outside hers.

'Are you gonna tell me what's bugging you?' Tom's quiet voice didn't fool her. Fee caught the sliver of anger running through his words.

'*We're happy to see you smiling again and if a woman did the trick good on you*.' As she repeated his father's words the colour drained from Tom's face. 'I'm glad to have served a useful purpose.' The instant she spoke Fee would have bitten off her tongue if she could.

'I'm not gonna sit here and listen to you trash my family. They're good, decent people who welcomed you into their home and don't deserve your scorn. I might, but they don't. Let's go inside and sort this out once and for all,' Tom challenged.

'I honestly am tired.' Fee wasn't lying and hoped he'd at least understand that much. 'How about we leave this until the morning?'

'It's your choice. I hope *you* sleep well.' His restraint was far more intimidating than being shouted and yelled at. If she didn't get away now she'd be tempted to soften towards him.

Fee reached for the door handle and for the first time he didn't run around to open it for her. She made her way towards the cabin steps and didn't dare to turn back around as she unlocked the door. Once she stepped inside Fee allowed herself to breathe again. She couldn't allow herself to think any more tonight or she'd go crazy. Slowly she got ready for bed and crawled in between the cold sheets, shut her eyes and hoped things would look better in the morning. It couldn't be much worse.

At three in the morning her insomnia returned with a vengeance and she dragged herself out of bed to make a mug of chamomile tea while craving good, strong coffee. She snuggled into a corner of the sofa and tucked a soft, red blanket around her cold legs, struggling not to think about how she could have been cuddled up in Tom's bed instead. Everything about him was so solid and *there*. There was no pretence. No false front. *Why'd you get so mad at him then?* He'd never made any promises or asked her for any. *Did you want him to?* Ever since Pierre's betrayal she'd been scrupulous about not letting herself get away with personal dishonesty.

You don't seriously think she's going to give up a top-notch career to bury herself in small town America surely? Or that I'd ever consider marrying again?

Why did his casual dismissal rankle? The combination of her unstable childhood and the awful sights she'd seen around the world helped her decide long ago that marriage and children weren't for her so why did she care if Tom never intended to marry again?

Fee wrapped her hands around her knees and rocked back and forth as large, hot tears trickled down her face.

Tom stared at the bottle of Jack Daniels. For two pins he'd

go over to Fee's cabin and bang on her door to demand she talk to him but he'd had all the rejection he could take for one night. He spread his hands on the table in front of him but all he saw was Fee stretched out in his bed this morning. A rough curse broke from his lips and he picked up the open bottle. Not bothering with a glass he took a long, deep swallow and allowed the smoky warmth to insinuate its way down his throat. The whisky pooled in the base of his stomach and eased the anger eating away at him.

Drinking's not the answer, son.

His father spoke those words to Tom six months after Gina's death and he'd sworn to never let it become a problem again. Tom shoved back his chair and took the bottle over to the kitchen sink. With a grimace he poured the rest of the expensive liquor down the drain, trying to picture his brothers' horrified faces if they could see him now.

There was no point in going to bed so Tom headed out of the back door and across the yard to his shed. Inside he turned on the lights and stared at the half-finished dolls' house waiting for him on the workbench. Lulu would be one excited little girl on Christmas morning. He'd finished the frame, walls and floor so tonight he'd work on the doors and windows. The painstaking work would be perfect for whiling away the long hours until morning. He only had about another three weeks to get it done because Mary-Jo needed the house completed by Thanksgiving so she'd have plenty of time to add the girly touches. His cousin planned to buy most of the furniture but Tom had told her he'd have a go at a few pieces.

For the next few hours Tom cut, sawed and sanded to his heart's content before laying each section out ready to paint. A yawn sneaked out of him as the first pink slivers of daylight sneaked in and he started to put all his tools away. When everything was back in place he locked up and wandered towards the cabin.

The loud squeal of tyres on the gravel road broke through

the silence and Tom glanced over in time to see Fee's rental car disappearing out of sight. *Where the hell was she off this early?* That was a dumb question. No doubt she couldn't wait any longer to reply to her father's email and under the circumstances wasn't going to ask *him* for help again.

He rubbed at the dull headache threatening to erupt and trailed indoors, pretty sure it'd be a long day.

Forcing herself to slow down Fee made a point of paying attention to the beautiful scenery around her. Trees shaded in the last colours of autumn gleamed in the pale, early morning sunlight and the hills beyond the horizon appeared to go on forever. All too soon the leaves would flutter to the ground and winter would wind its icy tentacles around the landscape until spring came around again.

Because of her mother's itinerant lifestyle the normal markers people used to indicate the passing of another year often slipped by them. Fee had never joined in an Easter Egg hunt, dressed up for Halloween, played with sparklers or eaten hot jacket potatoes on Guy Fawkes' Night and as for Christmas with its centuries old rituals that even non-believers enjoyed? Most years the 25th of December was little different from any other day. Was she foolish to have believed – however briefly – that a man who took these things for granted could ever really settle for someone who saw them as nothing more than a cultural curiosity? Or could she let loose the part of her that longed to share those common experiences?

Right now she could just keep driving and see where the road took her, the philosophy she'd taken as her mantra the day she left home at sixteen. The few things she'd left at the cabin wouldn't be any great loss but the idea of Tom finding her abandoned clothes and smelling her scent on them made that out of the question. No matter how they'd left things last night she couldn't be so cruel.

She glanced at the map to make sure she took the right

road towards Norris. Coming back here was part of a stupid, superstitious idea she had that it might help things to go smoothly with the man who was supposedly her father. Fee parked in the empty street and stared at the small, unlit building. *Idiot.* Why hadn't it occurred to her that the cafe would be closed at six in the morning? She'd check to see what time they opened and go for a walk while she waited.

There was a refreshing chill in the air reminding her that tomorrow was the first of November and Fee reached back into the car for the well-worn blue sweatshirt she'd hauled around the globe for years, tugging it on as she walked up the narrow path to the cafe. Fee stopped to smooth her hair back into place and was surprised to realise it grazed the collar of her white shirt. Sometimes Pierre would laugh and call her his boyfriend, making fun of her refusal to wear make-up and her total disinterest in clothes. She'd laughed along with him until she'd met his glamorous Parisian wife and realised she'd only ever been a diversion from his real life.

I'm a plain man, Fee Winter. I've never been one for fuss of any sort.

Tom's words sneaked back into her brain and she wondered if she was the one complicating things. He'd been honest with her from the beginning. As soon as she got back to Black Cherry she'd talk to him. Life was too short and precious to waste in misunderstandings.

'We don't open until seven, hon.'

Fee startled as the middle-aged bleached blonde who'd served them yesterday appeared at her shoulder. 'Oh, thanks. I'll wander around town for a while.'

'Desperate for your morning coffee fix?' The woman's welcoming smile forced Fee to be honest.

'No, I never drink coffee. I'm really here to use your Wi-Fi ... although I do intend to have breakfast.' She didn't want to give the impression she was taking advantage without intending to give the cafe any business.

The woman smiled. 'Come on in. I'm Brenda by the way. You can do your emails and whatever while I get the coffee on and start cooking.' Fee was ushered inside before she could protest and settled at a prime seat by the window. 'You have a look over the menu while I get organised.'

She did as she was told and selected scrambled egg whites with turkey sausage and Earl Grey tea. Left alone while Brenda bustled around in the kitchen she fished out her tablet and logged on. With Allain Dupre's message open Fee worked on composing a reply.

The cluster of bells hanging over the door chimed and she glanced up to see Tom standing there, haggard and grey-faced.

'We're not open yet, love, but you might as well come in too.' Brenda's shrewd glance at the two of them turned into a knowing smile. 'I'm guessin' you're together?'

He raised an eyebrow in her direction.

Fee nodded and gestured to the chair next to her. She kept her face blank and unrevealing while smiling inside. He wouldn't expect her to make this easy and she had no intention of disappointing him.

Chapter Twenty-Three

Tom considered turning right back around and walking out but before he could move the corner of Fee's mouth twitched and he realised she was struggling not to laugh. *Witch.* If she needed him to grovel he would. Whatever it took.

Ten minutes after she left Black Cherry he'd decided to go after her whether she wanted him to or not. He'd told himself it was because he thought she might get lost but deep down he knew that was a load of bull.

Tom pulled out a chair and sat down.

'Give me your order too, hon. It won't be long until the grill's hot.' The waitress gave him the sympathetic look he often received from older women who recognised a sad excuse for a man when they saw one.

He quickly scanned the menu. 'A couple of sausage biscuits, two eggs over-easy and a double order of hash browns please. And coffee.' The woman hurried off and he was left alone with Fee.

'Afraid I'd lose my way?' she asked with a sly smile. 'Don't answer you'll only incriminate yourself.' Fee thrust the tablet at him. 'Now you're here you can read that. Tell me if it's okay before I send it.'

Without saying a word he scanned over the email. To his surprise she'd agreed to visit Allain Dupre. 'Looks fine to me.'

'Have you ever been to New Orleans?'

He wasn't sure whether to take her question on a simple level or read any more into it so went for straightforward. 'Nope.' He needed to know where he stood but second guessing her wasn't going to help his quest.

'Right.' She dragged out the word. Glancing back down she touched the screen and sent her message. 'That's done.'

Tom reached across to cover her hand with his own. Her

slim, cool fingers always felt fragile to his touch although he knew that was far from the truth.

'Thanks.'

'What for?' he asked and her blue eyes appraised him. Tom caught a hitch in her breath before she spoke.

'Coming to find me even though I might've told you where to go.' The crisp, curt words made him smile. 'Sure of yourself, were you?'

'Hardly,' Tom scoffed. 'After last night I wasn't sure you'd even speak to me and having seen you in action with a dangerous knife ... let's just say I considered wearing a Kevlar vest in case you decided to give me a taste of Randy Watling's medicine.'

She burst out laughing and the girlish sound warmed his heart.

'I overreacted and I apologise.' Her frank admission stunned him. 'I thought about it from your family's point of view later and realised they were simply pleased to see you more ... contented.'

'Happy and smiling.' He grinned to prove his point. 'Pop was right.' Tom couldn't leave it there. 'But I was wrong to let them jump to conclusions about us. I've got no hold on you and we've made no promises. That's something neither of us want. Right?'

Fee prepared to lie. 'Of course not.' She managed a short, dismissive laugh. 'I'm not the settling down kind and you'll want a good Southern girl who's happy to stay in Pine Ridge.' She wanted to say she couldn't imagine anything worse but couldn't force out the cruel words. A huge part of her heart thought the idea sounded wonderful but the logical side of her brain assured her it'd be a huge mistake. She wasn't programmed to do "normal".

A shadow flitted across Tom's face before he nodded. 'Fair enough. As long as we know where we are.'

'We do indeed.' Fee plastered on a wide smile. 'We're grown-ups who enjoy each other's company and I'll be gone soon.' Why did a pit open in the bottom of her stomach when she spoke the truth out loud?

'I'll miss you,' he murmured, staring down at the table. A lump closed Fee's throat so she couldn't have spoken if she wanted to.

'Here you go.' Brenda appeared and set down plates of food in front of them both. Fee wasn't sure if she wanted to hug the woman for rescuing them or beg her to leave them alone. 'I'll be right back with your drinks.'

Neither of them said a word. Tom doused his hash browns with ketchup before taking a large forkful and cramming it into his mouth. Fee poked at her pile of pale, creamy eggs in revulsion.

'Tea for you, hon, and there's your coffee.'

Fee managed to thank the woman through gritted teeth. For several minutes the only sounds were made by him ploughing his way through his mountain of food. She pushed hers around the plate and wondered how soon they could leave.

'I thought you were supposed to eat regular meals?' His accusation startled her. Fee wasn't used to having anyone fuss over her. 'If you fade away I'll have nothing to grab a hold of.'

A heated blush warmed her face as she remembered the thorough way he'd explored every inch of her the other night. Fee scooped up some eggs before he could make any more embarrassing comments. The sausage was decent and she managed to eat about half of her breakfast. 'How's yours?' she asked, guessing it must have been okay by his empty plate.

'Pretty good. Not up to Aunt Ina's standard of course but decent enough.' Tom took a deep swallow of his coffee and sighed. 'Good coffee though. Should keep me awake long enough to drive home.'

Fee studied him closer and realised he was exhausted. 'Did you get *any* sleep?' The weary shrug he gave was his answer.

'What about you?'

'Not much. I ended up on the sofa about three this morning and dozed a bit.'

A mischievous gleam lightened his face. 'Sounds to me we might be a danger to other people if we drive back now.'

'Oh, yes, those thirty minute car rides are well known for pushing people over the edge. What do you suggest we do instead?'

He edged closer and Fee caught a hint of his crisp, pine soap. 'There's a motel up the road. We could check in there and ... rest for a few hours. For safety's sake.'

'Aren't you the considerate one?' She patted his hand.

'I expect you can check messages there too.'

'Another good idea.'

Tom smirked. 'I'm full of them.'

'Let's go before we fall asleep over the table.' She'd make the most of the day because they didn't have many left.

'I don't intend falling asleep anytime soon. Hope you don't either.' Tom's blunt statement made her hot all over and she briefly felt guilty for lying to him about where she wanted this relationship to go. 'I'll pay.'

The cafe was filling up now and she watched people stroll in and sit down at what she suspected were their regular tables. Brenda moved around taking orders, often asking if they wanted "the usual", and laughing along with people's conversations. What would it be like to truly belong somewhere? She'd spent her professional life chronicling communities shattered by war or natural disasters and never ceased to be amazed at the resilience of the human spirit when it came to rebuilding both physically and mentally. It was always the small things that made the difference like finding a treasured photo in the wreckage of a home or sharing a meagre amount of food with a long-time neighbour. Tom had the same sort of anchor keeping him steady and even when he'd strayed for a while it'd tugged him back and taken care of him.

'Hope you're not rethinking our rendezvous?' Tom's teasing voice disturbed her mental rambling. 'You looked pretty serious for a moment there. What's wrong?'

'Nothing. I'm fine.' By his wry smile Fee guessed he didn't believe her.

'Fair enough. Let's go and sample the delights of the Cottonwood Motel. You can follow me in your car.'

His casual response didn't mean he'd left it alone but she was pretty sure she could distract him from too much talking for quite a while.

Chapter Twenty-Four

'Please tell me you've never brought another woman here before or I'll doubt your sanity.' Fee glanced around the run-down motel room and couldn't help laughing.

Somehow Fee doubted the dark wood-panelled walls, orange lava lamp, garish psychedelic curtains and matching bedspread were even fashionable back in the seventies. She shuddered to imagine what the numerous stains were on the bright green shag carpet.

'Hell, no,' Tom insisted. 'We don't have to stay.'

She grinned. 'Oh, you're not cheating me out of this experience. When I write my memoirs this place will need a whole chapter to itself.'

'I swear I didn't have a clue it was like *this*. I've driven past before and it looked decent enough.' He stumbled over his words and Fee threw her arms around his neck.

'Trust me I've slept in much worse places. This would be considered luxury accommodation in many parts of the world. Anyway I'm sure you can make me forget my surroundings.'

A tempting grin creased his face. Tom rested a finger on the curve of her cheek before trailing down to skim the top button of her shirt. 'The question is ...'

'What?'

'I was wondering how clean the sheets are judging by the rest of the place.'

'The sheets?'

'Yeah, you know those things people make beds with.'

She slid her hand down to rest on his belt buckle and Tom exhaled a sharp, audible breath. 'Do you *really* care because I don't?'

'I thought British people were supposed to be very particular about those sorts of things, honey.' His voice roughened.

Fee pressed her mouth against his and Tom plunged them into a long, wonderful kiss.

'All right. I get the hint.' Tom's soft drawl made her skin tighten all over.

'Good.'

For a big man he moved fast. Zips. Belts. Socks. Shoes. He got everything out of the way in record time.

'This has to go.' Tom ripped the offensive cover off the bed and tossed it in a heap on the floor. 'I don't want to burn my eyeballs out while I'm making love to you.'

For several lingering seconds she swept her gaze down over him. Tom didn't have a young man's body but he was strong and comfortable in his own skin. He'd been around for a while and had the marks to prove it the same as she did.

'Do I pass muster?'

It helped to know she wasn't the only one with insecurities.

'Absolutely. How about me?'

'You're so beautiful it takes my breath away.' The rasp in Tom's simple words made her throat tighten. 'I love that what I see is what I get. No artifice. Nothing hidden.'

Except my heart. I daren't let you near that. I've seen what caring too much does to people. 'Can I love you now?' he whispered and smiled at her shy nod. Tom swept her into his arms. With a couple of strides he placed her gently on the bed.

Fee pulled him down to her.

Fee hated to wake him but needed to get to the bathroom. Shaking him had no effect and neither did gentle pokes in his ribs. 'Tom,' she called in his ear. He jerked awake and stared at her in obvious confusion. 'I need you to move.'

'Yeah, right,' he mumbled, shifting enough for her to wriggle out of the bed. After freshening up she sneaked back into bed and his arm automatically slid around her again.

He idly stroked her hair. 'It's grown.'

'I've never had it this long since I was a child,' Fee

murmured. 'Short is easier to maintain with my lifestyle. I've taken the scissors to it myself many times.'

'When you're working is it wiser not to be too ... obviously female?'

'In some ways. When I started out a lot of the male photo journalists still resented women doing their job. Things are largely different now.'

'What's the hardest part of the job?'

'Seeing people hurting and not being able to do anything but document their pain.' Fee's voice broke and Tom eased her around in his arms so they lay face to face.

'But if no-one did your job the rest of us would never know what was going on. You've done some amazing work but there's no shame if you decide you've had enough. Maybe it's time to pass on the torch.'

'Perhaps.' She wasn't sure how to vocalise her confusion and guilt.

'I get that it's hard when it's all you've ever done. I do understand. I grew up knowing I'd be a cop. Following in my father's footsteps was all I wanted.' His chest heaved with deep, gulping breaths. 'Gina's death killed the dreams we had as a couple but also took away everything I thought I was about.'

'You came through it though.' Fee wished she could make him see how strong he was.

'In a way.' Sadness dulled his rich, brown eyes. 'But I can't do the love thing again no matter how much I—'

'Don't.' She stopped him short. 'You don't need to be kind just because we had sex.'

Deep frown lines creased his forehead. 'Is that all it was to you?'

What did he want from her? Honesty might destroy whatever was going on between them but should she take the chance?

Chapter Twenty-Five

I've got no hold on you and we've made no promises. That's something neither of us want. Right?

Fee's heart raced. This beautiful man had brought her back to life but he'd made himself perfectly clear from day one. Taking several steadying breaths she knew what she had to say. 'No, Tom, that isn't all it was for me. But I didn't read too much into it either.' Something flared in his warm eyes and she couldn't decide if it was relief or disappointment. 'I need to check my emails before we go back to Black Cherry.'

For a few seconds he stared hard and then blinked. 'Fine.'

Fee slipped out of the bed and pulled her clothes on, purposely keeping her back to him until she was fully dressed. 'Let's hope the internet connection is more up-to-date than the decor.' She flashed a bright smile.

'If they aren't you'll be resorting to tin cans and a piece of string.' Tom played along and Fee ached to kiss him all over again. 'I'm going to risk the shower.' He tossed back the sheet and met her gaze without a hint of embarrassment. Tom strolled across the room, collecting his abandoned clothes as he went and disappeared into the bathroom.

Fee sagged against the wall in an effort to catch her breath.

She settled in the only chair and got her tablet out of her bag. At least the internet connection lived up to its promise and the reply she was waiting for popped in. Had she been too rash in offering to go and visit? Fee wasn't sure how she'd feel if Allain rejected her now.

Wonderful. Tell me the dates you'd like to travel and I'll send a plane ticket. Stay as long as you like. We've a lot to talk about. Allain.

Before she could overthink her reply Fee tapped in a couple of brief sentences and hit Send. She'd suggested flying to New

Orleans on Saturday and returning on Tuesday. If things didn't go well she could bail and explore the city instead, but if they got on okay it should be the right amount of time for a first meeting.

Tom flung open the bathroom door and emerged fully dressed. 'Did you have any luck?'

'Yes, thank you. No tin cans needed.'

He gave her a cautious smile. 'Anything from Allain?'

Fee nodded and briefly told him the details.

'Are you sure it's wise to meet him alone?'

'Why not? It's clear from everything I've seen online that Allain is a respectable businessman and we're talking about New Orleans not the remote mountains of Afghanistan. You're being ridiculous.'

He didn't have any idea of the kind of situations she'd found herself in over the last fifteen years and managed to survive on her wits and quick thinking. In comparison this should be child's play.

This wasn't the sort of man he prided himself on being. Tom was pissed because she'd coolly dismissed their lovemaking as nothing more than a pleasant interlude although he'd asked for it with his stupid half-assed comment about love. The one he hadn't had the guts to finish.

'Are you offering to come with me?' Her eyes flashed in a definite challenge.

'I've got new guests checking in on Saturday to see to.' Fee's satisfied smile made him want to call her bluff.

'Exactly. I suggest you abandon the alpha male chest-beating attitude and recognise the fact I can survive a few days in the wilds of New Orleans without a bodyguard.'

Tom hated the way she made him sound childish. He turned away without saying another word, picked up his keys and wallet from the bedside table and checked around for any more of their belongings. 'Let's go.' Tom stalked out of the room and headed for his truck. He hopped up into the driver's seat and watched Fee stalk across the parking lot to her own car. After they pulled out onto the road Tom kept sight of her in his rear view mirror as they drove back through Pine Ridge and up the mountain to Black Cherry. When he parked outside his cabin she stopped next to him and rolled down her car windows to speak to him.

'If you don't mind I'm heading back to my place.' Fee's quiet request as they pulled into Black Cherry annoyed him. Tom wished she'd shout and rant at him so he could yell back. Anything to get this aggravating politeness out of their systems.

'Of course. I'll be real busy the rest of the week. I've got cabins to get ready and a lot of odd jobs to catch up on. I hope your trip goes well.' Fee nodded and he couldn't be a complete moron any longer. He jumped out and ran around the front of her car, unable to resist the urge to touch her one more time. Tom smoothed his hands around her face. 'If you need *anything* call me. Guests. Family. I'll leave it all if you need me.' It was as close as he could get to spelling out how important she was to him.

She opened and closed her mouth several times without any sound coming out. Fee jerked from his grasp and quickly drove away from him.

Tom stood rooted to the ground until she was safely inside her cabin. With a heavy sigh he locked the truck and dragged up to his own cabin. When he slammed the door shut behind him he knew it was a damn good job he'd poured the whisky down the sink the other night.

Fee told herself it was for the best that she was getting away from here for a few days. She went through the motions of making a sandwich she wouldn't eat and sat at the kitchen table. Opening the mindfulness book she was supposed to be reading Fee only lasted a couple of minutes before pushing it and the plate of food to one side.

If she stayed inside for the rest of the day she'd go crazy and walking around the lake wasn't an option if her aim was to avoid Tom. Today's weather was unseasonably sunny and mild and she had a half-decent camera so she didn't intend to waste either one. On the way back from Norris she'd spotted several interesting old houses and barns and got an idea in her head of a collection of shots of abandoned structures – places that once meant so much to the people who built them but outlasted their purpose. It was a different way of telling the story of a particular place and one she was curious to explore.

You see things the rest of us don't, cherie. I don't know if that's a blessing or a curse. Remembering Pierre's last words to her sent a wave of grief flooding through Fee. He'd given a typical Gallic shrug, kissed her and breezed out of the hotel only to be blown to pieces because his mind was on her instead of his surroundings. In such an intense lifestyle one moment of inattention was all it took to lose everything. She couldn't live that way anymore.

Fee pulled the abandoned plate back in front of her and picked up the sandwich. She needed to take care of herself because there was no one else to do it for her and she didn't need there to be. Pierre's love proved to be false. Her mother's casual indifference would never change. The appearance of her possible biological father was interesting but nothing more. As for Tom ... he'd been a friend and lover when she needed one but that was as far as it could go.

She took a large bite of her sandwich and forced herself to swallow. Once she got the first mouthful down the next was easier and before she knew it her plate was empty. One step at a time. Dr Michael had tried to tell her it was the only way but she hadn't been willing to listen. Maybe coming to Black Cherry hadn't been the worst decision after all.

Tom hunched over his desk and contemplated the radio in front of him. He itched to call his father but had no real excuse.

Hank would sense his mood and demand to know what was wrong. A tiny smile made its way across his face as he knew who he could visit. His grandmother would call him an idiot but she'd also ply him with whatever delicious cake or pie she had in her kitchen and give him a dose of much needed TLC. Just because Fee was self-sufficient and didn't need anyone the same didn't apply to the rest of the human race. Maybe one day she'd understand that relying on other people to help her through life wasn't so terrible.

Whistling tunelessly to himself he grabbed a sweatshirt from the bedroom. The work he needed to do could wait until tomorrow morning. He had a grandmother to sweet talk.

Chapter Twenty-Six

Brandishing a bunch of her favourite scented pink roses Tom rang his grandmother's bell and opened the door at the same time. She never locked it despite his father berating her at regular intervals. 'It's only me,' he called out, looking in through the living room and not spotting her anywhere.

'Well if it isn't my long lost grandson.' Betty Mae Chambers carefully made her way down the narrow stairs stopping half way to catch her breath. 'I thought you'd forgotten where I live.' She waved a yellow duster in his face.

They both knew he'd seen her only the week before but in her book that *was* a long time. Keeping a close watch on all her brood was his Mee Maw's reason for living.

'Your daddy talked about you when he popped in last night.'

Tom wasn't stupid enough to ask what exactly had been said. 'Are you feeling better now?'

'I'm fine. Don't you start fussin'. I get enough of that from your daddy.'

'These are for you.' He thrust the flowers at her.

'I didn't think they were for Sooty.' His grandmother's reference to the overweight black cat she doted on made Tom grin. She lifted the flowers to her nose and sniffed. 'All right, you've grovelled enough. I'll let you stay a while and you can tell me why I'm being honoured by your presence *and* roses.'

Other grandmothers might simply be pleased to get a visit but he should've known Mee Maw would guess he wasn't simply being considerate. Talking to his father might have been the easier option. So much for sweet talking.

'We'll sit in the kitchen. I'm guessing you smelt the caramel cake and that's why you've come sniffing around.'

At least he'd hit the jackpot on the dessert front. Mee

Maw's caramel cake was renowned and she'd won multiple blue ribbons at the Tennessee State Fair before she stopped entering to give other people a chance. Her words not his. 'Pure good luck. I admit I was hoping for a little something sweet but didn't know I'd be totally spoiled.'

'Being charming doesn't suit you, Thomas Michael Chambers,' she retorted, bustling off in the direction of the kitchen leaving him to follow. 'Pour the coffee while I fix us some cake.'

'Let me take care of doing it all to save you—'

'I don't have one foot in the grave despite what that new doctor says.' She wagged her finger. Ever since she'd been warned to take it easy because her heart was weak the family had fought a daily battle to stop her overdoing things. She pretty much ignored them all and said that at nearly ninety she didn't expect to have many more years left but wouldn't spend her remaining time sitting around in a rocking chair. 'I'm right with the Lord and when he's ready for me I'm not gonna argue with his timin'.'

Tom glanced away or she'd see the emotion filling his eyes with tears. Everything his grandmother said made complete sense but he couldn't imagine life without her. He obeyed orders and saw to the coffee, adding plenty of cream but no sugar to both of their drinks. He set the cups on the table, sat down, stretched out his legs in front of him and waited.

'Eat up, boy and we'll talk after. We don't want to curdle the icing.'

He dug his fork into a massive slice of cake and savoured a mouthful of the soft yellow sponge covered in smooth caramel. This recipe was the downfall of many an amateur baker because the icing had to be stirred patiently and cooked at the perfect temperature for it to set. Tom remembered Gina's hopeless attempts to recreate his favourite cake, the last of which resulted in him eating runny caramel icing with a spoon.

'What's wrong? You look as though your mind's on the moon.'

He dredged up a smile. 'Sorry. Nothing's wrong. It's great.'

'You know what happens to liars – remember Pinocchio.'

Tom guessed he might as well tell her the truth or else she'd pick at him for the next hour. 'Satisfied?' he asked when he finished talking about Gina's culinary disaster.

'I guess your daddy was wrong.'

'In what way?'

His grandmother's eyes narrowed, a sure sign Tom was about to get a rollicking.

'He told me you'd met a decent girl and she'd shaken you out of your self-pitying mood.'

Tom normally tried to argue the point with her but he didn't bother. Recently he'd begun to see himself as others did and it wasn't pretty.

'Maybe this woman's done you some good after all.' Her satisfied tone made him wince. 'You're not answering back with your usual nonsense. It's an improvement.' Betty Mae blew on her hot coffee before taking a sip.

He could never stay cross or miserable long around his grandmother. Mee Maw's small, old-fashioned house tucked away here at the far end of the town behind the Presbyterian Church was always his refuge. When he'd been in a fight with one of his brothers or got on the wrong side of his parents her door was always open. She didn't always side with him but by the time he'd vented his anger to her, been fed and listened to whatever advice she had to dole out things never seemed as bad.

'I hoped you might've brought Miss Winter to meet me.' The slight note of censure in her voice got to Tom because it was exactly what he'd planned to do before Fee got all mad at him. 'You've done something idiotic to put the girl off, haven't you?'

She never hesitated to spell out her opinion in her plain-spoken way. Tom sighed and gave in. He launched into the whole sorry tale minus the motel incident.

'I don't get it, Mee Maw.' He couldn't hide his frustration any longer. 'Fee agreed she didn't believe in long-term commitment. She's lived a nomadic life and has no desire to change. I told her I had my own reasons for not intending to marry again and she appeared to understand. I thought we were both good with being adult about the relationship.'

His grandmother shook her head. 'You've got no more sense than a bag of rocks. Which one of you put all that nonsense into words first anyway?'

'I guess I did.'

Betty Mae leaned back in the chair with a satisfied smile. 'Enough said. She told you what she thought you wanted to hear and you fell for it like a typical dumb man.'

'What am I goin' to do?' Tom pleaded and a broad grin spread across her face. There was nothing Mee Maw loved better than being *asked* for advice instead of having to force it on her stubborn family.

The morning went well but Fee missed having someone to talk to about how it'd all gone. *Be honest. You miss Tom, not just some random person to talk to.* She'd taken a ton of great photos along the back roads between Pine Ridge and Norris and uploaded them to her laptop back at the cabin. She'd been particularly lucky and met a young couple at one of her stops. They'd bought the derelict building in an auction and shared with her their plans to renovate the old tobacco barn. The photos she'd taken of them in front of their future home were really eye-catching. Fee loved the contrast between the vibrant, attractive couple and the grey, worn-out building.

She'd checked her emails at the cafe where she'd eaten lunch and received another from Allain with her flight details. Her misgivings about going to New Orleans were growing deeper at the idea of meeting Allain face-to-face. What could they possibly have in common? The few nights he spent with her mother forty years ago might have resulted in her birth but that hardly made him her father. Despite Tom's irrational reaction Fee didn't consider herself to be taking a big risk. She kept coming back in her mind as to why Allain was so keen to meet her but suspected she was overthinking the whole thing. Of course he was curious – who wouldn't be? She'd done her research and there'd been no red flags surrounding Allain Dupre. He owned several high-end restaurants including the world-renowned Bayou Blues on the Louisiana Gulf coast, devastated by Hurricane Katrina but now back at the top of its game. He was a wealthy philanthropist and a member of one of New Orleans' oldest families. He'd been recently widowed after a long marriage but she hadn't seen any mention of children. She'd scrutinised several newspaper photos of him but they hadn't told her much.

They were both tall with lean, muscular body types but Fee didn't have Allain's startling emerald eyes. Her straight black hair was identical to her mother's so his silver blonde waves hadn't staked a claim there. Fee suspected she'd hoped to see either an unequivocal mirror image of herself or a man so radically different there was no way they could be related. Instead it was as ambiguous as these things usually were. Allain must want to know for certain as much as she did, but it was what they'd do with the knowledge that'd woken Fee up over the last few nights drenched in sweat.

She needed Tom's calm, quiet presence to help reassure her although yesterday he'd been far from his usual laid-back self and she still wasn't sure what had set him off. Fee thought it might've been her comment after they made love. Like so many men he wanted things both ways: to mean something to a woman without meaning too much. Negotiating relationships was like tightrope walking without a safety net which was why Fee usually stuck to keeping men as good friends instead. If occasionally she chose to add "benefits" to the package it was her decision. She'd seen her mother fall in and out of love quicker than most Hollywood celebrities and had been determined not to follow suit.

Fee calculated the time difference and picked up the phone.

'Freebird!' Her mother answered on the first ring. 'Is everything alright?'

'Of course. Why wouldn't it be?' There was a barely perceptible hesitation before Maddy spoke again.

'You don't make a habit of ringing me, do you?'

Fee wanted to be offended but it was the truth. 'Can you tell me anything more about Allain Dupre because I'm flying to New Orleans to meet him tomorrow?'

'Really?'

'Yes, really. Okay?' She resented being challenged as if she was still a small child.

'I've been having second thoughts. Maybe it's not such a good idea.'

'Why not? You were encouraging me before.'

'I suppose it's me being silly. Anyway I told you everything.' Maddy hesitated. 'You go and enjoy yourself.' Fee got the distinct impression her mother wanted to say a lot more.

After they said goodbye Fee plugged her phone in to recharge and walked outside to sit on the porch. She hoped she wasn't about to make a fool of herself.

Chapter Twenty-Seven

Tom wiped his sweaty hands on his jeans and glanced around the small Knoxville airport. If his grandmother was wrong he was about to make the biggest fool of himself. He'd taken a chance and bought a seat on the earliest flight out of Knoxville to Charlotte and on to New Orleans. If Fee didn't check in he'd be stumped.

He'd worked non-stop all day and barely finished in time to shower and change and race to the airport. Of course he hadn't been able to keep his plans quiet because he'd needed his family's help and everyone had given him their two cents worth. In the end his younger sister, Rayna, who taught at a year round school and had a week off for their equivalent of the normal fall break, volunteered to help him out. She insisted that looking after a dozen or so guests would be easier than dealing with a classroom full of third-graders. At eight months' pregnant she intended spending as much time as possible with her feet up. Her husband, Billy, would stay with her every night and all the way through the weekend plus his father promised to do frequent radio checks to make sure Rayna was okay.

In the end they'd shooed him out after insisting they were perfectly capable of reading and following the ten pages of instructions he'd given them.

Tom spotted Fee's gleaming black hair and air of purpose as she strode down the hallway in his direction. He briefly considered sliding behind the pillar in case she hadn't noticed him but stood his ground.

'Please tell me you're meeting someone or going anywhere other than New Orleans.' For a few seconds Fee's accusatory tone made him doubt his grandmother's wisdom.

No woman likes a dishonest man. Tell her where you stand and how you feel. After that it's up to her.

'That'd be a lie, sweetheart, and I'm not doin' that any more.' Tom's heart thumped as her eyes flared with surprise. 'How about we go on through security and find us a coffee shop?'

'Fine,' Fee snapped and hurried away, leaving him to follow along.

It could've gone worse. She might have slapped you.

After going through the usual rigmarole involved in travelling these days Tom led the way into a small cafe near their departure gate.

'I'll get our drinks if you tell me what you want.' The disdainful look he received suggested she'd be more than happy if he bought a glass of poison and drank it down in one gulp. If this was a woman in love she sure had him fooled.

'Water will be fine, thank you.' Fee left him standing there and went to sit at a table in the corner, taking out her phone and not looking at him again.

While he waited for their drinks to be fixed Tom watched her. As neat and self-contained as always, nothing about Fee suggested extreme emotion one way or the other. Tom guessed she used this outward persona while working along with her camera to keep a necessary distance between her and her subjects. The only way he'd get through to the real woman underneath was to break it down. Fee would make it as hard as possible but Tom was through with being a dismal coward.

With an extra shot of espresso in his coffee he was ready. *Bring it on, Fee Winter. You've met your match.*

The determined glint in Tom's eye as he marched towards her, brandishing two cups, dried up the challenge she'd been about to make and Fee took the one he thrust at her without saying a word.

'You want to know why I'm here and on your flight?'

She shrugged as if it didn't matter to her one way or another but the corners of his mouth twitched. Plainly she hadn't hidden her interest well enough. *Damn the man.*

'Play it whatever way you like. I don't care. I'll tell you and if you want me to leave and not go to New Orleans with you I'll respect your choice.' A stony cast darkened his face. 'I won't like it, but I'm not goin' where I'm not wanted.'

Fee was intrigued by this new more forceful version of Tom.

'I've been a moron. At least that's what my grandmother called me when I told her about you.'

She squashed down a smile.

'You've stirred up feelings I didn't expect to feel again and it scared me.' His honesty took her breath away. 'I'd mixed my guilt and grief over Gina with everything else. Might as well have been wearing a damn hair shirt.' Tom's angry scowl broke out the bubble of laughter hiding inside her and Fee giggled, gulping and struggling to breathe. He glared as though she'd stabbed him through the heart but all of a sudden his deep, rich chuckle filled the room and made everyone turn and stare. 'Don't do anything to make me feel better will you?' Tom seized hold of her hands.

From the first time he ever touched her there'd been something about his quiet, warm strength that spoke to her closed-off heart.

'Tell me right now if I'm way off base.' His bluntness touched her and Fee leaned in to kiss him. Tom sighed and rested his forehead against hers.

'No, you're not,' she whispered.

'Good. I'm not sure how I would've stood it.'

Fee swallowed hard. She needed to give him something in return. 'I care for you, Tom, very much but I'm ... scared. My mother fell in and out of so-called love at regular intervals and it never lasted. The closest I've come to trusting any man with my heart was Pierre and you know how that ended. I'm not a good bet for any man.'

'I'll take the odds I'm being offered. I've always been a gambling man. Me and my brothers love a good poker game.

I buy far too many lottery tickets and loved Las Vegas the one time I went.'

'That only proves how little we know about each other,' she joked. 'I can't even imagine you *in* Las Vegas let alone enjoying it.'

'Hey, because I live in the backwoods of Tennessee doesn't mean I'm an ignorant redneck.' Tom's effort to sound offended was belied by his cheeky smile. 'I do get out of Pine Ridge occasionally and even own a passport.'

'Wow, I'm impressed,' Fee teased, knowing they'd strayed away from the difficult topic of love and she was happy to keep it that way a while longer.

'You're changin' the subject, pretty lady.' Tom's voice turned serious and his deep-set eyes bored into her. 'You've got a lot of love to share, Fee, we both do. Are you willing to give it a go and see what happens? I am if you are.' The wobble in his voice betrayed the fact he wasn't as assured as he might seem. A slow smile crept across Tom's face when she nodded. 'I promise you won't regret it.'

Pressing her fingers against his lips Fee shook her head. 'Don't promise me anything, that way I ...'

'Stop right there,' he ordered, pulling back to glare at her again. 'If I want to make you a promise I will and you can like it or lump it. I hope I'm an honourable man, Fee, and if you haven't come across many of them before it's not my fault.'

Tears pricked at her eyes and she quickly apologised.

'Oh, sweetheart, I didn't mean to yell.'

'You didn't. I ...'

He looked so contrite she could've kissed him. 'All I was trying to say was that I promise never to deliberately hurt you.' Uncertainty crept into his voice. 'Is that enough for you?'

Fee nodded. 'I'm happy to promise the same, if that's enough for you?'

'Sure is.' Tom beamed and seized hold of her, drawing them into a passionate kiss and sending tingles all through her body.

He let go and glanced at his watch with a rueful sigh. 'Darn. We need to go to the gate.'

Everything slammed back and she remembered what they were doing and all the other things she'd been worried about before spotting Tom lounged against the wall and scanning the crowd for her.

'What's wrong?'

'It's not you. Honestly. I suppose it's thinking about meeting Allain ...' She stopped right there. Beginning with another lie wasn't any way to make progress with Tom. 'That's not the complete truth. I rang my mother yesterday and we talked about Allain. She sounded worried about something. I'm not sure ...'

'They're calling our flight,' Tom interrupted as an announcement came over the loudspeakers. 'We'd better go.' He squeezed her hand. 'I'm not putting you off, sweetheart. We don't have long in Charlotte to catch our connecting flight and we may not get the chance to talk properly until we get there.' He frowned. 'Is Dupre meeting you at the airport?'

Fee nodded, and hitched her backpack on again. 'It's okay. We'll talk later.' It wasn't okay really but she'd left it too late to start the discussion. 'Come on.' By his hesitation she knew it wouldn't take long for Tom to sit her back down and insist on talking and to hell with the flight. But if she didn't go now she might lose her nerve completely.

Chapter Twenty-Eight

Tom gave Fee a quick thumbs-up from the back of the plane when she glanced back at him over her shoulder as they touched down at Louis Armstrong International Airport. The people in front of her started to move so she had to move too. He kept his eyes on her as she made her way off the plane.

Out at the security gate he hung back and watched from a distance as Fee hesitated for a second but then waved and walked towards a man in the waiting crowd. She held herself stiffly as he attempted to give her a hug and Tom couldn't imagine what she must be feeling. It was hard to get his head around the idea of Fee never having known her father but he was trying – all part of his grandmother's advice. She'd trotted out the old "walk a mile in another man's shoes" adage when he shared Fee's story.

Allain Dupre seemed to be trying to persuade her about something but she kept shaking her head. It took all of Tom's fading self-control not to rush over and interfere. Fee knew he wasn't planning to leave until she did which meant all she had to do was turn around and call him over if she needed help. He wasn't happy with her decision not to introduce him to Allain right away but she'd suggested that seeing them arrive together might be off-putting. Tom had agreed to find a hotel room as long as she promised to ring when she got the chance.

The two walked away together and he didn't let himself move. Tom could follow them without being seen if he chose to but refused to break their agreement. Planting his feet in place he gritted his teeth and waited until they were out of sight.

Tom glanced around and spotted a sign for hotel bookings. He'd get a room in the closest hotel to Dupre's house in the Garden District and to heck with the expense. If it wouldn't get him arrested he'd camp on the doorstep. Once he was settled he'd call Mee Maw and give her an update. She'd had a new sparkle in her eyes when he left and threatened to contact the local *Pine Ridge Gazette* newspaper to offer her services as an agony aunt, convinced she'd found her calling in life.

Once he had a room sorted Tom headed out to the taxi rank. He scanned around but didn't spot Fee so guessed Dupre must have brought his own car. There was nothing more he could do except get to the hotel and wait on her call.

Being patient chafed like a pair of new shoes but there was no choice.

Fee wished she hadn't phoned her mother yesterday because the extra layer of worry made the meeting with Allain harder. No doubt she'd struck him as uptight and unfriendly but hopefully he'd put it down to simple nerves. He'd suggested they stop for dinner at one of his restaurants but she'd refused. The last thing she wanted was to have to deal with the whole food issue straight away plus the added strain of possibly being introduced to people he knew. Fee had claimed to be tired and said she would rather get something to eat at his house.

'I'm looking forward to sharing my beautiful city with you, *cherie*. New Orleans is unique.'

The way he pronounced the city's name, making it sound like one word, made her smile. She loved listening to Allain's smooth Cajun drawl but it wasn't always easy to understand and they'd already joked about the vast difference in the English they both theoretically spoke. She'd tried to hide her surprise when they emerged from the airport to discover a large, black limousine with a driver waiting on them.

'It's about ten miles from here to the French Quarter and my house is on the down river end of St. Charles Avenue.'

Despite everything Fee's interest in being in a new place rose. St. Charles Avenue was renowned for its ornate mansions, most of which were built in the early twentieth century for the wealthy elite of New Orleans. As a designated Historic District it was a mecca for tourists and guaranteed to make any photographer happy. It would be an interesting contrast to the abandoned barns and houses she'd spent her time photographing yesterday.

'In the morning we could take a ride on the streetcar so you can get your bearings and wield your camera.' His frank pleasure in her company made Fee guilty about the ambiguity of her own reaction. It wasn't hard to see why her mother was attracted to Allain all those years ago. Although he must be around sixty he was still a charming, handsome man.

'That would be great.' She struggled to infuse her voice with some warmth.

'I know this is tough for you.' His quiet words struck her heart. 'It's not easy for me either if that's any consolation.'

The promise of honesty she'd made to Tom came back to haunt her and Fee knew she owed this man nothing less. 'When we get to your home I'd like to talk properly.'

'Of course,' Allain agreed and began to point out various landmarks along the way making it easy for them to slip into ordinary conversation about the city. 'This area was very fortunate during Hurricane Katrina and escaped any serious flooding.'

Fee noticed one of the distinctive streetcars making its way down the centre of St. Charles Avenue. A myriad of lights twinkled and shone from inside the extravagant houses, all of them built in differing architectural styles.

'It's a pity you're too early to see our Christmas decorations. Even the streetcars are lit up. We don't do quiet here.'

They halted in front of a grandiose red brick house guarded by the intricate wrought iron gates and railings unique to New Orleans.

'My great-grandfather chose the Colonial Revival style with Corinthian columns because he liked to make a show,' Allain said with a touch of humour. He gestured to an over-the-top white building across the other side of the street. 'I think it was his effort to compete with the Wedding Cake house. Of course it failed and that one's always top of the viewing list. *C'est la vie.*'

'Yours is still very impressive.'

Allain gestured to his driver that they were ready and immediately Fee's door was opened so she could step out onto the pavement.

'Thank you, Charles. I won't need you first thing in the morning. I'll call.'

'I hope I'm not interrupting your normal work schedule?' Fee asked.

'Not at all.' He smiled. 'I'm the boss. I can go in when I want or not at all.'

She wasn't deceived by his laid-back attitude and couldn't imagine he planned to retire anytime soon. The next hour passed in a blur as he gave her a tour of the stunning house.

'You must be hungry by now? I know I am,' Allain declared.

'Yes, I am,' Fee conceded.

'Good. My cook left us a pot of her outstanding Jambalaya. I hope you like your food spicy?'

There was no point pretending because she didn't want to make herself ill. Fee explained about her ulcer and the restrictions it placed on her diet. 'I'm sorry. I've heard so much about the Cajun and Creole foods but most are off-limits for me.'

'My dear. You have nothing to be sorry for.' He frowned. 'How about a poached egg on wheat toast with a little smoked salmon?'

'That sounds delicious but will it suit you?' Fee asked and laughed when he assured her he'd doctor his up with plenty of hot sauce.

The kitchen ran the whole width of the house and resembled the set of a TV cookery show with its massive high-end appliances, acres of marble countertops and gleaming copper pans hanging from a metal rack suspended from the ceiling. She perched on a bright red leather stool at the breakfast bar and sipped a glass of sparkling water while Allain worked on getting their meal ready. He'd turned down her not-very-insistent offer to help after she'd declared herself willing but not very able.

'What's your mother doing these days?' Allain asked

It would sound awful to admit they hadn't seen each other in years but she couldn't pretend everything was fine between them. 'That's not an easy question to answer.'

He set down the box of eggs and turned around. 'Why not? Is something wrong with her?'

'Not as far as I know.' As simply as she could she told Allain about her difficult childhood and the way it'd affected her relationship with her mother. 'I suppose she did the best she could,' Fee said with a shrug, struggling not to sound bitter.

Allain's smile disappeared leaving deep-set frown lines cutting grooves into his narrow, lean face. 'I'm sorry.'

'It's not your fault,' she said hurriedly. 'You may not want to hear this but I'm pretty sure if you'd married my mother it wouldn't have lasted. She's never stayed long with any man so I've no reason to believe you'd have been different.' The sudden pallor under his tanned skin hinted at his distress and she wished she could retract her words.

'If you're trying to make me feel better about leaving you're doing a lousy job.' His throwaway comment made her laugh out loud. 'You're so like your dear mother.' A broad grin spread across Allain's face.

Fee wasn't sure how to respond without sounding rude.

'I meant it as a compliment, *cherie*.'

No doubt he did but as far as she could see the worst aspects of her character came from Maddy.

'Remember I was an idealistic young man when I met her.' Allain's voice softened and she sensed him drift away to another place and time. 'She was a hell of a way to celebrate turning twenty-one. I'd never met anyone like Maddy.' His emerald eyes shone. 'Never did again either. My late wife, Ellen, was a wonderful woman, but she wasn't your mother.'

An awkward silence hung between them and Fee took another sip of water.

'Not much of a host, am I?' Allain suddenly asked. 'You must be starving. I'll get on with cooking our eggs.' He turned away and quietly went back to work. Soon he shared out the food between two plates and returned to join her. 'Would you care for a glass of wine?'

She regretted she couldn't indulge because it would help to smooth out the rough edges of conversation. 'My ulcer wouldn't be happy.' Fee felt the urge to share something of herself with Allain. 'I overindulged in alcohol and pain medicine when I was working to deal with the stress and I've made a life choice to avoid both now.' She plastered on a smile. 'My doctor warned me I could forget celebrating my fortieth birthday if I didn't. I'm not sure I'll be hanging the flags out either but that's not his fault.' Her self-deprecating remark fell flat as Allain looked so sympathetic tears pricked at the backs of her eyes. 'Let's eat,' she declared and picked up her knife and fork. Fee exhaled quietly when he didn't say another word and followed her lead.

Half-way through eating the front door slammed.

'Papa, where are you?' A girl's high-pitched voice rang out. 'In the kitchen?' The swing door flung open and a stunning blonde, all long, tanned limbs and scarlet high heels ran into the room. She stopped dead at the sight of them.

Papa? Fee waited for Allain to say something, anything, but he remained chalk-white and silent.

Chapter Twenty-Nine

Tom groaned as he read Fee's text. How the hell did she think he'd sleep tonight now?

More complications. Meet me at Cafe du Monde in the morning at eight. Love Fee.

Talk about cryptic. He hoped Dupre hadn't rejected her. Underneath her layer of bravado he'd sensed Fee needed to make a connection with the guy. Tom wanted to rush over right away and reassure her she could do without Allain Dupre with his flashy house and million dollar restaurants.

Let me come to you now. Please. Love Tom.

He sent the terse reply and the phone beeped with an immediate answer. Tom knew what it'd say before he glanced at the screen. A polite refusal. *Be like that you stubborn woman.* For two pins he'd go around to Dupre's house and throw rocks at Fee's window to make her talk to him but there were multiple problems with his crazy scenario. The first was that it'd probably end with Dupre calling the cops on him. The second, and most important, was that Fee would flay him alive. Neither appealed.

He'd call for room service and get something to eat because it was that or head into the city and find a bar which was a lousy idea. An hour later he stretched out in bed after stuffing himself with crawfish étouffée. The spicy Cajun shellfish dish, served over boiled rice, was his new favourite food. He smiled at the idea of trying to persuade Aunt Ina to add it to the Mockingbird's traditional "meat and three" Southern menu.

Tom closed his eyes and tried not to think about Fee but at six in the morning he gave up. He took a long, cold shower in an effort to feel less corpse-like. When he stepped out of the hotel his eyes adjusted to the half-light as the first golden slivers of dawn crept into the morning sky. Setting off down

St. Charles Avenue he started the nearly three mile walk towards Decatur Street. If nothing else it should work off some of his energy. Tom was relieved Fee hadn't dragged them here in the height of the summer when he'd heard the humidity was so high as to drench anyone stupid enough to linger outside for more than a few minutes.

Tom didn't pay a ton of attention to all the fancy houses although he imagined Fee would have a field day with them through her camera lens. When he turned onto Camp Street the ordinary homes there appealed to him much more. A few houses sprouted Christmas decorations already but most were clinging on to fall with bright orange pumpkins on the front steps and seasonal wreaths hung on the doors. He'd read in a guide book about the metal wrap-around awnings signifying the corner grocery shops that'd long since gone and got a kick out of spotting one still in place. Once he reached Chartres Street the French Quarter really began and the number of hotels, restaurants and bars increased. He was tempted to stop for coffee but pressed on and walked through Jackson Square. Tom wasn't in the mood to play tourist and headed straight for the Cafe du Monde.

Any place selling coffee twenty-four hours a day, 364 days a year got a gold star in his books. They only closed once a year on Christmas Day or if a hurricane got close enough to threaten the city. Tom wasn't used to walking so far on hard tarmac and sank into a metal chair at one of the street-side tables. Fee wouldn't be here for half an hour and the overwhelming smell of hot dough frying and sugar tempted him to order a plate of beignets. Tom craved his coffee strong and black this morning and inhaled the first cup in short order. The touch of chicory blunted the edge of the dark roast and he gave silent thanks to the Acadians who'd brought the recipe with them from Nova Scotia. He selected his first beignet and sank his teeth into the soft square doughnut sending a cloud of icing sugar over the table and himself.

While he ate he studied the square and admired the old cathedral at one end and the ornate buildings around the edges. Tom guessed they'd once been family homes but now were divided into ground-floor shops and restaurants with apartments over them. The residences were all fronted with intricate wrought-iron balconies draped with hanging baskets overflowing with extravagant dark green ferns. There was a distinctly foreign air about the area and Tom enjoyed the contrast with Pine Ridge.

Few people were around this early and Tom stretched out his legs, put his hands behind his head and rested his tired eyes.

'Haven't you got anything better to do, cowboy?' Fee gave Tom's arm a quick poke. She'd sneaked out of the house so she wouldn't have to explain herself to Allain. After last night's debacle she'd had enough drama.

Tom's eyes flew open and he leapt to his feet. He threw his arms around her and pulled her against his warm, solid body. 'I've been so damn worried about you I haven't slept a wink.'

'I need coffee. Now.'

'Are you okay to eat here? It's not exactly health food.'

'You can help me out with the beignets and it'd be great if they could make the coffee with skim milk. I'll have a glass of water too.'

'No problem.' He gestured to a passing waiter and quickly placed their order. 'Come over by me. I've missed you too much to just stare at you across the table.'

Fee didn't object and sat in the chair next to him. The mild weather was perfect for sitting outside and Tom's fingers stroked her hand in a quiet, soothing rhythm. Out on the street things were starting to come to life as the locals headed off to work and the first tourists began to meander around. A musician was setting up his saxophone next to them and getting ready to play for tips.

'Interesting place, isn't it? If they didn't have such god-awful humidity for months on end and get pounded by hurricanes at regular intervals I can think of worse places to live.'

'I take it you don't plan to move here anytime soon?' she teased and was rewarded by one of his wide, sexy smiles. 'Not even if you could bring Pine Ridge with you?'

He shook his head violently. 'Nope. Not goin' to happen.'

The waiter appeared with a loaded tray and set down their food and drinks before leaving them alone again.

Fee stared at the three golden beignets dredged in icing sugar and before she could be tempted pushed two straight onto Tom's plate. She took a sip of coffee. 'I miss this so badly sometimes. This is nice and mellow but I still mustn't drink it all.'

'You've got more willpower than I'd have, sweetheart.' Tom chuckled.

'Pain like stabbing knives in your stomach will do that to you trust me.' Her dry observation made him wince. 'Hey, it's okay.' Fee squeezed his hand. 'I'm learning to manage and staying clear of alcohol and the painkillers I used to rely on helps the most.'

'You're a strong woman.' His eyes, as dark and decadent as the richest chocolate, rested on her. 'I already had one plateful of these before you came,' Tom admitted, picking up a beignet and giving it a rueful smile. 'It's time you explained your mysterious text.'

The swift change of subject threw her for a second and Fee took a small bite of warm doughnut before setting the rest back down on the plate. She fiddled with the paper napkin, screwing it up into a tiny ball and unravelling it again before proceeding to tear it into shreds. Stumbling over her words she told Tom about the meeting at the airport and Allain's house. Fee didn't do too badly until she reached the part about her mother and Allain's reaction to the story about her childhood.

Tom laid his fingers on her cheek and she leaned into his familiar touch. 'You're being too hard on yourself again.

None of this is your fault.' The knot of tension gripping at her stomach eased. 'I'm not convinced Allain comparing you to your mother was so terrible.' He smoothed her hair behind her ears and pressed a gentle kiss on her mouth. 'I'm pretty sure you got most of your beauty from her plus she's obviously a very focused, independent woman and that's nothing to be ashamed of.'

'I've never thought about it that way before,' Fee murmured. 'All I've ever seen is the lack of intimacy we have with other people …' His eyebrows rose and she couldn't help grinning. 'I'm not talking about sex.'

'I know, honey, but my wicked mind wouldn't listen.' His expression turned serious again. 'You shouldn't put yourself down. You might not be at ease around large, close families like mine but you did a damn fine job the other night. Not everyone has to be loud and over-sharing. There's nothing wrong in being more of an introvert.' He smiled. 'Every family needs one or two and it'd be a crazier world than it is if we were all the same.'

'You're a good man.' Fee rested her head on his shoulder and sighed. He'd already given her a lot to think about and hadn't heard half the story yet.

'Caught you.'

Tom jerked around and a young, blonde woman screamed right in his face, her stunning features marred by hot anger. Curse words sounded the same in any language and he guessed these were in the local Cajun dialect. Everyone around them stopped eating and drinking to stare.

'Excuse me, ma'am. Do we know you?'

'She does.' The woman pointed an accusing finger at Fee. 'Are you her accomplice?'

'Accomplice?' Tom asked. 'What the heck are you talking about?' He held out his hand but she didn't shake it. 'My name's Tom Chambers.'

'Would you care to join us, Lisette?' Fee broke her silence. 'I'd rather not broadcast our private business.'

'I guess you don't want everyone knowing you're a money-grabbing fraud,' Lisette sniped and pulled out a chair to sit down. She waved away the waiter who was hovering around their table to take her order.

'Tom is my … boyfriend,' Fee said with a shy smile before glancing at him. 'This is Lisette Dupre. Allain's daughter.'

Daughter? Of all the guesses running through his mind that one hadn't made the list. 'Pleased to meet you.'

'I can't imagine why,' she snapped. 'Your little scheme is over. If you think I'll stand by and let you fleece my poor father when he's still grieving you can forget it.'

'Lisette came to visit her father last night,' Fee explained with a tremor in her voice. 'He, um, explained who I am and it was rather a shock.' What she didn't say came through clearly and Tom could only imagine how the volatile girl reacted to the news of an unknown half-sister.

'It's all a pack of lies and we both know it,' Lisette interrupted. 'Papa agreed to a DNA test this morning. I assume you won't object.'

'Of course not. Why should I?' Fee's willingness took the other girl by surprise. 'I don't need his money and I've managed for nearly forty years without a father and done quite well for myself. Trust me, I don't have any agenda.'

'I guess we'll see about that won't we?' Lisette pushed her chair back and stood up, glaring at them both. 'I'll be staying with my father until you leave.'

'Making sure I don't steal the silver?' Fee quipped.

'You won't be laughing soon,' Lisette threatened and stormed off.

Tom waited for Fee to say something – anything rather than the blank stare she was giving him now.

Chapter Thirty

'I'll say it again you're an amazing woman.' Tom's warm, open smile brought Fee close to tears. 'You've made yourself the person you are today and no DNA test will change that.'

The urge to run away from him and the whole mess swept through her and Fee didn't know how she stayed seated. She'd never intended to upset anyone by coming here. After last night's debacle Lisette had disappeared upstairs to sleep in her old bedroom. Allain explained the reason Fee hadn't seen any mention of Lisette when reading about him was because his wife had been fanatical about maintaining their family privacy. Ellen had rarely accompanied him to social events and their daughter was never allowed to. It'd hurt Fee when Allain assured Lisette his relationship with Maddy was unimportant. Part of her understood he was a father protecting his daughter but what about *her* feelings?

The last twenty-four hours had shifted her perceptions and made her re-examine what she was doing to Tom.

This was a man whose reason for living revolved around his large, extended family and who had enough research material on his ancestors to write a book. He'd brought back to life the cabins his forebears built when they settled in Tennessee, and Black Cherry meant everything to him. The idea of him loving a woman who wasn't sure who both of her parents were and whose idea of a settled home was staying somewhere for more than a couple of weeks was totally crazy and always had been.

'You're doin' it again, honey,' Tom remonstrated. 'Jumping to conclusions. My brain's in pretty good workin' order and I'll make my own decisions.'

'I didn't mean ...' her voice trailed away because she couldn't lie. Everything tumbled out and in a flash the warmth left his face.

'Is that really what you think of me? That I can't love my family and where I come from and you? That's bullshit.' Bitterness laced his words.

'Strong feelings often blind us to the truth, Tom. Don't get me wrong. Our … relationship has been wonderful. It's helped me get over a tough time.'

'Glad to hear I've been of use.' She couldn't blame him for sounding churlish.

'You know that's not how I meant it.'

'Do I?'

Fee sucked in an audible breath. 'Be real, Tom, we have nothing in common. Can you really picture us living happily ever after? The situation with Allain has simply helped clarify things for me.'

'Oh good.'

'Sarcasm doesn't suit you. You're too nice.' She managed a tight smile but he didn't respond. 'I'm sorry to have dragged you out here for nothing.' Big, fat tears filled Fee's eyes and he pulled out another clean white handkerchief from his jeans pocket and passed it to her.

'Please. No crying. I'm a man and we don't do tears well.' He struggled to crack a joke. 'Anyway if we're nit-picking you didn't drag me out here. I came of my own accord because I knew meeting Dupre would be difficult and wanted to support you.'

Fee knew she should thank him but could only manage a brief nod. 'I'd better go or Allain will wonder where I am.' Tom stared at her in quiet disbelief. 'Will you go back to Black Cherry today?'

He tried to read her mind but failed, unable to decide how she wanted him to reply. *If you're not sure what she means ask the woman outright.* Turning his grandmother into a Tennessee version of Dear Abby had been a mistake because now he couldn't get her opinions out of his head.

'Do you want me to?' Tom couldn't make it any plainer. He sat back in the chair and sipped his cold coffee. Anything so he might not appear quite as desperate. Fee couldn't meet his eyes. *Good. If I still bother her that much I've got a chance.*

'It might be for the best.' Her cool words contrasted with the way her trembling hands clutched at her handbag strap. 'I'm really sorry, Tom.' Fee's voice broke.

Before he could stop her she pushed the empty chair next to her out of the way and took off running.

'Where have you been?' Allain hurried out from the kitchen as Fee limped back into the house. 'We might not be sure I'm your father yet but I can still worry.' His attempt to joke about their situation made everything worse.

'I'm sorry. I woke early and walked down to the Cafe du Monde.' She left it at that, wondering if Lisette was back but not comfortable with mentioning their acrimonious meeting to him.

'It's a long way with a bad knee,' he commented, 'and before you ask your mother mentioned your injury and I've been reading about you online. Call me nosy if you like but I was curious what kind of woman my ... uh, you were.'

'Don't believe all you read.' She hated how she either came across as a saint or totally mad. 'I'm sure you wouldn't want me to believe everything I've seen about you?'

His warm laugh filled the room. 'Touché. You got me there, *cherie*. I usually come across as either a greedy business tyrant or a male version of Mother Teresa for the little bit of charity work I do.'

"Little bit of charity work" was a complete misnomer. He was a philanthropist on a grand scale but also did a lot behind the scenes which only got revealed when someone broke his request for anonymity. There was a lot to admire about him and remembering the merry-go-round of her mother's boyfriends Fee couldn't help hoping Allain did turn out to be her father, even if having Lisette for a half-sister was the price she'd have to pay.

'Did you have any breakfast?'

'I tried the famous beignets and café au lait. They were delicious.'

'Really?' Allain's eyebrows rose. 'Was that a good idea?'

Why hadn't she simply said she went out for a walk? She hated being dishonest. 'I didn't eat much,' Fee murmured. 'I'm rather tired so if you don't mind I'm going upstairs to rest for a while.'

'No problem, but ...' He shuffled from one foot to the other and couldn't quite look at her. 'If you could be downstairs again by ten I'd appreciate it.' Allain hurried to explain that his doctor was coming to do the DNA test and would have the results back before she left. She hated that he felt awkward about asking her to do something which made complete sense. If Lisette hadn't demanded it Fee would've suggested the test herself.

She touched his arm. 'That's fine. We both need this.' Fee wanted him to know this wasn't only for his sake. 'I'll see you in a while.'

Before he could say anything else she left him alone and retreated to her bedroom.

She wouldn't be able to lay all of this to rest until she visited her mother. *What about Tom? Are you going to pretend he means nothing to you?* Fee wasn't clear what else she'd do when she returned to Black Cherry but meeting Tom's grandmother would top the list. She'd never been a person to put things off and had soon tracked down Betty Mae Chambers' phone number. As soon as she said her name and what she wanted Fee could sense the older woman's satisfaction. Within minutes she received an open invitation to visit. Mission accomplished.

We have nothing in common, Tom, be real. Do you really picture us living happily ever after?

If she thought he'd give up easily she was way off base. He'd do whatever it took to prove he loved her.

Tom's head spun as his family all tried to speak at the same time. He'd landed back in Pine Ridge in time for Sunday supper and dropped his bombshell in the middle of eating chicken pot pie.

'Sell? You've spent ten years restoring the goddamn place,' Sandy exploded. Thankfully the older kids were outside playing so his brother only received a stern glare from their mother instead of a swat around the head for his bad language. 'Why're you doing this?'

'A woman. Always is.' Mikey's dry comment cut through the roundabout argument that'd been going on ever since he'd announced his intention to give up Black Cherry.

'Are you doing this for Fee Winter?' Sandy spat out her name.

'Yes and no.' He held up his hand to stop them questioning him any more. 'I only went to Iraq because if I'd have stayed I'd have gone mad with grief. Leaving now is different.'

His father touched Tom's shoulder. 'I'm not convinced you're making this choice for the right reasons.'

'Maybe I need to see if I can survive outside of this comfortable little bubble we've got here. Did you ever think of that?' Tom pulled away. He meant every word. He thought he'd become too cosy in his quiet life where there were no demands on him and few challenges. Fee had opened his eyes to wanting more.

'What if she turns you down?' Chloe chimed in, hoisting her youngest child on her shoulder.

'Then I'll simply do it for me.' The room went quiet and Tom stared around at them all, waiting for the next smart remark, but no one said a word.

'I've got an idea that would give you a break without cutting your ties completely.' Billy broke the silence. 'Rayna's enjoying being at Black Cherry and nobody wants to see the land go out of the family so how about we manage it for you until you're sure you want to sell?'

Tom's mind raced. Although the land belonged to him because of the way his grandfather's estate was shared up he hadn't cared for the idea of it going to strangers. 'But how would you manage? Your job's in Knoxville.'

Billy grinned. 'You'd have to agree to getting phones and internet access put in. I can't do my accounting work by sending smoke signals. Rayna's tired of teaching and would be happy to combine looking after the baby with doing the domestic stuff around Black Cherry. I'd fit in the rest and only take on as much work as I needed to.'

Tom's father chuckled. 'Called your bluff, hasn't he? You've got no excuse now.'

The hollow in his stomach deepened and Tom put on a cocky smile. 'Of course not. Sounds perfect.' Everyone joined in the conversation again but he didn't have much more to say. What if he was making the biggest mistake of his life?

Chapter Thirty-One

'Oh, hello. I was looking for Tom.' Fee frowned at the younger, dark-haired man sitting at Tom's desk. He swung the revolving chair around and scrutinised her closely.

'You must be Ms Winter.' His soft drawl marked him out as local but she still didn't have a clue who he was. Getting to his feet the stranger held out his hand. 'Billy Robbins. Tom's brother-in-law. I'm married to his sister, Rayna.'

'Right,' she said, shaking his hand. 'Is Tom sick?'

'Nope, he's fine, ma'am. Just gone to Knoxville for the day. I'm getting a touch more practise in for when me and my lovely wife take over for a while next week.'

Fee's head spun. 'Take over? Why, where's Tom going?' This time Billy's intense stare made her shiver.

'Not sure he's decided yet.' Billy shrugged. 'Did you need something?'

She struggled to think up a good reason for coming in. 'Um, a light bulb. The one outside my front door isn't working.' An absolute lie but the best she could manage under the circumstances. She had rushed over here with two things pressing on her mind neither of which she could share with this stranger. Fee had been desperate to plead for Tom's forgiveness over her thoughtless behaviour in New Orleans and to share her devastating news about Allain. When the DNA results revealed he couldn't be Fee's father she wasn't certain who was more shocked.

'No problem. I'll come on over with you now.' He grabbed a bunch of keys off the desk and opened a cupboard by the window. 'I'll bring a selection of bulbs. Not sure which one we need.'

None. For a second she almost admitted the truth but slammed her lips shut and gave him a grateful smile. 'Thanks. I appreciate it.'

They left the cabin and walked along the path together leaving Fee open to being interrogated in the typical, polite Southern way. All Billy's questions were hidden under a discreet layer of old-world courtesy. Fee picked her words with extreme care because every answer she made would no doubt be spread around the Chambers family, and by default the whole of Pine Ridge. She raved about the beautiful scenery and talked about her photography while giving nothing personal away.

'You've paid for another week. Are you thinking of staying on for the holidays maybe? It sure is pretty here at Christmas.'

'I shouldn't think so,' Fee said with a brief laugh as though the idea had never occurred to her. 'Why? Has anyone enquired about booking my cabin?'

'Not yet. Just thought I'd ask.'

They reached her cabin and Billy stepped onto the porch to try the light switch. Of course it worked perfectly because there was no reason for it not to.

'Light bulbs are unpredictable things sometimes.' *Like women*. The unspoken words made Fee cringe. 'I'll leave you to it.' Billy nodded and half way back down on the path he turned around to shout over his shoulder. 'I'll tell Tom you stopped by when he returns.'

He carried on walking, whistling as he went, and Fee knew she'd been rumbled.

Tom fiddled with his London plane ticket. He'd bought it to travel on the same day Fee was due to leave but with an open-ended return date. How would she react when he told her? At this moment his priority needed to be hurrying back to Black Cherry so he could take over from Billy. He'd worry about Fee later.

As he pulled off the main road and drove slowly on the rough gravel towards his cabin a welcome sense of peace surrounded him. Thank goodness Rayna and Billy saved him from doing something terminally stupid. How he could even have thought of selling was beyond him. This was Chambers' land and his name on the deed did nothing more than make him the caretaker.

'About time too,' Billy grouched half-heartedly as he walked into the office. 'Your sister's been pestering me on the radio for the last thirty minutes. She's got supper ready and I'll get the sharp end of her pregnancy temper if I'm late.'

'You implying Rayna's turning into a witch?' Tom teased.

'You said it. I didn't.' Billy rolled his eyes. 'I won't be up until the afternoon tomorrow if that's okay? I'm going into town in the morning to sort out the internet and phone installation.'

'Yeah. No problem.'

Billy unhitched his leather jacket from the hook by the door and tugged it on. 'By the way, your lady came by.'

'Fee?'

'Got more than one have you?'

'Course not,' Tom protested. 'What did she want?'

Billy grinned. 'I'd say you. She claimed her porch light was out but when I took a new bulb over hers worked fine. I think she made up that little tale when she found me here.'

'Did she ask for me?'

'Sure did. I kinda thought she went pale when I mentioned Rayna and me taking over this place but could be wrong.'

Tom persisted with his questions and found out exactly what his brother-in-law told Fee. 'You did great. Off you go and pamper my sister.'

Once he was alone again Tom fixed himself a cup of steaming hot coffee and strolled out onto the porch.

'Are you up for company?' Fee materialised out of the fading light.

He forced down the urge to spring to his feet. 'I guess.'

'I met Billy earlier.' She came to sit down next to him.

'So I heard.' Tom wasn't going to make this easy for her. 'I was coming to tell you later. And the other guests of course.'

'Were you?' she asked. Fee's eyes brightened with unshed tears and he couldn't keep up his indifferent front any longer.

Tom sighed. 'Oh, Fee. I can't pretend I don't care about you. Go away and leave me be if you feel the way you did in New Orleans.'

'I made a huge mistake out there about a lot of things.'

The sadness in her eyes struck him deep in the gut. 'Allain?'

Fee shook her head unable to say the words out loud. Tom held out his hand and she couldn't resist shifting over to sit on his lap. She rested her forehead against his chest and relished his steady heartbeat thumping under the frayed blue check shirt.

'He's not my father,' she murmured. 'You should've heard Lisette gloat when we got the test results. Allain was devastated.'

'And you?'

'It hurt,' she admitted. 'At first I think I followed up the possibility more to keep my mum off my back but ... after I met him I came around to the idea.'

'Do you regret going?'

She forced herself to think before she replied. The truth was she didn't have any regrets. 'No.'

'Good. You shouldn't.'

She trailed her finger over his chest. 'But I do regret what I said to you. Are you doing something stupid now because I was a total idiot?'

'Nope. I'm doin' it because ever since I met you I've gone all off kilter. I didn't realise I'd turned into a bore.'

'I never said you were boring,' Fee protested. 'What's wrong with being contented? I wish I was.' He stared at her in disbelief. 'I'm envious, you fool.'

'But you've travelled the world and seen so much. Your job is a constant challenge and nothing about your life is predictable. I'm not saying I'd care for it long-term but I need shakin' up.'

'Oh, Tom. I'm not saying don't leave Pine Ridge for a while but I think you'll discover you already have a great life.'

'But if you're not a part of it none of the rest matters,' Tom whispered and his eyes shone. 'I haven't done anything drastic. I've got a plane ticket to London leaving the same day as you, and Rayna and Billy will run this place until I get back. How about we go from there?'

Fee softened into him and he wrapped his arms around her, giving a big squeeze. 'I suppose that's reasonable,' she admitted. 'I need to visit my mother. I can't give her this news over the phone and ...' She didn't know how to put into words her need to make one last effort with Maddy.

'No excuses needed, honey. She's still your mother.'

His simple acceptance loosened something inside Fee and she didn't try to hold back her tears. Tom tenderly removed her glasses and set them down on the table before pulling out another of his crisp, white handkerchiefs to wipe her eyes. 'I don't want your family to blame me for luring you away,' she sobbed.

'Come with me tomorrow. I need you to meet someone important.'

'Who?'

'My grandmother.'

Fee's face burned with embarrassment. 'I'm already having coffee with her in the morning.'

'Really?' He couldn't hide his amazement.

No matter which way she phrased this he'd think she was sneaking around behind his back. *You were.*

Fee threw up her hands. 'Okay. You've got me. I knew you'd asked her for advice and when things ... went badly for us in New Orleans it struck me the best way to work things out with you was to winkle some information out of your grandmother.' For several interminable seconds a deadly silence filled the room.

'Women.' Tom burst out laughing. 'You're all the same.'

Fee didn't argue.

'She's been at this a whole lot longer than you, honey.' A mischievous grin stretched over his face. 'She'll chew you up, spit you out and wipe the floor with you while leaving you convinced she's a sweet old lady who wouldn't hurt a fly.'

'Are you saying I shouldn't go?'

'Nah, you go ahead.'

'I'll tell you everything she says. Don't worry.'

'Hey, I'm not worried,' Tom said. 'You're back in my arms and haven't tossed out my ideas as complete crap. It's all good. This morning I was pretty much convinced you'd never speak to me again.'

'Would you still have gone to London?'

He gave a long, slow nod and she let herself smile.

'Good.' Fee snuggled back into his embrace and didn't say another word.

Chapter Thirty-Two

Fee changed from a long sleeved black T-shirt into a black cotton blouse before tugging that off and yanking on a thin black jumper. She'd got into the habit of wearing all black when she was working because it didn't show the dirt and everything could be washed in together. Looking at her wardrobe now, all her clothes struck her as dingy and well-worn. After seeing her pale, narrow face reflected back in the mirror she even considered buying a tube of lipstick.

Mrs Chambers would have to take her as she found her. This wasn't a job interview for the position of Tom's new wife. *Admit it. You want her approval.* Tom's grandmother was important to him and therefore to Fee as well.

She brushed her freshly washed hair, pleased to notice it was thicker and shinier these days. Fee tugged on her black cord trousers and added a pair of black trainers. Before losing her nerve she hurried outside and stopped dead. Tom leaned against her porch steps and he dragged his warm gaze all the way from her head down to her toes.

'Do I pass inspection?'

'Yeah. I'd say so.' He reached out and pulled her down to him for a hug. 'Thought you might care for a lift into town.'

'Haven't you anything better to do?'

Tom lowered his mouth and she forgot the question as his kiss soaked into every bone in her body. Easing away he brushed a rogue strand of hair away from her face. 'Come on, let's get you to the witch's lair,' Tom teased. 'I'm sure the cauldron's bubbling by now.' Before she could protest on his grandmother's behalf he kissed her again. 'I needed to pick up a few things in Pine Ridge anyway.' He took hold of her hand and they strolled down to his cabin. Fee waited while he went inside to fetch his keys. 'All set.' Tom waved them in the air. 'Pops wants me to stop by and see him too.'

'What about? '

'He didn't say.' Tom shrugged.

She got in the truck and rested her camera on her lap. They set off and half way down the mountain Fee yelled at him to stop.

'What's wrong?' He slammed on the brakes and screeched to a halt by the side of the road.

'Nothing. Why should there be?' Fee jumped out and focused her camera on the breathtaking scene spread out in front of her.

'I thought either a herd of stampeding bulls were heading our way or you were having a heart attack.'

Fee hurried to explain about the effect of the vibrant colours juxtaposed with the effect of the morning fog on the top of the mountains. 'Oh, my gosh, I'm so sorry.' She slapped a hand in front of her mouth. 'I didn't mean to scare you. I won't do it again.' If they were to have any sort of future together she must learn to be more considerate.

'Don't apologise. If you can endure listening to me drone on about the Chambers' family history for hours on end I'm damn sure I can put up with you takin' pictures right, left and centre.' Tom rested his hand against her cheek. 'It's called compromise, honey. All the best marriages have it in spades.' He cleared his throat, shifting from one foot to the other. 'I mean ... well, um ...'

'I know what you mean,' she whispered, certain he wasn't the only one blushing. 'I really want this with you, Tom, but I don't know if I'm capable of doing it and can't bear the thought of hurting you.'

'You know what I've decided?'

Fee shook her head, pretty sure it was a rhetorical question.

'For too long I was stupid enough to believe I could protect myself from more heartbreak by living a safe, quiet existence.' He caressed her face and his intense gaze stared right into her soul. 'I'm tired of safe. You've turned the light back on in my world and I want to enjoy every moment. If it ended tomorrow I'd be devastated but I wouldn't regret a second.' He brushed his lips over her mouth, teasing them both. 'I'm hopin' it'll be a lot longer but I'm willin' to take a bet on you, Fee Winter.'

'Wow. How did we get to here from me taking a photo?' Tom silenced Fee's attempt at a joke with another kiss.

'There's a ton more I want to tell you but not now.' He checked his watch. 'Being late for coffee at Mee Maw's isn't a good idea. Not if you want to impress her.'

'And why would I want to do that?' She tweaked his nose. 'Men are so vain. You think this is all about you.' It was of course, and they both knew it, but a little humour helped to smooth over the emotions swirling between them.

Tom gave a teasing smile. He knew exactly what she was doing. 'Take your picture and let's go.'

She turned away and raised the camera again, steadying her hands with a couple of deep breaths. Five minutes later she was done and swung back around with a broad smile.

Every time she took his breath away. What you saw was what you got with Fee and he loved that about her. *Loved? Yeah, you love her you moron.* Happiness bubbled up inside him.

'I'm ready.'

Yeah, so am I. Tom resisted the urge to speak and simply nodded. He could easily be tempted to say things that weren't right for here and now.

'We'd better be going.' He caught a glimpse of Fee's smile as she turned away to stare out of the window.

'Drive carefully,' Fee murmured and her tinkling laughter filled the cab.

Somehow he made himself concentrate on the road and got them there in one piece. Tom stopped outside his grandmother's house.

'I'll walk over to see Pop and get my shopping done. By the time I come back she should've finished interrogating you.' Tom helped Fee down from the truck and drew her into his arms for a long, slow kiss before letting go. 'There. That should cement things for Mee Maw.'

'Do you think she's watching?' Fee's cheeks flushed.

'Nope,' he said with a laugh. 'I don't *think* she's watching, I *know* she is.' Tom loosened his hold and held her at arms' length. 'Good luck. Not that you'll need it.' A touch of uncertainty pulled at her lips and he ached to kiss her again. Instead he swung her around and gave her a slight push in the small of her back.

Fee's spine straightened under his fingers and she walked away from him. He headed down the street because to be caught out watching her all the way in would imply he was nervous and Tom refused to give his grandmother that satisfaction.

Before she could press the bell the door opened and Fee took a step back, almost tripping over a clay pot full of cheerful yellow chrysanthemums.

'Careful, dear. I don't want to have to explain to my grandson why you ended up in the hospital with a broken leg.' The tall but slightly stooped woman smiling at her had Tom's rich brown eyes, warm laugh and soft drawl. There were a few stray hints of auburn left in Mrs Chambers' wavy grey hair and by her unfussy elegance Fee guessed she'd been a beautiful young woman. She shot out her hand but was pulled into a hug instead.

'You'll have to get used to our Southern ways if you're goin' to marry our Tom so you might as well start now,' Betty Mae declared. 'Don't bother to deny it, hon. It's in your eyes. Come inside and we'll talk.'

Fee smiled and followed the other woman in over the front step like a lamb being led to the slaughter.

'I bought some of the chamomile tea Tom told me you drink.' She led the way in through a narrow hall which opened out into a sunny, well-lit kitchen at the back of the house. 'Tasted like cat's pee to me when I tried it but I'm sure it's mighty good for you.'

'It's an acquired taste,' Fee said with a laugh. She looked out of the window at the small well-tended garden. 'Do you do all this yourself, Mrs Chambers?'

'I used to, my dear, but these old bones won't let me bend well enough any more and the doctor keeps tellin' me to take it easier because my heart's not what it was. I tell him it's nearly ninety years old so what does he expect. Hank lines up one of the boys to do my yard work if he hasn't got time himself. My Tom does the lion's share.' She fixed Fee with a stern look. 'And you can stop calling me Mrs Chambers right now. My given name's Betty Mae but you can call me Mee Maw same as they all do.'

'Does that mean I've passed the first test?' For a second she wondered if she'd gone too far but Betty Mae's face cracked into the same wide generous smile Tom gave her the first day they met.

'I believe you might do.' Her eyes sparkled. 'Ask me again before you leave and I'll tell you for sure.'

'Fair enough.'

Tom's grandmother didn't comment and carried on getting their drinks ready. She took the lid off a large plastic container and the beautiful cake she revealed made Fee's mouth water.

'I fixed us an angel food cake. The recipe's made with egg whites and no fat. I hope that's alright?'

Her thoughtfulness touched Fee and she swallowed hard before nodding.

'I'll slice up some strawberries to have along with it.' Betty Mae sheepishly confessed she usually added a large dollop of homemade whipped cream and Fee was able to joke that at least her digestive problem kept her slim. Tom's grandmother suggested they had their tea out on the patio to enjoy the sunshine.

'Would you like me to carry the tray?'

'Certainly not. You're my guest,' Betty Mae retorted and Fee didn't dare say another word as they left the kitchen. 'Sit yourself down.' Her hostess gestured towards the small, white wrought-iron table and four chairs arranged in the middle of the patio. Pots of late-flowering pansies, colourful deep-coral sedum and white chrysanthemums were spaced out all around the edge and their warm fragrance filled the air. Fee made herself comfortable while Betty Mae sorted out their cups and plates, laying a lace-edged white napkin at each of their places along with a well-polished silver cake fork. 'Right. Dig in and tell me what you think.'

'And then?'

'Then *you'll* tell me all about yourself and *I'll* tell you about Tom.' Betty Mae's gentle smile didn't fool Fee for a moment. 'Deal?'

'Deal.' Her firm response garnered another approving nod but deep inside Fee was afraid Betty Mae would stop smiling when she heard the truth about Fee's life.

Chapter Thirty-Three

'Higgins is dead? You sure?' Tom leaned on his father's desk, unable to get his head around the news. Last night Gary Higgins was spotted in Mississippi and when the police gave chase he crashed the stolen car he'd been driving into a wall.

'Killed outright, son.'

'Shit.' Tom slammed his fist on the desk. Piles of papers toppled over and his father's full mug of coffee spilled all over them. 'The bastard should've been locked back up for violating his parole. It's not goddamn fair.'

Without a word Hank took down a roll of paper towels from the top of the filing cabinet and started to clean up the mess. Tom's initial fury seeped away and he sunk back into the chair. His father walked out around the desk to rest a comforting hand on Tom's shoulder.

'Nope. It's not.'

The straightforward sympathy finished him and Tom slumped forward and rested his head on his bent arms giving in to the rush of emotions swamping his body. Bitterness. Relief. Hatred.

'It's okay, son, let it out.' His father patted his shoulder. 'I won't tell your brothers.'

Tom managed a weak smile. 'You'd better not.' He wiped at his face and dragged a handkerchief from his pocket to blow his nose. 'I wanted … I don't know what I wanted but it wasn't this.'

'Yeah. I know,' Hank agreed before hesitating.

'Go on, spit it out. You don't normally have a problem with saying what you think.' His wry comment pulled a smile out of his father.

'I'm not sorry about Higgins. This ends it.'

Tom started to protest but Hank raised his hand in the air to silence him. The commanding gesture worked when they all were children and it did the trick again now. He shut up.

'I know you'll never forget but now you don't have to go

through life looking over your shoulder, wondering where Higgins is and eaten up because he's not behind bars. Gina's at peace. Take your freedom and make the most of it.' His father's voice cracked and it took the last remnants of Tom's self-control to hold himself together.

'I will. Fee's at Mee Maw's house having coffee and I'm off to join them.'

'They'll sort you out,' Hank ventured. 'When are you leaving town?'

They chatted about his plans which had expanded from simply going to visit Fee's mother to travelling some around Europe while they were that side of the pond. His father's only request was that he return home in time for Christmas.

'No problem. I've got to get Lulu's dolls' house finished and I'm not gonna miss her seeing it for the first time,' Tom replied.

'Good. Now get on with you. Some of us have work to do. Your mama's planning to have a big family get-together before you take off for foreign parts. She'll tell you when.'

There was no question of being *asked* and Tom wasn't stupid enough to argue. He got to his feet and stuck out his hand to his father but Hank pulled him into an unexpected hug. The last time that happened was at Gina's funeral and the significance wasn't lost on him. He hugged his father back and without another word they let go of each other.

Tom walked out of the office and stopped for a moment out on the street. He took a few steadying breaths of the crisp, clear air. He needed Fee. Now.

Fee glanced up as Tom stepped out onto the patio and panicked. 'What's wrong?' His eyes were suspiciously pink and if she didn't know better she'd guess he'd been crying.

His grandmother glanced between the two of them.

'Sit down, Tom. I'll fetch you some coffee and cake.' Betty Mae's gentle request got him to move and he dropped down into the chair next to Fee.

'*You're* frightening *me* this time. Did your father give you some bad news?' Fee asked, grabbing hold of his hands.

The hint of a smile tugged at his mouth. 'I thought it was at first but he helped me see it wasn't.'

Fee searched unsuccessfully for the right words to tell him he was making no sense but he leaned in to kiss her before she could speak again. Tom launched into a long, convoluted story about Gina's killer who'd apparently died in a traffic accident. Her first instinct was right and when he admitted to crying Fee choked up. Strong men rarely cracked but when they did it broke the hearts of those around them.

'Hey, I'm supposed to be the one who's upset not you,' Tom teased, playing with a strand of her hair. His eyes pleaded with Fee to pull herself together for his sake so she sucked in a deep breath and forced out a bright smile. 'Much better,' he declared and kissed her again.

'That's enough messin' around in the middle of the morning, Thomas Michael Chambers. Eat this instead of that dear girl.' Betty Mae deposited a plate loaded with cake and strawberries in front of Tom along with a mug of coffee. 'After you finish that you can tell me what's goin' on.'

'Angel food cake. You're a wonder.' He dug his fork in and speared a large piece. 'Fee, why don't you go ahead and tell Mee Maw everything? That way she won't have to wait until I'm done eatin' to satisfy her curiosity.'

'Are you implying I'm a gossip?' The older woman bristled and Fee hoped he'd turn his charm on before his grandmother smacked him.

'Not likely. I value my life,' Tom declared.

Before they could go back and forth all day Fee interrupted and started to do as Tom had asked. Betty Mae made exclamations and pithy comments all the way through the story.

'It's not Christian to say this but some people don't deserve to take up space on this earth and that man's one of them. Of course I'll add him to my prayers tonight. The wicked man's gonna need it.' Betty Mae calmly sipped a fresh cup of coffee while she made the blunt summing up.

'Thanks, Mee Maw,' Tom whispered and kissed his grandmother on the cheek. When he turned back towards Fee there was a new sadness touching his eyes. 'There's somewhere I need to go.' He hesitated for a second. 'I need to tell Gina and I wondered if you'd come with me. The cemetery is about a five minute drive but I need to go to the flower shop first.'

Fee struggled against the urge to run away. Those days were part of her past. Loving wasn't always going to be easy. 'Of course.'

He gulped down his coffee and pushed away the empty plate. 'Mee Maw. Do you mind if we go now?'

'What a damn fool question. '

'Before we go let me take your picture together,' Fee suggested. 'It's so pretty out here.' She picked up her camera and encouraged Tom to move his chair closer to his grandmother before quickly framing the shot. 'Perfect.'

Betty Mae set the dishes back on the tray. Fee smiled to herself when his grandmother made no objection to Tom taking it right out of her hands.

This time out by the front door Fee initiated the hug. 'So?'

The old woman's eyes danced with amusement. 'You'll do fine. Tom's not a rash, flitting around sort of boy. You'd better appreciate him and if I ever hear you've messed him around you'll have me to deal with.' Betty Mae mitigated her sharp retort with a mischievous smile. 'Even if I've passed on I promise I'll come back and haunt you.'

'I don't doubt it for a moment.' Fee laughed.

Tom opened his mouth to protest but they both stared him down until he gave up the idea and stood there, waiting until she joined him. They walked down the path hand in hand, waving back at his grandmother as they went.

'You sure you're okay with doing this?' As soon as the words left his mouth Tom regretted them. 'Sorry,' he murmured. 'I don't mean to be stupid.'

'I know. It simply comes naturally to some people.' Her face softened. 'You've had a tough day so I'll let you off this time.'

'Thanks. I don't deserve you.'

'Something we both agree on at last. Now let's get to the flower shop.'

He chose the usual bronze chrysanthemums tied with a gold satin ribbon. Out at the cemetery Tom left his cleaning supplies in the truck and walked with Fee along the rough gravel path, the pale November sun warming their backs.

'This is a lovely spot.'

'Yeah. Her parents chose it.'

'Are you close to them?'

'Not any longer.' He shook his head. 'They blame me. Gina was their only child.'

'That's tough. Are those her favourites?' Fee pointed to the flowers and he nodded. Tom hunkered down on the grass and gathered up the flowers he'd put there on the anniversary of her death before replacing them with the fresh ones.

Quietly he told Gina what had happened to Gary Higgins and how he hoped she could be at peace because he was, finally. Without looking at Fee he described her to Gina, catching Fee's quick intake of breath when he struggled to explain how much he loved her. 'I hope you don't mind?' he asked, smiling as a warm breeze touched his face. 'I'm goin' away for a while but I'll be back.' Tom rubbed his fingers over Gina's name etched into the cold marble and sighed.

'Are you good now?' Fee asked. He stood and pulled her into his arms, burying his face in her fresh, silky hair.

'Yep.'

'Is it time to go home?'

Hearing her call Black Cherry home warmed his heart. 'Sure is.'

'I might even make you one of my famous sandwiches if you're lucky,' Fee teased.

'I can't get any luckier.'

Chapter Thirty-Four

'Oh, Tom, it's beautiful.' Fee ran her fingers over the tiny doorframe. The dolls' house was a beautifully crafted piece of carving and she couldn't help thinking that no one had ever done anything as wonderful for her when she was a child. She swallowed hard, desperate not to give in to more tears. Between them they'd shed more than enough of those today. Fee had completely broken down telling Betty Mae about her mother after the older lady encouraged her to talk. Tom's grandmother was better than any therapist on the face of the planet and all she'd really done was listen. 'Lulu's a lucky girl.'

'No. I'm the lucky one.' Tom's gruff voice gave him away and Fee didn't dare turn around. Children were one topic they'd avoided until now. His broad hands circled her shoulders and she couldn't resist any longer, meeting his gaze straight on. 'It's okay.'

Fee's head dropped onto his chest and she rested against his steady heartbeat. 'For lots of reasons I don't think I can …' her breath trailed away.

He shifted his right hand to the centre of her back and worked his fingers in gentle rhythmic circles. 'I love you, Fee. *You*. Not any random woman who can give me a child but you.' Tom lowered his mouth to hers and trailed his tongue around her lips until she sighed and gave in to his exploration for several wonderful moments. 'No one comes without baggage especially at our age and I've got enough to fill the cargo hold of a Jumbo Jet. Remember I've got enough nieces and nephews, plus more on the way, to satisfy my desire for children.'

'I'm not exactly young and my health isn't the best.' Were those feeble excuses?

'There's always adoption.' Tom fixed his dark eyes on her and Fee shivered.

Taking a step backwards she let her arms fall to her side. 'Tom. I ...'

'Don't say it.' He shook his head. 'Not today. After we've seen your mother we'll talk again.'

Would she be taking the easy way out by going along with him or was it only common sense?

Tom grasped her face in his broad, warm hands. 'Don't you dare tell me you're giving up. I expect better of you. Fight for us. I am.' This time his kiss wasn't gentle and his hard, uncompromising body pressed against hers. The shard of desire he ignited took her breath away. 'I'm gonna send Billy on home to Rayna and take you to my bed.' He couldn't have made his intentions any clearer if he'd shouted them from the mountaintop.

'Oh. Yes, please.' Her polite comment drew out the hint of a smile at the corners of his mouth.

Without another word he led her back outside.

Tom wanted to beat himself around the head. He'd almost lost Fee twice now. Once at the hands of Randy Watling and again a few minutes ago because he'd stupidly spoken too soon. He'd almost been dumb enough to tell Fee what a wonderful mother she'd make but that was the last thing she'd want to hear. From day one he'd known Fee didn't share his dream of a large family and it hadn't mattered. Convincing her she was more important to him than any mythical children would be an uphill task. *You're still hoping she'll change her mind. Admit it.* A corner of his heart still clung onto the vision but he swore to himself never to raise the subject again. He could live without having children but didn't intend on living without Fee.

'I think the phones and internet were connected today so Billy will be a happy man.'

'Will it change things?' Fee asked.

'I'm not sure.' He shrugged. 'It'll make running the business easier but take away part of the timeless quality I enjoyed being able to offer guests. Everything's a compromise isn't it?' Her shrewd eyes narrowed and Tom yearned to assure her he hadn't meant the words personally.

'I'm sure your ancestors debated the virtues of candles versus oil lamps and whether to buy a length of factory-made fabric instead of spinning their own,' Fee observed. 'How about I leave you to speak to Billy and come back later? I need to throw some clothes in the wonderful, new-fangled washing machine.'

'You're telling me not to be a stick-in-the-mud aren't you?' Tom seized her in a massive bear hug.

'Never.' Fee wriggled in his arms but he tightened his grasp.

'Good. If you aren't careful there'll be no fun later.'

She laughed in his face. 'Oh, yes. And who's that going to hurt most?' Fee glanced at him from under her long dark lashes, fluttering them against her pale, perfect skin.

'Go and do your laundry. Come back at six.'

'Say please,' Fee whispered, rubbing her finger back and forth over his unshaven jawline.

'Go,' Tom rasped and a streak of triumph flitted across her face. It seemed she was learning to enjoy the power she wielded over him. Tom decided to keep to himself how much he loved it too.

'Later.' With a quick wave she raced off, her heels barely touching the ground as she hurried along the path.

For a few moments he stood outside the office until he could wipe the satisfied smile from his face. He didn't need his brother-in-law teasing him for being a lovesick sap.

'Finally. I thought you'd forgotten about me,' Billy declared, swinging the chair around to face him. 'I wanted to give you a run-down on the new systems before I beat it.'

Tom glanced at the clock. 'What's the hurry? It's only just gone four.'

'Yeah. I know but Rayna's in a touchy mood. Tired of being

pregnant I guess.' He sighed. 'Did you go into the cafe this morning?'

'Nope.' He wasn't about to go into how he *had* spent his morning. No doubt the Pine Ridge gossip brigade would spread the news fast enough.

'Luke Durham injured his shoulder in their last game and is out for the season so he's back in town for the holidays. Aunt Ina caught him sniffing around Mary-Jo and got the mother-lion claws out. Mary-Jo's ordering her to butt out of her business. Says she'll be twenty-one in a couple of weeks and she'll talk to who she wants.' Billy rolled his eyes. 'Never a moment's peace with this family. Y'all are better than any soap opera.'

Tom suppressed a smile. Billy was an only child and grew up with his older parents in a quiet Knoxville suburb. Before she agreed to marry him Rayna insisted on moving back to Pine Ridge and Tom had witnessed multiple noisy arguments between the two over the lack of privacy Billy experienced living in the small community. 'Glad we keep you amused.'

'Sure do.'

'What's Pop saying about Durham?' Tom knew his father thought the boy was a jerk.

'He's a wise man and leaving it to the women.' Billy tossed him a sharp look. 'You'd be smart to do the same.'

Tom's dislike of Luke Durham was well known. The way the Durham family "dealt" with Lulu's birth had made him sick to the stomach although the boy himself was essentially harmless. 'Yeah. Yeah. I'm not goin' to challenge him to a fist fight. Apart from anything else Fee would kill me.'

Billy grinned. 'You tamed as well?' Tom didn't need to reply because they both knew the truth. His brother-in-law shrugged and started to tell him all about the new internet and phone connections. 'The only phones are here in the office, your bedroom and one in the communal room. Cell phone coverage is a bit patchy so don't promise guests it'll work everywhere.

The internet's pretty decent in here and in the closest cabins but loses strength the further it gets from the router. You might consider putting a computer in the communal room.'

'Sounds good.' Tom took off his denim jacket and hung it up. 'Off you go and rub Rayna's feet and feed her ice cream or whatever she's fancying.'

'Brussels sprouts.' Billy screwed up his face. 'If I never see another sprout it'll be too soon. They've got to be boiled to death as well.' He hauled himself out of the chair and found his computer bag. 'Our house smells like a rancid swamp.'

Tom slapped his brother-in-law on the back. 'It'll all be worth it when Billy Junior arrives. Now go.'

They said goodnight and once the door closed Tom sank down into the chair. He leaned on the desk and stared at the computer. Suddenly the door swung open and he glanced up. 'Hi Pop, what's up? You should've called on our fancy new phone line.'

'I've got some news I couldn't tell you over the phone, son.'

An icy hand clutched Tom's heart as he took note of his father's haggard face. He wanted to order him not to say another word.

Chapter Thirty-Five

'My washing is doing its thing and I saw Billy's car was gone so I ...' Fee's voice trailed away as she glanced at the two men. 'What on earth's wrong?'

'It's my mama.' Hank's anguished voice made the bottom drop out of Fee's stomach. 'Her heart ...' He couldn't carry on.

'Pop stopped by when he was out on patrol and found her on the patio. He thought at first she'd fallen asleep in the chair but ...' Tom wiped at his eyes. 'We all knew she had a bad heart but no one thought it'd come this quick.'

'Was our visit too much for her?'

Tom snatched hold of her hands. 'Mee Maw saw us happy together.' He swallowed hard. 'I'm damn glad we went and she'd say the same.'

'I'd better go, son.' Hank interrupted. 'Got a ton to arrange. I'm guessin' we'll go with Thursday evening for visitation and Friday afternoon for the funeral.'

'As soon as that?' Fee couldn't hide her surprise.

'Yeah. That's the norm here. We do the visitation piece for people who can't get to the service and those who want a chance to talk with the family. It'll last a couple of hours and we'll do that in the church hall. How long do y'all wait for your funerals?' Tom asked.

'At least a week and a fortnight isn't unusual.'

'Mama left me very specific instructions and she went over them with me only last Sunday. Almost like she knew.' Hank blinked back tears. 'I'm guessin' this will sound mighty strange to you but my mama was a huge football fan and she insisted that her funeral mustn't be held on a Saturday when the University of Tennessee plays at home in Knoxville. That's the case this week so Friday it is.' His raspy voice broke. 'She said people would resent giving up their tickets to the game and would be searching for a TV to watch or following the score on their cell phones. She wanted their full attention.'

'Oh, right. Well you can't disobey her orders.' Fee struggled to smile.

'We'll come down in a while to be with y'all.' Tom rested his hand on Hank's shoulder and something about the role reversal touched her. The two men walked outside together and their murmured voices drifted in through the half-open door before his father drove off.

Tom's boots dragged across the wood floor and he hurried to wrap his arms around her. 'Mee Maw would insist she had a good long life with so many blessings she couldn't count them.' His eyes glistened as he fought with his emotions. 'But it doesn't make it any damn easier. What am I goin' to do without her, Fee? She nagged me after I lost Gina about wasting my life and I regret—'

'Don't.' Fee fixed him with a stern stare. 'Regret is a complete waste of time. The best way to honour your grandmother is to make every day count.' She rolled her eyes. 'Goodness. I'm starting to sound like a combination of my therapist and your grandmother.'

'She is ... was a wise lady and I'm damn sure she's in heaven now laughing at me and sayin' it's about time I realised she was right all along.' His voice wobbled. 'I'd better change into some decent clothes before we go to town then I'll fix us a snack. I'm sure there will be a ton of food in the house by the time we arrive but there won't be much suitable for you to eat.'

Fee almost said she wasn't hungry and couldn't imagine being so anytime soon but sensed he needed something to do.

'It's an old tradition in the South to bring food to people who they think need nourishment whether it's because they're sick, just had a baby or are in mourning. After Gina died my kitchen was covered in food but I couldn't force down a single bite.'

It broke her heart to hear him say that one night he tossed it all in the trash when he couldn't bear the constant reminders of his loss staring him in the face every time he fetched a glass of water.

'By tomorrow morning there'll be at least four variations on the standard green bean casserole, mounds of fried chicken, baked ham, devilled eggs and pies and cakes too numerous to mention. Make sure you stay away from Dolly Robinson's oatmeal raisin cookies.' Tom eked out a smile. 'You might think they're a safe choice but you'll risk breaking a tooth. You'll easily recognise them because she incinerates them to a lethal shade of charcoal black.'

'You're exaggerating.'

Tom held up three fingers. 'Scout's honour.'

'I'll let you feed me.'

Tom drank in the sight of Fee across the kitchen table. She'd eaten every scrap of the wholewheat tortilla stuffed with lean turkey and salad he'd made. He polished off one too, figuring it wouldn't do him any harm. In the back of his mind he knew he'd indulge in more food later so it wasn't complete altruism on his part.

'By the way, we're still goin' to Europe next week as planned.' He thought he'd better put that out there before she got the idea to cancel their trip.

'But surely you ...'

'Mee Maw knew we needed to go.'

'If you're sure, I'm not going to argue. Tomorrow I'll have to go shopping and buy something for the ... funeral. I don't have a skirt or dress with me here.' She shrugged. 'Actually I don't actually own either.'

'How about I take you in the morning?' The words tumbled out of his mouth before he stopped to think. Gina only took him clothes shopping once and then refused to ever repeat the experience. She'd called him grumpy, impatient and morose. And those had been the kindest words she chose – the rest didn't bear remembering.

'Really?' Her eyebrows rose to the ceiling. 'The combination of you and shops was one of the things your grandmother warned me about.'

'Dare I ask what the others were?'

'She said if I was having any difficulty getting to sleep to get you talking about the Chambers' family history and I'd be out like a light in five minutes. Apparently I'm to cover my ears when you're watching football and your team is losing because you've got a foul mouth. Do you really want me to go on?'

'Probably not.' His dry comment made her smile. 'You hit it off didn't you?' Tom couldn't hide his wistfulness.

'Yes and I've never experienced that before. I tend to get on better with men because I'm not girly. My mother's the same way.'

Working out how to reply was tricky. Tom sensed Fee was searching for a way to change without betraying who she was deep inside.

'It's okay.' She patted his hand. 'I don't expect you to wave a magic wand and solve all my problems in one go. You're doing pretty good so far. Let's not push our luck.'

'So are you goin' to take me up on my offer to go shoppin'?'

Fee's shrewd blue eyes bored into him. 'I do believe I will.'

'Great.' *Liar*. 'Right let's get goin'.'

For once they didn't talk on the drive down to Pine Ridge and Fee only broke the silence when he drove past the Mockingbird Cafe.

'I see Mary-Jo's been busy.' Every trace of Halloween had been eradicated apart from the orange plastic pumpkins which were doing double duty for the cafe's new Thanksgiving theme. Straw scarecrows and Pilgrim cut-outs were dotted over the front and linked together with bright fall leaves. Flashing orange and yellow lights completed the transformation.

'Yep, she sure has. Mee Maw always says Thanksgiving is her favourite holiday.' Tom gripped the steering wheel so hard he was surprised it didn't buckle. 'I mean used to say.'

'Why did she love it so much?'

He pulled into the only parking spot left anywhere near the house and realised they were the last to arrive. 'She said it combined her two favourite things in life – plenty of good football to watch and the chance to feed her family. We always went to her house on Thanksgiving Day.' Tom swallowed hard. 'We've all helped out with the cooking over the last few years when she couldn't manage as well but …'

'It still won't feel right not to gather around her table.'

Fee's simple statement punched him in the gut.

'No, it won't.'

'I'm sorry.'

'Yeah, I know and that means … everything to me.' He pulled her to him for a few precious moments. 'We'd better get inside before Mama sends out a search party.'

The second they stepped into the house Lulu came barrelling out of nowhere wearing her Halloween pirate costume and brandishing a plastic sword.

'Uncle T did you know Mee Maw's gone to heaven and she's an angel now with wings and a halo?' She bounced up and down. 'I want wings and a halo too. If I ask Santa Claus will he bring me some?'

Tom swept her into his arms and buried his face in her red curls. He'd break down if he tried to answer and the last thing he wanted was to scare her.

'Mama says it's only fifty days until Christmas and she's made me a thing to count them on. Is fifty a lot, Uncle T? I want it to be Christmas now!'

'It'll go really quick if you're a good girl.' Fee promised.

'Do you want to see my new dolly? She cries and wets herself.'

'Wow, that's awesome. I'd love to.'

Laughter bubbled up inside him at Fee's disingenuous statement.

'You go and be with your family.' She whispered close to his ear. 'They need you and you need them.'

He caught the fleeting touch of envy and despite being swamped by grief Tom knew she was right. Fee never sought sympathy but he felt it anyway. Later he'd try to put it into words.

Chapter Thirty-Six

Foolishly he'd thought a black dress was a black dress but boy was he ever wrong. For a woman who claimed no interest in fashion Fee was being mighty picky in Tom's opinion although he hadn't been stupid enough to say so.

'How about this one?' She emerged from the changing room and twirled around. If he told her the dress was great to get this ordeal over with she'd pick up on his indifference in one second.

'Oh, yeah. Great.'

'It's the same one I showed you five minutes ago that you said had an ugly neckline. Pretty amazing.'

He threw his hands in the air. 'Okay. You win. I'm hopeless at this.' Tom went for complete honesty. 'You look damn beautiful in anything to me and one black dress is much the same as the next.'

'I'll need to buy some heels to wear with the dress.' Fee frowned.

'You could borrow some. There's enough females in my family surely someone must have a pair to fit you.' Tom pulled out his wallet. 'I'll pay. You get your stuff.'

'I'm perfectly capable of buying my own ...'

He gave her a hard kiss. 'I know you are but let me, please.' If nothing else it might make up for his uselessness.

'If it's any consolation I hate shopping too.'

'It is.' Tom grinned.

Five minutes later they were back in his truck.

'What's the plan for the rest of the day?'

'I need to catch up with some work in the office for an hour or so and then I've got to go tidy up Mee Maw's garden. She insisted we have the funeral tea at her house instead of the church so I'm delegated to get it straight while Mama and the girls swoop in to clean.' Should he take it for granted Fee would come with him? Taking her for granted could have negative connotations but he was pretty sure she'd want to be there.

'What on earth is going through your mind now? I can see the wheels turning.' Fee nailed him. 'Whatever "this" is we're in it together. From my perspective it'll take some working out because I'm clueless about ... long-term relationships.'

Tom swiftly poured out everything rattling around his brain.

'Silly man, of course I'll come with you. That's not "taking for granted" in a bad way. It's doing things together.'

Before they went any further he should explain more about his marriage but Tom didn't know where to start. *If you want to tell her something do it outright. It's always best. Hard maybe but for the best.* His grandmother's advice resonated and he wished he'd listened to her more often.

'Spit it out.'

'What?'

'Whatever is putting the frown on your face.'

'Okay.' Tom exhaled a deep, long breath. 'I respect you for never asking much about Gina but it's time you knew a bit more.' Tom hated to watch her smile disappear.

'I'm not sure I ...'

He touched his finger to her lips, stopping whatever she'd been about to say. 'Please. I need this and so do you.' Tom hurried on before he could lose his nerve. 'I loved Gina dearly in many ways. We were best friends since we were little kids. I was a year older and looked after her at school and stuff.' Tom sighed. 'Anything going on around Pine Ridge she tagged along with me and by the time we were in high school we'd somehow become a couple. I hate to say she worshipped me because it sounds vain. Gina was beautiful and all the other boys envied me.'

'You were flattered.'

Tom shrugged. 'Sounds lame, but yeah, I was. She never had any ambition to go to college. All Gina wanted was to settle down and have a whole brood of children. '

'With you.'

'Yeah.'

Fee rested her head on his shoulder, giving comfort without speaking.

'Gina worked in her father's real estate business while I went to college and the police academy. She never asked why I didn't propose, but something kept holding me back until after I graduated and had my badge.' His family wouldn't admit to pressuring him but he'd felt it anyway, plus even more from Gina's parents. Tom tried to explain to Fee how it'd been.

'What did your grandmother think?'

Tom cracked a smile. 'She was the only one who questioned whether I loved Gina the right way. Being Mee Maw she dragged me to one side in the middle of our engagement party.'

'Great timing.'

'Oh, yeah. She asked me if I'd met Gina then instead of years earlier would I have asked her out and considered building a future with her. I lied and said yes, but she knew the truth.'

'She would.' Fee's wry comment made him laugh. 'And then the wedding treadmill started.'

Tom nodded. 'It sweeps you along. Soon I had a beautiful woman as my wife and a job I loved. Life was good.'

'Did you make her happy?' Fee wasn't certain how she hoped he would answer.

'I think so at first, but she needed me to be everything for her and ... I let her down. She resented the fact I was ambitious because it took me away from her and she was lonely. We argued a lot and I took on more overtime to avoid going home.' Tom's pain resonated between them.

'If Gary Higgins hadn't come along what do think would've happened to you both?'

Tom flinched at her bluntness. Fee knew she'd asked the

question he'd let destroy him for the last sixteen years.

'I don't know. But I hate the fact I got my freedom at the cost of Gina's life.'

Fee wrapped her arms around him. 'It didn't free you though, did it?' He shook his head and shudders ran through his body. 'You need to let go. Nothing can change what happened. The only way any of us survives is to learn from our mistakes and move on.'

He eased away and stared down at her, his deep brown eyes full of love. 'I'm not the only one beating themselves up here. I'm ready to make a fresh start if you are too.'

Fee's heart raced. What exactly was he saying?

Chapter Thirty-Seven

His timing was lousy. Who on earth proposed to one woman after spending the last half hour pouring out every detail of his less than perfect marriage?

'I'm gonna say what I want to despite everything I've just told you.' Tom rushed on. 'I'm not expecting an answer right away, but think about it. Please.'

'What? You haven't asked me anything yet.' Fee's gentle remonstrance stopped him in his tracks.

'Oh. Right. Yeah.' This wasn't going well. He'd better get it over with before he screwed up any worse. 'Marry me. No man's ever goin' to love you more than I do.' Tom's proclamation came to an abrupt halt.

'Yes.'

'Yes what?'

'Um. Yes, please.' Fee's mouth curved in a wide smile.

'Just like that?' he croaked.

'Just like that.'

He'd expected a ton of questions and a plea for more time but she'd yanked the rug out from under his feet again.

'Say something, Tom, or I'll start to think you regret asking me.' The laughter in her eyes told him she was joking. 'Please don't start fretting about rings or weddings either. There's time enough for all that and anyway I don't really do jewellery,' she murmured.

Tom smoothed his hand over her hair, playing with the shaggy ends that'd grown out in the last few weeks. 'You love the silver bracelet.'

'That's different.'

'Why?'

'It's simple.'

'Who says an engagement ring has to be fussy? Hang a

metal washer on a string around your neck for all I care. As long as the world knows you're mine it's all good to me.'

'So now you're trying to be cheap,' Fee teased.

Tom pulled a white handkerchief from his pocket and waved it in the air. 'I officially surrender. Tell me what you want and we'll do it. End of story.'

'One thing I must say and please don't take this as a criticism of Gina but we're two very different women. I'm too independent to *need* a man to have a good, productive life. I am certain it'll be a better and more complete one with you because of the love we have for each other.'

He only wished he could express his feelings half as well as she did. 'Do you want to tell everyone today?'

'I don't think so. I don't want to seem disrespectful.'

Tom couldn't help smiling. 'We'll do whatever you want but I'm pretty damn sure Mee Maw is up in heaven takin' credit for this big time.'

The triumphant grin plastered all over her face made everything worthwhile. He silently thanked his beloved grandmother for making him see sense.

Fee should have known Tom's mother would guess their secret. Sarah took one look at them as they walked into the house and beamed. She clapped her hands together and shouted for everyone to come out to the hall.

Sarah wormed the whole story out of Tom while they all listened.

'Some people might say you're rushin' into things but this good man snatched me from under Bubba Watkins' nose and had me down the aisle before I hardly knew his name.' Sarah pointed at Hank who turned the colour of a boiled beetroot. 'We've rubbed along together for nearly forty-six years so I guess it worked.'

Fee's therapist would tear his hair out. She'd done the precise opposite of everything he'd advised and never been happier.

Hank held up his hand to silence all the congratulations going around. 'Don't mean to break things up but we've got work to do.'

This was why she'd wanted to keep the news to themselves for now. She didn't blame Tom's father for being cross.

'Wipe that sad look off your face.' He wagged his finger at her. 'My sweet Mama thought the sun shone out of Tom and she loved you already. She was happy as a clam that you'd found each other and told me so on the phone ...'

'When?' Tom asked.

'Right after you left her. She wanted to make sure I was going to stop by later for a hunk of angel food cake.' Hank struggled not to break down.

'Thanks for telling us that.' Tom slipped an arm around his father's shoulder. 'It means a lot. And you're right, we do need to get busy. I don't want Mee Maw to torment me because I left a weed in her precious flower beds.' His gruffness betrayed the emotions shimmering under the surface of his weak smile.

They all returned to their assigned jobs and Fee was handed a clean yellow duster and told to go into the living room and help Rayna.

'Do you mind dusting Mee Maw's thimble collection while I do the glasses?'

'Good grief. How many are there?' She stared in horror at the glass-fronted display cabinets dotted around the walls.

'At last count I think she had around five hundred.' Rayna grinned. 'Tom built the cabinets for her. He's good with his hands.'

'He certainly is,' Fee agreed. 'Have you seen the incredible dolls' house he's making for Lulu?'

Rayna shook her head. 'I'm sure it'll be amazing.'

'It is. Makes me wish I was a little girl.'

'Me too. My all-time favourite present was the roller skates I got when I was six. I managed to skin my knees before Christmas dinner and rip my new dress. Mama sure was mad.'

She laughed. 'What was your best present?'

'Um, nothing really stands out.' She remembered the disappointing Christmases of her childhood. Holidays always took a back seat to the latest man in her mother's life or the plight of whatever endangered species Maddy was passionate about that particular week. She often overheard her school friends discussing what they wanted for Christmas but avoided joining in because the chances were the day would be just like any other for her. The first and only "normal" Christmas dinner they had was at Will's house in Cornwall one year when he cooked roast turkey with all the trimmings. It had amazed her on Christmas morning to wake up and find a stocking stuffed with presents at the foot of her bed.

'Tom says y'all are going to visit your mother next week and then travel around Europe.'

Fee began to take the thimbles out onto the table one shelf at a time ready to be dusted so she could put them back in the right order. 'Yes.'

'Does your mom live in London?'

'No.' Fee hoped Rayna would get the hint it wasn't something she wanted to discuss.

'You'll be goin' back again for Christmas I guess?'

'I shouldn't think so. She's used to my work taking me away.' That sounded better than admitting the truth.

'But you're not working at the moment.'

Fee's head throbbed. Would Rayna never give up? 'Why did your grandmother collect thimbles?' She tried to change the subject.

'Mee Maw never travelled much but thimbles are small and relatively inexpensive so she'd ask anyone who went somewhere interesting to bring her one back,' Rayna explained. 'I suppose you think I'm being nosy but we'd all like to know more about you.'

She sighed and laid the duster down. 'So you got stuck with the job.'

I don't blame you or the rest of the family but it still hurts. The Chambers family were close and Tom falling head over heels for a woman they knew almost nothing about was bound to make them curious.

'What do you want to know?' Fee pulled out a chair and sat down, picking the duster back up to work while she talked. 'Three guesses. Everything?'

'Heck, Fee, do you blame us?'

'No. But don't you trust Tom's judgment?' Fee brushed off Rayna's attempt to apologise. Struggling to keep her voice steady she rattled through a condensed version of her life story. More than anything she hated the idea of the Chambers family feeling sorry for her. She'd had an unsettled childhood but other kids had a hell of a lot worse. 'That's it. You can tell everyone I'm an emotionally stunted nomad who's never lived in one place for more than a few months or sustained a relationship with a man long enough to send out Christmas cards together. I can't cook and I never wear make-up or high heels.' Fee blinked back tears. She'd been stupid enough to believe they'd accepted her as she was. 'Now you know everything Tom does.'

'Fee. I never meant ...'

She calmly laid the duster back on the table and walked out of the room. Fee ignored Rayna's shouts for her to come back and raced out of the front door. She hurried off down the street with no plan in mind other than to get away. Halfway down the street she stumbled on a crack in the pavement and fell down on her bad knee.

'Going somewhere?' Tom appeared out of nowhere and helped her to stand back up. 'We're going home.'

She leaned into him and savoured Tom's solid, warm strength. Fee imprinted it on her brain for when they were apart. Soon enough she'd have to say things neither of them wanted to hear.

Chapter Thirty-Eight

Tom surreptitiously glanced at Fee, pale and silent and wanted to kick himself for not being one step ahead of his family. It didn't take a genius to guess what Fee intended on saying to him when they got back to Black Cherry. He'd come close to wringing Rayna's neck when he found out what had been said but catching up with Fee was more important. Later he'd deal with his family.

Outside his cabin he slammed on his brakes and got out of the truck, running around to open her door. 'Don't even think about running off. We're goin' in here and you'll listen to me first for a change before you say another word.'

Fee didn't look at him as she got out and headed for the steps. Tom left her sitting on the sofa and disappeared into the kitchen to fetch them both a glass of ice water. He returned and set her glass on the table before taking his own over to the recliner.

'I don't know every detail of what was said because I was too worried about you to stand still and listen to Rayna but I got the gist. This is all my damn fault.' He stifled her attempt to protest. 'I should've sat them down and told them everything weeks ago but I figured it was your business and it'd come out as they got to know you. I'm an idiot and you'd be within your rights to smack me.' Fee's solemn face gave him no clue as to what was going through her mind. 'They love you. They don't care if you've got a huge close family or none and the fact you haven't lived in the same house your whole life is irrelevant.' Tom tried to smile. 'What they hate is the fact I didn't spell out every detail in the first place. They're nosy.' He risked moving across to sit next to her and caught a new sparkle in her eye that wasn't there before. 'As a family we're very protective of each other. Too much sometimes but I kind of think it's better than too little.' He left it at that because the last thing he wanted was to imply her life was less complete than his own.

'It is.' She took hold of his hands. 'I overreacted. All poor Rayna did was ask a few questions including where my mother lived. I should've given her a straightforward answer. It wasn't a big deal but I made it one.'

'Are you unsure of me? Of us?' Tom hated asking but needed to know. 'Have I rushed you into something you're not ready for?'

'I'm totally ready but I need to sort things out with my mother one way or the other before we make our own plans.' A wry smile tugged at her mouth. 'It would've been nice to know who my father is but that's life.'

'Shame about Allain.'

'Yes, it was.' Her quiet answer tore at him. This was one thing Tom couldn't fix. 'Are we good now?' he asked.

'I'd say we are.' A slow, captivating smile crept over her face. 'Can we leave seeing your family again until tomorrow please? I need to apologise hugely to all of them, but especially Rayna.'

He yearned to say *they* should be apologising to *her* but kept his mouth shut. If he interfered she would gut him and hang him up to dry.

'That's right. It's my place to sort it. Not you. Hate it don't you?' Fee's spot-on summing up made him wince. 'You can do something useful and get some ice for my knee please.'

'What about some painkillers?'

She shook her head. 'Been there. Done that. Not a good idea. I know you're talking about something innocuous but I'd better not. Ice and elevating it will do the trick.'

'Maybe you should go to bed and rest.'

'Going anywhere near a bed with you doesn't usually involve resting,' she retorted. 'Perhaps my own cabin would be wiser.'

'No way. What if you need help in the night?'

'Oh, I give in. I'll take up residence in your bed and let you fuss over me. Just for tonight.'

Forever sounds better to me. By the way her eyes widened Tom knew she'd read his mind. He wanted to cheer but satisfied himself with kissing her and whisking her off to his bedroom.

As the pale morning sun sneaked into the room Fee lay in Tom's arms and wished the next couple of days over with. A few weeks ago it took all her courage to walk into the Mockingbird Cafe and order a sandwich. Now she was expected to stand by Tom's side while the whole town came to pay their respects to his grandmother. She'd be stared at. Questioned. Talked about. This could be tougher than any war zone.

'I can't imagine tryin' to get through this without you,' Tom whispered. 'If it gets too much for you let me know and I'll whisk you out of there.'

Fee nodded and snuggled back into his warm body.

'How's the knee?'

She flexed it gently. 'Not too bad. I'll know better when I get up.'

'Make sure you sit down when you need to, okay?'

'Yes, Doctor Tom,' Fee teased.

'I'm looking forward to meeting your mother. How did she react to the idea of us visiting? I forgot to ask.'

'I haven't actually told her yet.' She made an effort to sound casual. Tom eased her around to face him, deep frown lines etched into his face.

'Are you crazy? You're planning to turn up on the doorstep unannounced?' Plainly he couldn't believe her. 'Won't she want to get ready? My mother spends days cleaning the house and baking a ton of food when she's expecting visitors.'

After he met Maddy maybe Tom would fully understand

how different their upbringings had been. Domesticity was never her mother's forte, which was why Fee didn't have a clue about how to make a home. Meals were sporadic. Cleaning was something done by people with small minds and nothing better to occupy their time. And irons were only seen in historical dramas on the television.

'I'm being an idiot, aren't I?' Tom frowned.

'Yes, but I'll keep you anyway if you can put up with my quirky ways.'

He wrapped his arms around her. 'If you want to spend your time taking photos while I cook and clean it's fine by me. I'm well-trained. Doesn't bother me.'

'You mean that don't you?'

'Yeah. Why wouldn't I? I'm not gonna lie to you, Fee, ever.' A mischievous smile tweaked the corners of his mouth. 'Unless I'm trying to surprise you in a good way and I assume that's allowed?'

She nodded and swallowed down the tears threatening to bubble over. She'd never known love could be this way.

'Think you can compromise and at least send your mom an email?'

If it made him happy she'd send a handwritten ten-page letter. 'Of course.'

Tom kissed her and any logical thoughts that'd been lurking in her head flew away.

Chapter Thirty-Nine

Tom glanced at his watch and checked his appearance in the mirror. He adjusted his black tie and smoothed down a stray curl of hair. The new silver photo frame on his dresser caught his eye again. It contained a beautiful photo Fee had taken of him with his grandmother the day they visited and was something he'd always treasure.

'Will I do?' Fee emerged from the bathroom and planted herself in front of him. Tom cleared his throat but couldn't find the words to express how beautiful she always looked to him. 'I'll take your silence as a "yes".'

'We'd better go.' He took hold of her hands to stop her fiddling with her hair. Fee's hands were one of the first things he'd noticed the day they met. There was a strength and elegance about them; the fingers long and slim and her nails short and unadorned. Fee wriggled free and picked up the clean handkerchief he'd laid on top of the dresser. 'You'll need that.'

Tom pushed it down into his pocket and tucked her hand into the crook of his elbow to walk out through the cabin together. He'd survived last night's visitation by a hair's breadth, overwhelmed by the number of people who came and today's funeral service would be worse. His father had aged ten years in these last few days and that was hard to watch. The comfort of family and friends helped but in the end they were all alone with their grief.

Fee hitched up her dress to clamber into the truck and caught her heel on the footboard.

'This is why I usually dress the way I do. I don't know how people manage this all the time.'

'Practical is good.' He managed a half-smile. 'But I like this too.'

'I thought you would.' She buckled her seat belt. 'I'm relieved I sorted things with Rayna last night.'

Before visitation started at the funeral home Fee had apologised to his sister and the rest of the family. She'd brushed off their attempts to do the same and courageously laid out her life for them all to hear so nothing was hidden now.

'I've never felt this sense of ... peace before.'

He squeezed her hand and they sat silently for a few moments before he dragged in a deep breath and turned on the engine. 'Time to go.'

Fee's head whirled with trying to remember the names of all the people she'd been introduced to. They'd all be confused if she told them today's funeral for Betty Mae reminded her of one she photographed a couple of years ago in a small African village. Everyone there came to mourn an old lady who was considered to be a wise woman and much revered. The predominantly black clothes worn here were different to the vivid patterns loved by the Africans but the sentiments were the same. Both were about celebrating a life well lived and in the middle of tears there'd been a lot of laughter and the sharing of many well-remembered stories.

Across his grandmother's crowded house Fee spotted Tom and his strength nestled deep inside her. Loving Tom so completely was something she'd never expected to happen and occasionally it still caught her out in the best possible way. She suspected her mother would size him up as conventional and boring but she'd be wrong. He'd been through the hell of his wife's tragic death and survived it, using the love of his family and his own inner strength to claw back from the dark edges. There was nothing weak about this man. *Her* man.

He's not a rash, flitting around sort of boy. When he chooses he thinks carefully and takes his time. You'd better appreciate him and if I ever hear you've messed him around you'll have me to deal with. Even if I've passed on I promise to come back and haunt you.

She covered her mouth with her hand and bit back tears.

'You doin' okay?' Tom appeared in front of her and she managed to nod.

'I'm sad I didn't have more time to get to know your grandmother.'

'Yeah me too.' He brushed a light kiss on her cheek. 'Doesn't matter if you're rollin' in money it's the one thing no one can buy. Let's go see Mama and Pop for a minute then head for home.'

'You don't need to rush off for my sake.'

Tom rested his forehead against hers. 'I've had enough too and my folks will be grateful for someone to make the first move because it'll give other people the hint to head on home themselves.'

Fee registered the strain carved into every plane of his face. She brushed a fleck of dust off his jacket and re-adjusted his crooked tie. 'Can't have you looking scruffy. Mee Maw wouldn't approve.'

Tom laughed when Fee mentioned looking forward to a peaceful evening. 'We're leaving tomorrow and I've still got a ton to do.'

'I'll happily help you with anything if you need me but if not I'll go outside to get a few evening shots around the lake.'

'I'm not gonna ask if you've packed because I'm guessin' it'll take you all of five minutes.' She had mocked him kindly for starting a list of things to pack a week ago and fretting over it every day since. Right now everything was laid out on his spare bed ready to be fitted in the new backpack she'd insisted he buy, saying it would be easier to travel with than a suitcase. 'Off you go and do your thing. I'm gonna clear up the office paperwork first ready for Billy and Rayna. I'll probably go do some work on Lulu's house afterwards. I want to get the kitchen furniture finished up if I can.' He touched her hand, stroking his fingers over Fee's warm, silky skin. 'You'll be here when I'm done?'

'Of course.' Her lips turned up in a wicked smile. 'I'll be in bed waiting.'

Tom fought to dampen down the shot of desire flooding his body.

'Hell, Fee,' he rasped. 'You look so damn cool and controlled. Did no one before me ever see underneath the mask?'

'No.'

'You're all heart and passion deep down. I'm guessin' your mother showed so much of her own it made you lock yours away to protect yourself.' He kissed her but kept it gentle. 'You can let it all out now. It's safe with me.'

'I know,' she whispered. 'It's one reason I love you.'

Tom held her tight. 'Love you, too.'

The contrast between the vibrant, laughing woman standing in front of him and the closed down person she'd been a short while ago was mind-blowing. He wondered if she realised how far she'd come and not simply in air-miles. 'Later.'

'Later,' she said and left, glancing over her shoulder to give him another smile full of promise on the way out of the door.

Fee stared at her empty backpack on the bed. She'd never been one for looking back. Make a decision. Stick to it. Go forward. That had been her mantra for so long but the idea of facing her mother again for the first time in years brought a lot of long-suppressed memories slamming back. The strange thing was they weren't all bad. She'd had a freedom many children would envy because Maddy believed Fee needed to learn for herself rather than simply be ordered to do things a certain way. It'd helped her develop an independent mind that stood her in good stead for her career and made it easier to deal with the transient nature of the job.

It would be interesting to discover what her relationship with Tom looked like outside of Pine Ridge. They'd avoided any deep discussions about where they saw their future leading but at some point it couldn't be stepped around any more. She loved Black Cherry and Tom's wonderful family but still harboured doubts about her ability to settle. Fee suspected he had concerns too, but neither of them wanted to speak them out loud and spoil the magic.

What if they were making a huge mistake and this was nothing more than a high-octane holiday romance with a touch of therapy thrown in for good measure? Maybe she'd arrived on the scene as Tom was becoming receptive to the idea of moving on from his tragic marriage. The whole thing could be nothing more than coincidence – the stars aligning and all that nonsense.

Her phone buzzed and she answered without checking to see who was calling.

'I got your email and I can't believe you're coming,' Maddy babbled. 'I can't wait to see you and the mysterious Tom of course.'

Fee was taken aback by her mother's enthusiasm and tried to inject a note of caution. 'If you don't have room for us to stay we'll book into a hotel. It's not a big deal.'

'Don't talk nonsense. Will's house has plenty of space.'

'Will?'

'Don't tell me you've forgotten him? I know it's been a long time, but ...'

'Will Sawyer? Are you in Cornwall? I assumed you were at the last address I had for you in London.'

'We'll talk when you get here. Let me know which train you'll be catching and we'll come and meet you.'

Reuniting on a station platform sounded a terrible idea but Fee needed to be careful how she phrased her refusal. 'I'm not sure when we'll come to Cornwall. Tom might like to spend a day or two in London first. How about I give you a ring? We can always get a bus or taxi from the station if we need to.'

'Do you remember Will's address?'

'Yes, unless it's changed. I assume you mean the house in St. Ives where we used to stay? I'm surprised you're back there.'

'Why?'

Because you always mocked Cornwall and said it was the dullest place on the planet. 'I didn't think you cared for it much.'

'People change.'

If Fee didn't get off the phone she might change her mind about going at all. She said a quick goodbye and hung up with her heart thumping.

Chapter Forty

Fee should've guessed Tom would be one of "those" – the people for whom travel was akin to planning for World War III. For her it was second nature to go with the flow and expect the unexpected but Tom fretted from the moment they left Black Cherry, early enough to account for a multi-car pile-up, a major earthquake and unspecified medical emergencies along the way. By the time they made their connection in Charlotte she was surprised his hair hadn't turned white. Any nerves she had about their upcoming meeting with her mother were buried under the desire to simply get Tom there in one piece.

'I'm driving you crazy, aren't I?' He squeezed her hand as they took their seats on the London flight. 'Sorry. I'm okay with short flights but I don't do well with the long distance stuff.'

'No, you don't.' She didn't sugar-coat it. He'd have to get over this if they were going to make a go of things together. The fact she wanted to explore other work options didn't mean her desire to see and experience other cultures had lessened. She hoped she'd still be travelling when she was ninety with camera in hand.

'I guess I should've warned you.'

'That would've been nice,' she admitted. 'They do say couples learn more about each other on holiday than anywhere else.' Fee broke into a wry smile. 'I'm not sure it's encouraging in our case.'

'Once we get there I want you to take over.' Tom's grim determination made her smile. 'I won't say a word. You tell me what to do and I'll do it.' He sounded like a man telling the dentist to go ahead and pull all his teeth without any anaesthetic while promising not to scream.

She kissed his cheek, smelling his familiar pine soap. 'I totally understand flying these days can be a hassle but a positive frame of mind works wonders. Ninety-nine point nine per cent of the other passengers are decent people not terrorists.' She'd watched him sizing up everyone around them with his suspicious cop's mind. 'Caution is one thing. Fear, something entirely different.'

'In other words stop being a coward.' His thick eyebrows drew together and Fee sucked in a few deep breaths.

'Yes.'

Tom's slow, sexy grin exploded and a curl of lust tightened her gut. 'Fair enough.'

'It's that simple?'

'Probably not, but I'll work at it.' He stuck out his hand. 'Deal?' The second she placed her hand in his Tom drew her to him and leaned close to whisper in her ear. 'In return you can learn how to make my favourite German chocolate cake.'

The feminist side of her strove to be outraged but Fee remembered the crucial word compromise and bit back the cutting reply she'd had all ready. Would it really kill her? No. Plus it'd make him happy.

'Deal.' She held up a warning finger. 'I've never baked a cake in my life.'

'Mama will be happy to teach you.'

I'm sure she will. Fee sensed his grandmother hovering over them and laughing. If this carried on she'd be crocheting tea cosies and sewing her own wedding dress next.

Tom popped a kiss on her forehead. 'Don't worry. I've no desire to turn you into a Stepford Wife.'

She shuddered. 'My God, I hope not. You've got the wrong woman if that's what you're in the market for.'

'I've got exactly the right one,' he declared with a satisfied smile.

Tom called on his reserves of patience. She needed him to

handle the journey a lot better than he'd managed so far. He wasn't stupid enough to believe Fee wanted to hole up in Pine Ridge for the rest of her life. If he wanted a future with her, and he did more than anything, he'd have to learn to enjoy this side of her, not simply tolerate it.

'I recommend you snuggle right in here,' he wrapped his arm around Fee's slim shoulders and pulled her closer, 'and we'll try to take a nap.' He didn't complain about the lack of space or the cold blast of stale air blowing down on the top of his head.

'Good idea, my hero.' She burrowed into his chest and in a matter of minutes amazed him by going straight to sleep. Tom took several long slow breaths and concentrated on her alluring scent and the warmth of her body seeping into him. He'd try to take a short nap if it killed him.

Bright lights bothered his eyes and Tom rubbed at them, struggling to focus. The cabin lights were on full blast, flight attendants were bringing breakfast around the cabin and the pilot suddenly made an announcement about starting their descent into London soon.

'Goodness, Tom, I've never seen anyone sleep so heavily on a plane without the benefit of alcohol or pills.' Fee's teasing voice trickled into his awareness and he turned to see her smiling at him.

'You slept too,' he protested. 'You went out like a light.'

'For a while but I've had dinner, watched a good film and made friends with the lady across the aisle while you were off in Neverland.' She poked him gently in the ribs.

'At least one of us will be well-rested for the day to come.' When Fee was drooping with tiredness later she'd be glad he was alert and able to function. 'Remind me what we've got to do after we land.'

She ran over every detail again all the way through to their arrival in Cornwall late in the afternoon. 'It's not hard. Trust me.'

'I do.' He kissed her cheek. 'Heck. I need to move. I'm stiff as a board.' Tom stretched his arms over his head and all his joints creaked. 'God, I'm getting old.'

'Flying does that to everyone.'

He didn't argue although to his eyes Fee looked as fresh and clean as ever. Nothing about her said ragged or weary. Tom craved a pounding hot shower and change of clothes more than anything and was pretty sure the sight of him wouldn't impress her mother.

'Don't bother with the breakfast they're offering. A soggy croissant, insipid strawberry yogurt and a lousy lukewarm drink aren't going to help.' She wrinkled her nose. 'Wait until we land and we'll buy some decent bacon rolls and strong coffee for you before we get the bus to Reading.'

Tom shrugged. 'Fair enough but what about you?'

'Believe it or not they do sell healthy options too. I'll be fine.'

He wasn't stupid enough to debate the point and dragged out the landing card he still needed to fill in, feeling her fond smile on him the whole time.

How on earth could he sleep again? Fee pondered the wonder of it as Tom snored gently with his head pressed against the dirty train window. She supposed he wasn't weighed down with anxiety in the same way as her. As each station slipped away, the pain in her stomach intensified and she sipped on a bottle of water in an attempt to calm it down. Another hour and they'd be at St. Erth where they'd have a twenty-minute wait for the short connecting train to St. Ives.

A warm hand snaked around her back and Tom pressed soft kisses all the way up and down her neck.

'Mm. Much better,' he murmured and settled her into his arms. 'How about you give me a rundown on this Will Sawyer?'

Fee stiffened. Until now Tom had asked very little about her mother and nothing about the man she was presumably living with again. 'I haven't seen him in years but he was around a lot when I was a child. We often stayed with him.' She frowned and struggled to remember. 'I get the impression we went back to Cornwall when things went wrong somewhere else.'

'I wonder if the poor devil was always in love with your mother?'

'I've never thought about it.' The idea startled her. 'I loved his house because he had an enormous garden and it was only a ten minute walk from the nearest beach.'

'He was good to you?'

'Yes.' Fee nodded. 'He often took care of me when my mother was out running around saving the world.' She couldn't help smiling. 'He made me a birthday cake once.' She swallowed hard. 'Maddy forgot but he didn't.'

A thoughtful look settled in Tom's warm eyes. 'You don't suppose ...?' His question trailed away but it wasn't hard to guess where his mind was going.

'He's my father?' Fee put it into words and he shrugged. 'I suppose it's possible but Mum swore it'd been a lie when she told Allain the exact same thing.' There'd been an endless stream of different men in and out of Fee's childhood so maybe Maddy really *didn't* know who her father was.

'Just an idea.'

They both went quiet and she was happy to stay that way, needing to collect her thoughts. Fee peered out of the window as the train slowed. 'This is Camborne. The next stop is ours in about ten minutes.'

'Are you going to—'

'No.' She cut him off before he could finish. 'We'll get a taxi and I'll ring while we're on the way.' A shadow crossed his face but he held his tongue. Fee managed a brief, tight smile and prepared to face her past.

Chapter Forty-One

'Freebird?'

Tom's reassuring hand on her shoulder gave Fee courage and she put on a bright smile to face her mother. Maddy's appearance took her by surprise because the smart black trousers and dark red check blouse were a million miles from the bright-coloured hippie clothes she'd always favoured. At least her hennaed hair was the same, although even that appeared well cut instead of hacked at with the nearest pair of scissors.

Maddy ran down the path and seized hold of her hands. She checked Fee out from head to toe. 'When did you get to be so ...'

'Old?'

'I was going to say beautiful.' She touched Fee's cheek. 'You were always so serious and well ... plain.'

Thanks, Mum. Tom relied on his family to tell him the truth even when it was the last thing he wanted to hear. He held it up as a good thing but she wasn't convinced.

'I knew you'd grow into your looks one day.' She fingered Fee's hair. 'The style's softer than I remember. And jewellery?' Maddy lifted up the silver bracelet around her wrist. 'You'll be wearing red next.'

'On the phone you told me people change. Aren't I allowed to as well?' Fee challenged and her mother's familiar wry smile emerged.

'That's more like my spiky girl. Always sticking up for herself.'

I had to or I wouldn't have survived. Fee swallowed back tears.

'Aren't you going to introduce me to your young man?' Maddy asked.

She couldn't believe she'd almost forgotten Tom in the shock of seeing her mother again. Fee pulled him forward.

'Pleased to meet you, ma'am.' Tom's soft, deep drawl brightened her mother's smile even more.

'Call me Maddy, please, or I'll think you're talking to the Queen.' Her raspy laughter tugged at Fee's heart. She'd missed her mother's earthy good humour.

'I can see where Fee gets her beauty from ... and her uniqueness.'

Fee bit the inside of her cheek to stifle a giggle.

'I can see why my daughter's fallen for you.' Maddy's eyes shone. 'You'd better pick up those bags and come in.' She gestured to the luggage they'd set down on the path. 'Oh, Will, come and say hello.'

Out of the corner of her eye she noticed a man hovering at the front door of the house, shadowed from clear view. As he stepped forward and headed slowly towards them Fee caught Tom's quick intake of breath. 'Long time no see.'

The older version of Will Sawyer was taller and leaner than she remembered, his shoulder-length black hair streaked with grey and sharp, hawkish features softened with age. He pulled her into an affectionate hug and Fee smelled spearmint chewing gum on his breath. The remembered scent assaulted her senses and she fought against crying. He'd sneaked her endless sticks of gum when Maddy was going through her organic, sugar-free phases and called it their secret treat.

'I thought you were never coming home again.' Will's dark blue eyes glazed over and he draped his arm around Maddy's shoulder. 'We've both missed you.'

'Well, I'm here now.' A feeble response but the best she could come up with.

'Come in.'

Tom picked up their bags and gestured for her to go first. Memories of arriving here with her mother, tired and hungry, flooded back and Fee walked up the couple of steps and into the entrance hall in a daydream. She glanced down at the familiar floor where Will taught her to play hopscotch on the black and white tiles and wondered how she could have allowed herself to forget so much. The large Victorian house had been a sanctuary then and now it wrapped its comforting presence around her again.

'Neat place,' Tom commented.

'Thanks. We're happy here.' Will tightened his arm around her mother. The loving smiles they gave each other told her that Tom was right. What else had she missed?

Tom tried to sort things in his head. Fee's mother didn't match the image he'd formed of her and Maddy and Will were obviously a couple in every sense of the word. He was no geneticist but he would bet his bottom dollar Will Sawyer was Fee's father. Their bone structure was identical and when Tom met the older man's shrewd gaze it'd been like facing Fee in questioning mode.

He left their bags in the bedroom and hurried back down the elegant staircase to the now empty hall. Before Tom could go in search of Fee a door opened and Will came out frowning.

'Maddy took Fee off to the living room and she's asking her about Allain and the paternity test. Tell me what you know.' His blank, expressionless voice contrasted with the pain lingering in his bright blue eyes. 'Don't get bloody noble on me.' Will growled. 'I watched you put two and two together the moment you clapped eyes on me.'

'Maybe.'

'There's no maybe about it.'

'Why does Maddy think otherwise?' Fee's mother had been adamant.

'She's always had a thing about the man. First love. You know the sort of thing.'

Gina. Oh, yeah, he knew alright.

'Maddy convinced herself Dupre was Fee's father. She chose to forget the number of times we slept together before he was on the scene and again right after he left when she was upset.'

'She loves you now. I saw that too.' Tom tried to reassure him.

'I hope so but we both need her to let go of Dupre's ghost.'

'How about we join them?' Tom suggested. The knot of tension in his neck eased when Will turned away and strode out of the hall.

Fee watched as the colour drained from her mother's face.

'Really? Are you sure?'

'Yes, Mum. I was there when the test results came through. His daughter couldn't have been happier, but … Allain was upset.' Fee couldn't make herself ask the question burning a path through her mind.

Maddy's smile barely reached the corners of her mouth. 'Will must've been right all along.'

Say it out loud. Go on. I need to hear it.

'He's always believed himself to be your father but I refused to listen.' She couldn't meet Fee's eyes. 'I always wanted you to be Allain's. I suppose because …'

'You loved him.'

'I did,' she whispered, 'so very much.'

'What about Will?'

'Yes, what about me?' He rasped out the words and Fee's heart broke for the man who'd been more of a father to her than she'd ever given him credit for.

Maddy jerked around. 'I hadn't finished speaking, Will. I was about to explain to Fee that I'd been blinded by Allain's charming ways. His tantalising accent. The stories he told me about New Orleans. I was young and stupid.' She hurried across the room. 'I've been an idiot, Will. I needed to know I was loved but you never told me in so many words. You've always been my best friend – with benefits as they say these days – but I craved more.'

Fee gulped back tears as Will cradled Maddy's face in his

hands.

'Of course I love you, silly girl. I loved you from the first day we met in that appalling squat in Wandsworth. I'm not good at the romantic stuff. I wish I was.' He sighed.

Tom caught her eye and he beckoned her to join him at the back of the room. Maddy and Will wouldn't miss them. They sneaked out to the hall and made their way to the kitchen.

'Do you want me to put the kettle on?' Tom offered.

'That sounded very natural. Have you been practising?'

He put on an affronted stare. 'I'm tryin' to be considerate. It's well known you Brits use tea to soothe all difficult situations and I took a wild guess this might count.'

Fee slid her arms around his waist and hugged him to her. 'It does indeed. You saw the resemblance when we arrived, didn't you?'

'Sure did.'

The possibility of Will being her father never occurred to her before Tom threw out the idea on the train but it'd started her thinking and a lot of things made more sense now.

'Are you good with the idea? I know you liked Allain.'

'Yes. I'm more than good. Allain's a decent man but Will was part of my life when I was a child. I always hated to leave him when Mum took us away again.'

'He made you feel safe.'

She nodded through a haze of tears.

'Tell him so later. He needs to know you love him.' Tom nuzzled her cheek. 'We all need to hear it, just like your mom said.'

Fee exhaled a deliberate, heavy sigh. 'Fine. I love you. Alright?'

'It'll do for now,' he teased. 'Let's go and see how your parents are doing.'

'Gosh. That sounds peculiar.' She startled at his choice of words. 'I've never had "parents" before.'

'You do now.'

Fee couldn't help beaming. 'Your family will be pleased. This should make me a touch more normal.'

Tom's eyes darkened. 'I'm not goin' to say this again. I've never cared if you had a whole bunch of family or none. It makes no difference to me lovin' you.'

His honesty struck her to the core. He meant every word he said and she must never take that for granted. 'I know, sweetheart.'

'You better had.'

Fee stifled a laugh at Tom's attempt to sound cross. 'Yes, dear.'

She had lost one potential father but found the one she'd been too blind to see she had all along.

Chapter Forty-Two

'You sure we've stayed long enough?' Tom watched Fee tuck clothes into her backpack. They'd toured Cornwall from end to end over the last week and he'd fallen for the place big time. Hiking the rugged coastline and checking out a few of the sites connected with the Celtic history he'd discovered a new passion for, topped his list of favourites.

'We must be smelly fish by now,' she declared.

'What the heck are you talking about?'

Fee grinned. 'You must've heard the old saying about the resemblance between guests and fish – both stink after three days.' Her smile wobbled. 'I don't want to push my luck. Let's leave while it's going well. Anyway you want to see more of Europe and someone has a dolls' house to finish making before Christmas and that's rapidly creeping up on us.'

He backed off. Fee's effort to reconnect with her mother hadn't been straightforward. Many evenings he'd held her in his arms while she complained about how stubborn Maddy was. He'd smiled inside, thinking how Fee could be describing herself but wasn't stupid enough to say it aloud.

'Fair enough.' Tom hesitated. 'You sure having nothing planned or booked is goin' to be okay?'

Fee wagged her finger. 'You promised to give me at least two weeks. If I haven't converted you to spontaneous travelling by then I'll give up.'

He plastered on a bright smile. 'Fair enough.' They'd bought a couple of Eurail passes and were simply going to explore anywhere that took their fancy.

'Make the most of our comfy bed tonight because it may be the last you'll get for a while.'

'Don't worry. I intend to as soon as you finish packing.' His blatant declaration of intent made her cheeks turn rosy and he burst out laughing.

For the first time Fee was sorry to leave her mother. Normally she'd breathe a sigh of relief and vow never to go back but now she heard herself promising to return as soon as possible.

'Take care of her or you'll answer to me,' Maddy instructed Tom and Fee struggled not to burst out laughing. She wouldn't ask her mother who she thought had looked after Fee for the last twenty years when she'd travelled the world with little more than her camera and her wits.

'Yes, ma'am.' Tom's eyes gleamed. 'You'd better get ready to come to Tennessee for the wedding. We'll let you know when we've set a date.'

Fee swallowed down the tears burning her throat. It'd cracked the last part of the shell she'd erected around her heart when a serious, polite Tom asked Will for her hand in marriage after dinner last night. She'd been bemused when her new father launched into a whole raft of questions about Tom's background, family and financial stability. Afterwards she'd asked Tom if he'd minded and he stared as if she'd grown two heads.

Why should I? Any decent man would do the same. He's cared for you all your life even when he wasn't officially your father. Why would he stop now?

It'd made her love both men even more.

'We'd better leave before y'all drown in tears.' Tom grabbed her hand and led her out to the waiting taxi. This time she'd turned down Will's offer to drive them to the station because she thought it'd be easier to say goodbye here at the house.

Amid a wealth of hugs and kisses they finally left and Fee craned her neck to wave at her mother and Will until the taxi turned the corner and she couldn't see them anymore.

'Paris next stop?' Tom asked.

She easily got caught up in his enthusiasm and they chatted about where he wanted to go first. In Cornwall she'd relished photographing familiar places through Tom's fresh eyes. Redirecting her talent for observing people and their surroundings didn't seem the impossibility it had appeared to be a couple of months ago. She'd emailed her therapist to thank him and told him briefly about her progress and the effect going to Black Cherry had on her life, and not simply because of Tom.

'Do they have hamburgers in France?' he asked. Fee was all set to berate him when she noticed his broad smile. The other night she'd talked to Tom about being open to new experiences and different cultures and got a bit preachy about the whole thing – at least that's how he'd described her over-enthusiasm.

'You'll get escargots in a butter and garlic sauce and love them.'

'And you think chitlins are nasty?' Tom retorted.

'The rest of your family won't touch nasty pig intestines either. Your own mother said you were peculiar.'

He shook his head. 'Y'all don't know what you're missing.'

'I'm happy to keep missing them.'

'Fine.' Tom sighed. 'Take me to the snails.'

Several places they visited stuck in Tom's head but it wasn't for the reasons he'd expected. He appreciated the history and architecture all over Europe but what really spoke to him was the people. The artist they observed in a back street in Florence trying to capture the sun setting over the Duomo. A group of Parisian children laughing at Tom's inept efforts when they invited him to join in their impromptu street football game. His obvious enthusiasm for that particular side of travelling had the bonus of bringing him closer to Fee. Always in the background he'd been aware of her taking pictures and in the process fully returning to life, cementing the fact Tom had made the best decision in suggesting they take this trip together.

'Did you get a reply yet?' Fee asked, pointing to his phone.

'Yeah. About ten at last count. Even Lulu sent us a big kiss.'

'I take it they're happy we'll be back for Thanksgiving?'

'Let's just say the cooking's started already.' He chuckled and patted his stomach. 'Mama's trying out some new recipes to impress you.'

Fee frowned. 'I hope she isn't going to spoil everyone else's meal to please me.'

'No way. It's in addition to the ten million things she always fixes.'

'I don't want to hear them all, do I?'

'Nope. It'll make your stomach hurt to listen, honey.'

'Where do you want to spend the last couple of days before we go back to London?' Fee asked. They'd chosen to fly out of Heathrow on Sunday to get over their jet lag before Thanksgiving on the following Thursday.

Tom drank in the sight of her emerging from the shower with only a small, white towel wrapped around her before considering how to make his reply sound spontaneous. They'd treated themselves to this decent hotel in Brussels after he'd insisted his back was shot after too many nights curled up on hard train seats and scrunched into cheap hostel beds.

'Amsterdam.'

'Oh. Okay. That'll work. It takes less than a couple of hours on the high-speed trains. What makes you want to go there?'

He knew the reason but wasn't about to share it with her yet. 'I like the look of the canals and Anne Frank's story fascinates me.'

Fee crossed the room and leaned in over the bed, letting her scented heat surround him. She stroked his unshaven jawline and the rasp of her fingers made him shudder. 'You're a terrible liar.' A mischievous smile tugged at her mouth. 'Which makes me happy because I've met enough of those in my time.'

'Good.' Now he'd basically admitted to lying. 'Damn. You're good at this.'

'What?' Her hand trailed down his bare chest.

'Finding out information. The intelligence services should employ you.'

'A modern day Mata-Hari. I rather like the idea apart from the fact I'd have to seduce other men and that's not going to happen. So?' Her hand rested on the cord of his sweatpants. 'The truth. The whole truth. And nothing but the truth.'

'I give up. It's useless trying to surprise you. Amsterdam is famous for its diamonds, you annoying woman.'

A triumphant smile lit up her face. 'I knew it.'

'Then why'd we have to go through this?' he complained.

'Because it's fun and I've never had fun with a man before.' A touch of sadness ran through her words.

Tom lay back on the bed. 'Okay. I'm all yours.'

Fee's eyes darkened. The hotel room would be worth every one of the Euros it had cost him.

Chapter Forty-Three

'Simple and beautiful. Like you.' Tom's deep chocolatey eyes bored into her and Fee fought back tears.

Despite her shrewd guess about why he wanted to go to Amsterdam he'd still managed to surprise her. When they were in England he'd gone online and tracked down an old college friend who'd married a Dutch girl. He'd described Fee's taste in jewellery and been steered towards this ultra modern shop in the centre of the city. The platinum ring with squared off edges and single rectangular diamond set flush in the band was so perfect she could have designed it herself.

'We have matching wedding bands if you would care to see them?' The manager offered and Tom nodded his approval.

Fee slipped the unadorned platinum ring onto his finger and held it there, not daring to look up at him. He wrapped his other hand over hers and they stood that way for the longest time.

'Do they work for you both?'

'Perfect.' Tom's rough voice betrayed his emotions.

Before she knew it they were back out in the street and officially engaged.

'Sightseeing is going to be a let-down after this,' Tom joked, grasping her hands and kissing her fingers one by one. 'Should I take a picture and email it to the folks or would you prefer to surprise them?'

He was like a little boy wanting to show off his new Christmas bicycle and Fee couldn't help responding to his obvious joy. 'Show them now. They'll get a kick out of it.' She reached for her camera but he stopped her.

'You can do your fancy stuff later. I'm taking this one with my phone,' Tom declared and she backed off. Putting it politely photography wasn't one of his talents and this picture would no doubt be crooked and out of focus. She dutifully held out her hand and waited while he took a couple of photos, checked them out, cursed and tried again. 'Not bad.' He showed her for all of two seconds then whisked the phone away and sent the picture. Then he pulled her into his arms. 'I sure as heck don't deserve you but somehow I got lucky.'

So did I.

In the middle of settling into their seats on the plane in London, Tom turned to her with a big grin on his face.

'Did I pass the test?'

'You'll do. You only fretted a couple of times when we missed a train or couldn't get a room for the night and you did only insist on going to McDonald's once. But you redeemed yourself with this gorgeous thing.' Fee flashed her engagement ring under his nose.

'Don't overdo it.'

'We'll go somewhere more challenging next time.'

He rolled his eyes. 'I'm ready to stay home for a while although I'm prepared to do Cornwall anytime you like.'

Fee ran her fingers down his arm. 'Doesn't a warm Caribbean beach sound tempting in the middle of a harsh Tennessee winter? Think skimpy bikinis. Cocktails. White sand.'

'You're wicked,' he whispered.

She contented herself with a smile.

'I'm goin' to sleep.'

'Of course you are. See you in Charlotte,' Fee joked and threw a pillow at him.

The handmade signs were unmistakeable and the loud yells sealed it – their welcoming committee was here. Fee's plan to slip back to Black Cherry unnoticed faded away at the sight of Tom's family.

'Sorry,' he murmured. 'You'd think we'd been gone for a

year instead of a few weeks. They didn't make this much fuss when I came back from Iraq.'

Probably because you wouldn't have appreciated it then.

'Yeah. Yeah. I know.' Reading her mind again he laughed and kissed her, eliciting more whoops of joy.

The second they got through the security gate Fee gave herself up to being hugged by what seemed to be a hundred pairs of arms. Lulu's sticky hands grasped her face and the little girl plonked a wet kiss on her nose.

'I love you, ice cream lady.'

'Love you too, sweetheart.' Fee plucked her from her mother's arms. 'I've got something to show you.' She lifted her left hand and Lulu made a grab for her ring.

'Pretty. I want it.'

'Sorry, sweetie. It's a present from Uncle T and he wouldn't be happy if I gave it away.'

Lulu pouted. 'Not fair.'

'Do you know what a bridesmaid is?' They'd discussed wedding plans a little and decided on a quiet ceremony – all excepting this special little girl who'd helped bring them together.

'Yes. You wear a pretty dress and have flowers.' She grinned. 'And a ring?'

Fee laughed. 'All of those. Absolutely.'

'Have you set a date?' Sarah Chambers interrupted and the free-for-all started. Fee threw Tom a beseeching look.

'Mama, leave her alone. We're beat. It's great to see y'all but we need to get out of here and head for home. You can interrogate us tomorrow,' he said with a firmness that instantly stopped the questions.

Outside the airport they found Tom's truck waiting on the kerb with Billy in the driver's seat.

'Thought you'd prefer your own wheels.' He hopped out and tossed Tom the keys.

'You're a pal.' Tom seized them and held out his hand for

her backpack. With the luggage thrown on the back seat he gestured for her to get in. 'The welcome was great. We sure did appreciate it. We'll be down tomorrow evening for supper.'

'Think you're invited, do you?' His mother tried to sound aggrieved.

'Better be. I've had some damn good food over there but I'm cravin' some decent home cooking.'

Fee stifled a laugh as his mother's face softened.

'I suppose I'll come up with something,' she conceded. 'Now off with you and get some rest.' Sarah shooed them away and Fee was too tired to argue.

Jumping into the passenger seat of the truck she couldn't help remembering the first time she'd ridden along with him and Lulu into Pine Ridge.

'A lot's happened since then, honey,' Tom muttered as he got in beside her. 'Who would've thought?'

'Not me.' Fee declared. 'Although I have to concede a tiny part of me did register the fact you were …'

'Handsome. Charming. Witty. Sexy.'

'Oh, yes, all of the above.'

He ignored her effort at sarcasm. 'Exactly what I thought about you.'

'Not scared, weird and odd-looking?'

Tom placed his hands on her shoulders, turning her towards him. 'I could tell straight off you'd had a tough time but to me you were always beautiful inside and out. You needed to realise it yourself, that's all.' He stroked his thumb over her mouth. 'You believe me now, don't you?'

She sucked in a deep breath before nodding.

'Good.' He let go and placed his hands on the steering wheel. 'Time to go home.'

'It is indeed.'

Watching Tom going around his home, checking every room and touching things to reassure himself they were the same

Fee smiled to herself. She followed him outside and saw him frown at the diminished woodpile. Next he unlocked his shed and stepped inside.

'What still needs to be done?' Fee gestured towards the dolls' house.

'The outside's finished and inside I've got some painting to finish up. Then it's a question of getting the furniture and fixtures in place. Mary-Jo's got most of it bought but I told her I've made a few pieces.'

'You can start back on it tomorrow.'

'Yeah.' He pulled her into his arms. 'Right now I'm ready to celebrate being home and then sleep until I'm forced to wake up either by you or starvation.'

'Jet lag will have you awake early. Trust me.'

'Come on. Let's get out of here.' He grabbed her hand and they left, locking the door behind him. 'Tomorrow we'll see about gettin' a wedding license then buy you a dress and buy somethin' girly and fussy for Lulu.'

'Uh, we're not hanging around then I take it?'

'Did you want to?' he asked, frowning. 'Sorry. I should've asked.'

'It's okay apart from the fact I really want Mum and Will here.' She still found the idea of calling Will her father strange. One day when she'd tried to explain her reticence Will had told her he loved her regardless. She'd offered to do a DNA test but he'd insisted it wasn't necessary for his sake. After discussing things with Tom she'd made the decision to leave well alone.

Tom smacked his head. 'Sorry. I'm runnin' away with myself. We'll call tomorrow and see what suits them. Of course they must be here.'

'Stop fretting. I don't know about you but I could do with a good cup of tea.'

He screwed up his face. 'Not for me. I've drunk enough gallons of the stuff to float a ship. Between that and the thick espresso sludge in Italy I'm ready for a decent mug of coffee. I need to have a quick skim through the mail Billy said he'd left on the desk.'

'How about you start on the post and I'll make our drinks.'

'I knew I was marrying you for a good reason.'

Fee stuck out her tongue and flounced off towards the kitchen. With their two mugs ready she carried them into the office and discovered Tom sitting at his desk and staring at a thick blue envelope.

'This one's for you. From France.'

Fee's heart thumped as she reached out her hand to take it from him.

Chapter Forty-Four

The blood drained from Fee's face and Tom yearned to snatch the envelope back.

'Do you want to sit down?'

Silently she pulled the other chair closer and perched on the edge. With great care she eased open the flap and removed a sheet of paper and another smaller envelope. Fee finished reading the loose page and passed it across to him without saying a word. Tom slipped on his glasses and checked the signature first. Helene Marchand. Pierre's wife.

'How did she know where to contact you?'

'It's been forwarded from my London flat. You can see it's dated several weeks ago.'

He scanned over the brief, stilted lines, written in very precise English. Helene explained that the enclosed letter addressed to Fee was found among Pierre's possessions. Because it was without a stamp the authorities included the letter with the box of effects sent to his widow. In the last sentence she asked Fee not to reply or get in touch with her again.

'I'm guessin' she knows about the two of you,' he ventured.

'I'd say so.' Her fingers shook as she opened the other letter and started to read. Tom ached to do something, anything to make this easier for Fee.

'This was written the night before ... he died.' Fee's voice splintered into shards of pain and Tom crushed down a surge of jealousy. 'He begins by telling me he loves me because I'm a beautiful, intelligent, fearless woman.' Tom heard the catch in her breath. 'He goes on to say he wishes he could spend the rest of his life with me but then admits he's been lying and explains about his wife and son. He doesn't offer any explanation for our affair apart from wanting me too much.' Fee sighed and pushed the letter across the desk.

'Are you sure?'

'Yes. Please.'

Tom fingered the thin sheets of airmail paper. He disliked the idea of reading another man's love letter but she needed him to. By the time he reached the second paragraph he pitied and detested the Frenchman in equal measure. Pierre's love for Fee shone through but near the end of the letter he admitted that he couldn't justify breaking up his family.

'He loved you.' He forced the words out knowing she needed to hear them.

'But he didn't love me enough. This is very ... freeing.'

For you and me both.

'When you're finished working I'm ready for bed.'

'There's nothing that can't wait.' He pushed the pile of bills off to one side. Fee was his priority. Tom didn't intend to live with any more regrets. He put away his glasses and closed down his computer for the night. 'Come on let's go and work on our jet lag.'

Fee scribbled a short note on a piece of scrap paper and placed it on her pillow. Tugging on last night's clothes she snatched her camera from the bedside table and crept out of the room. This was her go-to method when she needed time alone to think. From the time she was an unsettled teenager Fee used photography to work through whatever was happening in her life.

With the sun inching up over the lake the sky flooded a glorious shade of purplish-gold, dappling the still, dark water and for a second she fought to catch her breath. Being present for the start of a new day always affected her because her experiences had shown her what a fragile gift that was. She concentrated on the views around her and with each frame she shot, the tension loosened inside her head. Taking her time she made her way around the lake and as she emerged from the trees Fee spotted Tom sitting on the bench.

'Working with wood has the same effect on me. Gets it out of my system and sorts out a lot of crap,' he commented.

She nodded, warmed by his gentle smile and grateful beyond words to have found such an understanding man.

'I appreciated you leaving the note. I know you're an independent person and we don't own each other, but ...'

'I didn't want you to worry.' Fee sat down by him, settling into his warmth as he draped his arm around her shoulders.

'You good now?'

'Yes. I need time alone sometimes to stay sane.' Fee smiled. 'Well. As sane as I'm ever likely to be.' She sensed him smile. 'I'm starving. Would you mind doing your chef bit again? Only I'm not up to facing the cafe yet.'

'Can't imagine why,' Tom joked. 'You mean eating while being interrogated by my family and any of the other customers who want to stick their oar in isn't your idea of easing back into the week?'

'Not exactly.'

They stood up and wandered off back along the path towards the cabins. 'Are you going to call home to let them know we're back safely?'

She stopped walking. 'Why do you call it home? I only lived there briefly and it was years ago.'

'Home to me is family, my people, not a building.' He shrugged and gestured around. 'In one way this land means a lot to me but deep down it's not the physical ground – it's the Chambers from generations ago who struggled over the mountains and found a refuge here. Your folks are home for you and where they are on the map is pretty much irrelevant.'

Fee slid her arms around his waist and rested her head on his chest. 'You're a very perceptive man.'

'I haven't always been. It's been a hard road. Still is some days.'

The past never left a person alone but wound around them and became part of the fabric of who they were. They were both long past the stage of being a clean slate where loving another person was concerned but that wasn't necessarily a bad thing.

'No one else would tolerate us, sweetheart,' he murmured. 'Good thing we found each other.'

Fee wasn't going to argue with *that* statement.

'Let's go eat before we both fade away,' he said.

'Good idea. I'll ring ... home before doing anything else.' The word didn't sound as odd now. 'You can put me to work once I'm off the phone. I know Billy and Rayna took care of things but there must still be a lot to do.' Tom's approving nod lightened Fee's heart. He needed to realise she was happy with Black Cherry being a large part of their future.

'There sure is. We've got several folks comin' in for the Thanksgiving holiday so two of the empty cabins need a freshen up. You could do that while I cut a stack of wood and do a few minor repairs Billy didn't get around to. We'll need to go into town for supplies before supper or else the stores will be shut.' Tom gave a quick grin. 'No rest for the jet-lagged here.'

'Obviously not.' Fee let go of his hand and ran up the cabin steps. 'Come on, lazybones.'

'Yes, ma'am.' Tom came to unlock the door and stood aside to let her go in first. As she stepped into his office Fee spotted the red light flashing on his phone.

'You've got a message.' It was stupid to assume something was wrong but she still crossed her fingers while he pressed the button to listen. Within seconds a satisfied smile crept across his face.

'We're off the hook for providing today's family entertainment. Rayna went into labour in the middle of the night and an hour ago provided my dear parents with their ninth grandchild – Billy Junior. Mother and baby are both doing well. Family supper is still on the agenda but we'll visit the hospital first.' Tom rang his mother back and Fee's stomach worked into a tight knot listening to the happiness in his voice. After several minutes he hung up and turned back around to face her. 'Great isn't it?'

'Wonderful.'

'But?'

'Surely poor Rayna won't want us all visiting today? The poor girl will be shattered.'

Tom's gaze narrowed. 'If we don't turn up she'll think it odd. It's a family tradition to welcome every new baby the day they're born.' He scrutinised her closely. 'If you don't want to go I'll make your excuses.' Fee couldn't explain her reluctance without sounding a monster. 'I know you haven't been around babies much but you won't have to hold him just make a few admiring noises. Nobody stays long.'

Fee touched her engagement ring for reassurance. 'Of course. I was only thinking of Rayna.' They both knew she wasn't being completely truthful. A shiver of unease trickled down Fee's spine. Would this tiny baby shine a light on the delicate subject they'd only tiptoed around until now?

For now she'd continue to hope that Tom didn't see past her fake smile.

Chapter Forty-Five

All day Tom sensed Fee's disquiet but something about the way she held herself apart warned him not to ask questions.

'Does four o'clock still suit you to leave?' he asked, resting his hands on the pile of paperwork he was dealing with.

'Yes. I'm going to get changed.' Fee hesitated. 'Don't we need a present or something?'

'We'll pick up some flowers and a stuffed animal on the way.'

A faint hint of a smile lightened her serious expression. 'Is that the standard offering?' He yearned to urge her not to overthink it all but instead nodded and let it go. 'I won't be long.' Fee dashed off to the bedroom.

No woman likes a dishonest man. Tell her where you stand and how you feel. After that it's up to her.

His grandmother's advice ran around his head, beating on his useless brain and ordering him to grab the bull by the horns and sort this out right now. Tom pushed the chair back and headed down the hall to his bedroom.

Fee turned around from fixing her hair in the mirror.

'Sit with me.' Tom dropped onto the bed. 'I won't bite.' With a caution he hadn't seen since their earliest days together she joined him, perching on the opposite corner and not quite meeting his gaze. 'Correct me if I'm barking up the wrong tree but you're frettin' about goin' to see the baby aren't you?' She shrugged but didn't answer. 'You think I'm gonna be bowled over by the sight of little Billy and start pressuring you to have kids when we get married. Did I nail it?'

'I suppose,' she murmured, staring down at her lap.

'Yeah, I love kids. Always have done. I practically raised the twins and hoped to have a whole brood of my own with Gina. But life happened and everything changed. I never thought

I'd give my heart away again until you appeared.' He risked touching Fee's arm and she finally looked right at him, her sky-blue eyes swimming with tears. 'I'm so damn lucky. We're lucky. End of story.'

'But it's not, is it?' Her anguished voice tore him up and Fee pressed her hand against his racing heart. 'In here you'll always resent me for depriving you of a family and I wouldn't be able to bear it.'

Tom's frustration ripped through him and he wanted to scream – not at her but his own ineptness at putting his feelings into words. 'Depriving me of a family? I've got a million of them if you hadn't noticed. Family is one thing I'm definitely not short of.'

'I'm selfish, Tom. I grew up selfish in order to survive my mother's haphazard parenting. In my job I've documented so much pain over the years – parents who've lost children or watched them suffer – often in horrific circumstances. I can't open myself up to that,' she whispered.

'But what about the joy?' he challenged. 'I've seen amazing pictures you've taken of newborn babies and toddlers taking their first steps. What about your prize-winning one of the Afghan father reunited with the son he'd thought was killed in a terrorist attack?' If he couldn't get through to her this way he'd no clue what to say next. 'Pain comes along with joy and love. It's how the world works. Swings and roundabouts, honey. Life's short and you gotta take the good with the bad.' The clichés rolled out one after another but by the way her face softened he guessed they might be hitting the bull's eye. 'Sure I'll cry when I hold little Billy because of the wonder of him. Doesn't matter if he's the ugliest kid ever. And yeah, I'll think his parents are lucky. But does it mean I love you any less? Course it doesn't.' He brushed a strand of hair away from her face and kissed her.

With a hitching sob Fee seized Tom, gripping his shirtsleeves and kissing him right back. 'I lost perspective today.' She laughed through her tears. 'Idiotic thing for a photographer to say but it's true.'

'I did the same over Gina. I forgot to appreciate the good stuff and there's always been plenty.' He stroked his hand down over her hair and a trickle of desire stirred in her core. 'We're a good pair.'

'We certainly are. Nothing's written in stone. Remember women are notorious for changing their minds.' Before she could take back the words that'd popped out before she had time to consider them Tom drew her to him.

'Shush. That's enough for now,' Tom whispered.

This special man had already broken down so many of her barriers the possibility that he'd crumble the one she'd thought would never fall wasn't out of the question now.

'Good. Let's get ready to go.'

Seeing the whole family gathered around Rayna's hospital bed awed her because from this fortunate child's first breath he was clearly loved. All the designer baby clothes, expensive toys and fancy cribs were worthless in comparison. Of course little Billy wasn't ugly. Naturally he had inherited his gorgeous brown eyes from his mother's side of the family and his adorable tufts of thick, black hair came courtesy of his besotted new father. Tom had already shed more than a couple of tears and it surprised Fee how moved she was by the classic, heart-tugging sight of her big, loving man cradling the tiny baby.

She kept waiting for someone to make the obvious comment that it would be their turn next but no one put their foot in it making her wonder if Tom had warned his family off. Fee tried to stifle a yawn but Sarah caught her with her mouth gaping open.

'Thomas Michael, you need to take that poor girl home. She's worn out.'

'Yes, Mama.' He gave a sly wink behind his mother's back.

'Come on, sleepyhead. Y'all should leave Rayna to get some rest. It's the last she'll manage for eighteen years.' His joke earned him a swat around the head from his father.

Before Fee knew it they were settled on Tom's porch and snuggled together in a warm blanket to keep out the chill November air.

'Do you fancy a Christmas wedding?' Tom mused. 'We might have snow on the ground if we're lucky. Think twinkling fairy lights, lots of candles and green stuff.'

'Green stuff?' Eloquence wasn't Tom's way but his heart was in the right place. 'I think it'd be perfect.'

'What about your folks?

'We talked about them possibly coming out for Christmas and I can't see any reason why killing two birds with one stone wouldn't work.' Fee hadn't been like so many women who spent years picturing their perfect wedding. All she really wanted was to click her fingers and be Tom's wife.

'Eloping is fine with me if that's the way you want to go.' Tom's casual comment took her by surprise. 'We could have a family party after. Whatever makes you happy.'

For a second she was tempted to take him up on the offer but refused to be selfish. 'No, thanks. Snow, candles, lights, Lulu and green stuff works for me,' she said.

'That's a deal. I promise to shower you with green stuff. Now and for the rest of your life.' Tom chuckled and swooped in for a sizzling kiss. 'As soon as Thanksgiving's over we'll set Mama loose.'

'Perfect.' *And so are you.*

Where the last couple of days disappeared Tom wasn't sure but somehow they made it to Thanksgiving Day and the Chambers' house was bursting at the seams. For the kids' sake they kept up the pretence of enjoying the holiday as much as usual but the gaping hole left behind by his Mee Maw was wider than the Grand Canyon. Chloe's cornbread dressing was good but didn't taste quite right. His mother reckoned there wasn't enough sage while Rayna insisted there was too much. No one had the heart to attempt his grandmother's caramel cake and Mee Maw's holiday fruit tea was replaced by a store-bought version because she'd never been persuaded to write the recipe down.

He squeezed Fee's hand. 'Do you want to bring up our wedding plans to lift the mood a bit?'

'With pleasure.' She gently tapped her water glass then resorted to shouting. 'Does anyone have any plans for the day after Christmas that they can't break?'

'Why?' His mother stopped in the middle of scraping the last spoonful of sweet potato casserole onto Mikey's plate.

'Because that's when we would like to get married.'

The noisy chatter eased off for a moment before immediately increasing in volume with a lot of yelled questions from those who were too far away from the main dining table to know what was going on. By the time everyone got the message a free for all ensued as they all tried to voice their opinion at the same time.

'Right you lot be quiet.' Hank held his hand in the air and Tom breathed a sigh of relief when his family got the hint and shut up. 'Tom, give us a few details.'

'We want a quiet, intimate ceremony at Black Cherry for immediate family only. The Sevier cabin isn't booked and should be the perfect size.' He nodded to Fee. 'Your turn.'

'Sarah, we don't want a lot of fuss but do you think you and the girls could take charge of the food and decorations?'

His mother beamed. 'Of course.'

'Where's Lulu?' Fee craned her neck and Tom's little niece jumped off Mary-Jo's lap to race around to them. 'Do you know what we need?' Lulu stuck her thumb in her mouth and shook her head. 'We need a bridesmaid who likes sparkly dresses and flowers—'

'And rings?' Lulu giggled.

'Of course.'

'I reckon I need a best man, Pop.' Tom chimed in. 'Are you up for the job?' Only in his head did he add the word – again. Yesterday when he asked Fee who would give her away she said it was an outdated notion but rang Will Sawyer to ask him anyway and he couldn't have been more thrilled.

'I can manage that.'

'My parents are planning to arrive in about three weeks to meet you all and help with the wedding.' Fee's voice wobbled. She'd been shocked when Maddy insisted on coming so early, explaining that she'd let her daughter down too many times.

For once he'd chosen the right words when he tried to ease her concerns.

As long as I end up married to you, sooner rather than later, the rest is irrelevant. I'll listen to the craziness during the day and shut the door on it all at night to be with you.

'We needed this today.' His father's smile struggled to reach his eyes. 'Y'all raise your glasses and let's have a toast to Fee and Tom.'

Amidst the loud cheers and whistles Tom's throat tightened.

'Mee Maw's not really gone. Take a good look around the room. She's here in every single one of these people who love you and each other,' Fee whispered in his ear.

Later he'd tell her how much she meant to him but for now Tom contented himself with giving her a long kiss to the satisfaction of his rambunctious family.

'Right that's enough sloppy stuff,' Mikey shouted. 'The game's about to start.'

'Not until the dishes are done.' His mother's order wiped the smile off his brother's face.

'Yep, that's right.' Mary-Jo grinned. 'Then you get to watch the kids while us girls do up the shop.'

Fee looked puzzled.

'Family tradition. While the cafe is closed for the day the Thanksgiving decorations come down and Mary-Jo turns it into Christmas.' He squeezed her hand. 'Do you mind helping?'

'I'm not exactly creative but I'll give it a try.'

'Thanks. I expect you can hang giant plastic candy canes with the best of them.'

'Will it be full-on Christmas from now on?'

'Oh, yeah. Thirty-three days and counting.'

'You're as bad as Lulu. Don't tell me you still expect a Christmas stocking at your age?

'Of course and if you're very good Santa will bring you something too.'

'I'm pretty sure he brought mine early although he could've tied a red bow around your neck to make you look more festive.'

'I'll see what I can do later,' Tom whispered.

'One more thing before y'all get crazy.' His mother held up a red velvet drawstring bag. 'I'm gonna start with Fee and we'll go around the table clockwise.'

'What—'

'It's okay, honey. This is to find your Secret Santa pal.' He explained that with the family growing so large they'd decided a few years ago to only give the kids proper Christmas presents. The grown-ups swapped names and bought that one person a gag gift. 'It can't cost more than five dollars and the more outrageous the better.'

'Oh, right. I hadn't thought about presents.' A shadow flitted across her face. 'I don't know—'

'Don't fret. We're doin' all this together remember?' The relief in her eyes lifted Tom's heart to his throat. Whatever it took he would always be there for her. Being thankful today was easy.

Chapter Forty-Six

For a full fortnight after Thanksgiving they enjoyed the lull before the storm. Fee helped Tom to add simple decorations to all the cabins that were booked for the Christmas season. They kept it natural by using fresh cut greenery, pine cones and shiny holly laden with plump red berries. It seemed there was an unwritten rule in Pine Ridge that it was compulsory to hang Christmas decorations on every available spot. The town turned into a colourful, brightly lit wonderland. Even the police department didn't escape despite Hank grumbling that it wasn't professional to have an inflatable Santa Claus wearing a jaunty uniform cap outside the door. She'd seen far more elaborate decorations in cities around the world but the joyful, unsophisticated nature of Pine Ridge's efforts appealed to Fee.

Every time they saw Lulu the little girl updated them on how many nights she had to sleep before Santa Claus finally came. They often joked that she would quite possibly burst with excitement long before the 25th of December.

But the previous week everything had changed when they collected her mother and Will from the Knoxville airport. They'd turned down Tom's offer of a cabin at Black Cherry or Sarah Chambers' guest bedroom on the grounds that they were used to being independent and would be fine in the Pine Ridge motel. Despite their differences Maddy and Sarah clicked the first time they met and united in their determination to thwart Fee and Tom's plans for a simple, quiet wedding. They tried to distract their mothers and eat up more wedding planning time by taking them on several sightseeing trips around the local area. Out of desperation they even braved the appalling traffic jams around Gatlinburg and Pigeon Forge to see the fifteen million Christmas light display in the Smoky Mountain Winterfest. Fee's eyeballs burned for days after that one.

'We've created a monster,' she sighed. 'You've heard the media's habit of mashing celebrity couples' names together these days? Well I think our mothers qualify. I can't decide whether Saddy or Marah sounds best.'

'Honey, hold onto the fact that when all this stuff is behind us we'll be married and that's all that really matters.'

'I know you're right but I didn't expect—' Fee succumbed to Tom's kisses and pushed tomorrow's wedding dress shopping expedition from her mind. She'd put it off up to the point where she thought Sarah and Maddy would kidnap her and drag her to the nearest mall. The fact it was now only five days until their wedding and she still had nothing to wear forced her to give in.

'Yeah well there's a lot we didn't expect, sweetheart.' Tom's lopsided smile warmed her heart. 'Most of it's good.' He nuzzled into her neck and his stubble tickled her skin. 'Whatever you buy I'll love it and love gettin' you out—'

'Behave yourself.' She slapped his hand away, the one exploring under the hem of her jumper. 'At least until later.' Fee sighed. 'Any minute now our wonderful parents will be arriving for dinner and we'll be back to talking about interesting topics like flowers and wedding cake.'

'Don't worry. I'll show you interestin' later.'

I'm sure you will.

Fee started to despair. She'd spent most of the day being herded around every bridal shop in Knoxville. Despite the fact she was within waving distance of forty, both women had similar visions of her in an elaborate white dress complete with veil. To please them she'd tried on a multitude of traditional wedding dresses until even Sarah and Maddy were forced to admit the futility.

'There's one more store Mary-Jo told us to check out,' Sarah announced with firm determination and Fee got the hint she'd better not object. 'She said the Bridal Bar has some cute dresses. If you can't find something there we'll be forced to go to Nashville tomorrow.'

The thought of enduring another round of shopping was chilling but the daylight was starting to fade along with Fee's enthusiasm.

'Get back in the car,' Sarah ordered.

Ten minutes later they stood on the pavement outside the Bridal Bar and Fee almost danced with joy. The mannequin in the centre of the window wore Fee's dream dress. The ice-blue, tea-length lace dress sprinkled with light-catching diamante, soft ballerina style skirt and scooped neckline was the first she'd been able to imagine herself wearing.

'That's the one.' Fee pointed and Sarah and Maddy exchanged unreadable glances before smiling and nodding. 'Fingers crossed it fits.'

'It will,' Maddy declared and for some nonsensical reason Fee believed her mother.

Five minutes later she stared at her reflection in the mirror and bit back tears. *I don't do pretty*. It'd taken Tom's generous love to make her understand she didn't have to make a choice between being strong and feminine.

'Come on. Don't make us wait any longer,' Sarah shouted.

She stepped out of the dressing room and the look on their faces was worth every aggravating moment of the whole day. Fee hoped Tom would be equally struck dumb.

Tom leaned against the door post and blew on his hot coffee, gazing out over the frost-tipped landscape. He strolled over to one of his terracotta pots and plucked a dead leaf from his favourite dark wine Lenten Rose. Sturdy enough to survive a cold East Tennessee winter but colourful enough to make a statement. He smiled at the idea Fee might describe him the same way. They didn't have any snow on the ground yet but the forecast and dull, grey sky held strong hints that Fee might get her hoped for white wedding.

As Lulu would say "Only three more sleeps, Uncle T". After he lost Gina, and himself for a long while, he was convinced he'd never marry again but now he couldn't wait to make Fee his wife.

'You're up early.' Fee wandered out to join him, tugging on a soft grey jumper over her pyjamas. 'You've finished the patio furniture haven't you?'

'Yeah.' He didn't apologise for leaving her alone in bed because he knew she understood. 'That's it for now. I won't get a chance to do any more. There's too much goin' on.' He could hardly wait to see his little niece's face when she saw the completed dolls' house for the first time.

'Why on earth would you say that? We've only got a school Christmas pageant this afternoon, the Pine Ridge Christmas carol concert at six o'clock.' She ticked them off on her fingers. 'There's a Christmas cookie swap at the church tomorrow morning which you still need to make cookies for because I've been reliably informed that shop-bought ones are totally not acceptable—'

'There are three dozen of my famous Reindeer Ears in a plastic box all ready to go.' Tom popped a kiss on the top of her head. 'You've forgotten to mention attending the midnight Christmas Eve service, filling our stockings and wrapping presents.'

'The positive spin to put on all of this is that assuming I survive the festivities we finally get to the best part.'

'Eating all of my mama's great food?' Tom knew he deserved the sharp jab in his ribs but he'd made her smile which was all that mattered. 'Oh you mean that weddin' thing we've got goin' on?'

'Yes, Thomas Michael Chambers that "wedding thing".'

'Roll on Christmas is all I'm gonna say.'

Fee stirred from sleep as Tom kissed her shoulder, his breath warm on her bare skin.

'Merry Christmas, sweetheart.'

'What time is it? It's still dark outside.'

'Six o'clock. I thought you were never goin' to wake up.' She watched him reach down to the bottom of the bed and drag up an overstuffed red and green knitted stocking with her name embroidered on the top.

'Are you sure you're forty years old and not four? I'm pretty sure Lulu isn't any more excited than you today.'

'Sure she is,' Tom scoffed. 'My bet is she woke Mary-Jo at least a couple of hours ago. When I was little Pop would threaten not to cook his Christmas morning chocolate chip pancakes if we woke them up before five but he never followed through. Go on and see what he's brought you.'

How could she not respond to his boyish enthusiasm? Fee pulled the gifts out one at a time and his, or rather Santa's, thoughtfulness touched her. Small packets of healthy nuts and dried fruit. Red, fluffy socks because her feet were always cold. Her favourite perfume. A pack of leather-bound notebooks. A beautiful antique silver travel alarm clock. In the toe of the stocking she discovered a sheer, red lace bra and a matching thong.

'I had no idea Santa was such a naughty man.' She dangled the lingerie from her fingers and watched Tom's cheeks darken. 'We need to leave by nine, right?'

'Yeah.' His raspy voice made her smile. 'Which gives us plenty of—'

'But you haven't opened your stocking yet.'

'I can wait.'

Fee dropped the incriminating items on the bed and fumbled around the floor for the dark green velvet stocking she'd hidden there last night. 'Here you go. I can't have you thinking Father Christmas forgot you.' It hadn't been easy to shop when she'd rarely had a moment on her own. He didn't seem to mind the rather generic chocolate, whisky miniatures and socks she'd tucked in there but his smile broadened when he reached the toe.

'I assume these aren't for me?'

'Yes and no. There's a scene in Poldark when Ross buys Demelza a pair of white stockings tied with satin ribbon and he … puts them on her.'

'Interestin'.'

'I thought so.'

'I sure hope Mama's whipped up extra cinnamon rolls this morning.'

'Why's that?'

Tom eased her back down on the bed. 'Because some folks are gonna work up a mighty big appetite by then.'

'I hope your folks won't think we're a bunch of crazy loons.' Tom tried not to fret. He'd run through the usual Chambers' family Christmas Day routine with Fee and knew she'd had a quiet word with Maddy and Will to warn them what to expect. Everyone opened stockings at their own houses before arriving at Hank and Sarah's by mid-morning. The rest of the presents were opened there and Tom warned her it'd be a free-for-all. There was no system and it was every man, woman and child for themselves. A huge lunch was served around one and once the men finished cleaning up they all gathered round to watch the classic Christmas film *It's a Wonderful Life*.

'They'll love every minute.' Fee gave a wry smile. 'Will's pretty normal really. Mum on the other hand …'

'Not so much.'

'I often think she wrote the book on crazy. One year we ate vegan nut loaf in a freezing cold caravan on a cliff in Dorset because Maddy was working with a group trying to save a beached whale. Another time she was going through a pagan phase and we celebrated the Winter Solstice instead.'

'Different.' Tom parked the truck and unloaded their presents from the back. 'We're lucky Mikey and Sandy are both off work today. That almost never happens. Of course Pop is on call but hopefully nothing happens to drag him away.'

'It'll be a house full.' He caught the hitch of concern in her voice.

'You'll do okay.' Tom winked. 'Think about tomorrow. That's what I'm doin'.'

The front door flung open and his father yelled for them to hurry on in before all the cinnamon rolls were eaten. He didn't need telling twice.

Across the room Mary-Jo gave a brief nod and Tom disappeared towards his mother's sewing room. The previous evening he'd set up the dolls' house and worked with his cousin to get the tiny furniture in place. This morning he'd sneaked in the miniature wreath he'd made to hang on the front door which had ended up being a joint effort because Tom needed Fee's slender fingers to fashion the tiny red bow. Mary-Jo was going to explain to Lulu that one of her presents was in a different room because it was too big to go under the Christmas tree. He stationed himself by the wall ready to plug in the dolls' house lights when Lulu opened the door. Tom crouched down out of sight.

'Merry Christmas, Lulu.' Mary-Jo's laughter alerted him and Tom pushed in the plug, quickly standing back up to catch her reaction.

For a second the little girl didn't move or make any noise. Tom watched her eyes widen.

'Is it mine?' The disbelief and wonder in her voice tied his heart in knots. Mary-Jo nodded and Lulu shrieked and jumped up and down, bubbling over with excitement.

'Uncle T made it for you.'

Lulu broke away from her mother and flung herself at him. Tom swept her up into his arms and succumbed to her wet, sloppy kisses. He was surprised her squeals didn't burst his eardrum.

'You want to take a look at your new house, pumpkin?' He softened his voice and started to tell her all about the different rooms as he carried her slowly around the table. When he set her down on the floor and Mary-Jo came to join them everyone else piled in to take a look and he eventually managed to extricate himself from the crowd. Tom slipped behind his mother to join Fee over in the doorway.

'I don't think she likes it much.' Behind Fee's broad smile Tom saw the little girl who'd never experienced this kind of Christmas. Maddy and Fee got along much better now but some hurts never went away. Forgiveness didn't mean forgetting.

'Nope. I guess I'd better take it back.'

'You'd have a riot on your hands. Lulu's got too many people on her side.' Fee's voice cracked and there it was again, the separateness and loneliness he'd recognised in her the day they met.

'So do you now, sweetheart.' Tom pulled her into his arms, aware of her heartbeat through the new red sweater he'd bought her. No black. They were making progress. 'Trust me.'

Her eyes glazed with tears. 'I do.'

'That's all we've got to say tomorrow and you'll be mine and I'll be yours,' he whispered. 'In case I haven't said it enough I really, really like you in red.' Fee's cheeks turned the same rich shade of scarlet as the sweater. Tom jumped as someone tapped his shoulder.

'Thomas Michael.' His mother's stern tone brought him back to being five years old and in trouble again for talking in church. 'I'm giving you advance warning now so don't bother to claim later I didn't tell you. When you leave here you'll take Fee back to Black Cherry, wait while she packs an overnight bag and bring her straight back here. You will not phone, text or otherwise pester the girl tonight. She needs her rest plus it's bad luck for you to see each other before the wedding. Her mama and I will take good care of her.' She nodded over at Maddy.

He heard Fee's hastily stifled giggle. 'Yes, Mama.' With a smile his mother left them to go and look at the dolls' house.

'Yes, Mama,' Fee mimicked him. 'You are a truly hopeless case.'

'I'm glad I amuse you.' His effort to sound offended failed because all she did was laugh harder. 'You won't find it so funny when you're sleeping alone in a hard, single bed tonight.'

'My only consolation will be in knowing that you're equally miserable,' Fee retorted. 'Your mother didn't actually define "straight back". You know I always take an extraordinarily long time to pack.'

'Yeah, putting a toothbrush in a bag takes ages.'

'It certainly does.'

'Uncle T. Uncle T.' Lulu tugged on his arm. 'The kitchen door broke. Fix it.'

Tom let go of Fee and flashed an apologetic smile. 'Of course, pumpkin.' For the women in his life he'd do anything and everything he could to make them happy. Tomorrow he'd make his promises to Fee in front of everyone and couldn't wait.

Chapter Forty-Seven

Tom hovered by the cabin steps and fixed his binoculars on the path around the lake. No way would Fee be able to resist. The delicate icicles hanging from the bare tree branches, crisp snow underfoot and a sky so blue it could've been created in Photoshop all combined to make Black Cherry a magical sight. The previous evening his mother and sisters descended on the Sevier cabin with an inordinate number of candles, flowers and the famous "green stuff". No doubt they'd transformed it ready for the brief wedding ceremony and informal reception afterwards. He'd spotted the convoy of four-wheel drive cars a while ago and caught a glimpse of Fee's dark hair among the gaggle of women heading into the Sevier cabin.

A tall, slender figure in black popped into his vision and Tom zoomed in on Fee's face.

'Get in here and chug this,' Mikey shouted from the doorway and waved a can of beer at Tom. 'Hurry up before I freeze my balls off.'

'Okay. Okay.' He grabbed the beer and followed his brother inside. The men were all sprawled around his log fire and the TV was blasting out a football game. A lot of sports trash talk bounced between them all while a plate of his mother's home-made sausage balls made their way around the room.

A brief flash of memory seared his brain. Tom recalled his scared twenty-three-year-old self, dressed in an ill-fitting rented tuxedo and waiting at the Pine Ridge Methodist Church for Gina to arrive. When his father asked if he was okay he'd barely managed to nod as she appeared at the other end of the aisle. Once she stood next to him, glowing with love and beautiful in a froth of white lace he'd pushed away his doubts and made himself think of the wedding night to come. It'd been an injustice to a woman he hadn't deserved.

'You good?' His father came to stand by him and rested his hand on Tom's shoulder.

'Yep. I sure am.' Tom didn't hesitate. 'Don't eat all the sausage balls, you useless bastards,' he shouted at his brothers. 'Pass them over.' He grabbed a handful and crammed three into his mouth. 'Who's winning?'

'Shouldn't you get changed?' Sandy probed.

'Won't take long. No penguin suits today, thank the Lord.' Fee had been very clear about wanting as little fuss as possible. 'Dark trousers. White shirt. No tie. Simple.' Everyone joined in hassling him so Tom decided it'd be easier to get dressed and shut them all up.

Fee succumbed to Sarah's urging for her to come inside and get dressed.

'He'll catch you in your jeans if you don't hurry up.'

She smiled to herself knowing he already had. Fee had caught the reflected light from his binoculars as Tom watched from the porch. She'd taken some amazing shots of the gorgeous snowy lake and they'd be part of a special album she intended to give him after this was over. Mary-Jo was their official photographer today and she'd rolled her eyes at Fee's detailed instructions about precisely what, and what not to take pictures of.

Fee had bought an elegant ivory leather album and written on the title in the elegant calligraphy script she'd perfected years ago when working for a wedding photographer.

Snow, candles, lights, Lulu and green stuff.

This would be their private joke.

'Everyone else is ready. The bedroom is empty so it's your turn.' Sarah's brisk instruction made it clear that Fee better not argue. 'Your mama and I are coming to help you.' At nearly forty she was quite capable of dressing herself but wasn't stupid enough to say so. The stunning result of the one battle she managed to win was hanging on the outside of the wardrobe. To go with the dress she'd bought pale blue leather ballerina flats and would wear the silver bracelet that had been Tom's first gift to her.

'Mee Maw would've lent you these to wear today but they're mine now so I get to do the honours.' Sarah opened a small black velvet box to reveal a pair of sparkling diamond drop earrings. Fee would never usually wear something as fussy but couldn't hurt her future mother-in-law's feelings. 'They were a wedding present from Tom's great-great grandfather to his beloved Arlene and have been worn by every Chambers' bride since then.'

Fee put them on and studied herself in the mirror, unable to stop smiling. 'They're beautiful.'

'Like you.' Her mother's half-whispered comment took Fee by surprise and as their eyes met her throat tightened around the words she couldn't speak. 'I'm so proud of you.'

'Time for champagne,' Sarah announced and poured out three glasses from the bottle she had ready on the dresser before passing them around. 'To Fee and Tom. Wishing you a long and happy life together.'

She only dared to take a small sip but the sweet bubbles sneaked into her bloodstream. 'Right. Let's do this.'

Tom's smile took over his face as Lulu, a sparkling silver fairy complete with wings, bounced down the impromptu aisle between the chairs tossing white rose petals over everyone and everything in her path. As he glanced behind her Tom temporarily lost the ability to breathe. Fee, beautiful in a pale blue and sparkly dress, beamed straight at him. She and Will started to walk towards him and as she reached his side Tom took hold of her hand.

He ached to tell her how beautiful she looked but contented himself with lifting her fingers to his lips for a brief kiss. Vaguely he registered the minister beginning the ceremony and Will doing his part as the bride's father. Neither of them needed any prompting to say the vows they'd written together. Tom heard his brothers sniggering when they reached the part about not considering themselves the marrying kind until they met but ignored them.

'I now pronounce you man and wife. You may kiss the bride.'

Tom swept Fee into his arms and she melted into him as his mouth crushed her soft lips.

He tucked her arm through his and they made their way back through their cheering guests to have photos taken while the room was changed around for the reception.

An hour later Tom decided he'd been photographed from every possible angle. Every time he breathed Mary-Jo stuck a camera in his face. Once he dared to grouch and Fee's glare had shrivelled him to the core. It clearly said that this was the one thing she was asking of him. After that he smiled until his face ached.

'Not long until escape time,' Fee murmured.

'Hallelujah.' Their bags were ready in his truck. Two tickets to the Bahamas and their passports were tucked in his wallet. She'd dropped tempting hints about the significant number of skimpy bikinis she'd purchased.

'Come with me a minute.' She tugged on his hand and dragged him towards the door. 'I need a breath of fresh air.'

Tom shivered as they stepped onto the porch, decked out in gleaming white fairy lights. 'No problem. I arranged the freezing temperatures specially.' He lifted her hand and spun her around. 'I love the dress.'

'I thought you would.'

He held her at arm's length and studied it properly. 'It matches your eyes and shines. Like you.'

'Goodness. I'll think I've married a poet if you're not careful,' Fee teased.

'Hardly. That's it I'm afraid.' Tom yanked her to him, crushing the dress but guessing she wouldn't care. Now he gave her the kiss he'd wanted to earlier, holding nothing back and drawing soft moans from the back of her throat.

'Not cold out here any more, is it?' Fee joked. She fumbled in the folds of her dress and drew out a small camera from the pocket. 'Selfie time. Smile.' Holding out the camera she did several rapid clicks. 'This is for our private album.'

'We have a private album?'

Fee's eyes sparkled. 'Of course. Can you guess the title?'

'Didn't know they had to have one.'

She shook her head. 'Ignorant man. It's *snow, candles, lights, Lulu and green stuff*.' Fee touched his cheek. 'You gave me everything today. It could be hard to live up to.'

'I'll do my best. Always. Every day.'

'I know. And so will I,' Fee promised. There was nothing more to be said.

Thank You

from Angela Britnell

Thank you for taking the time out of your busy lives to read *Christmas at Black Cherry Retreat* and I hope you enjoyed being a part of Fee and Tom's story. If you could take a few moments to leave a review on a site like Amazon or on Goodreads to encourage other readers to discover my stories that would be wonderful.

About the Author

Angela was born in St. Stephen, Cornwall, England. After completing her A-Levels she worked as a Naval Secretary. She met her husband, a US Naval Flight Officer while being based at a small NATO Headquarters on the Jutland Peninsula in Denmark. They lived together in Denmark, Sicily, California, southern Maryland and London before settling in Franklin, Tennessee.

Angela took a creative writing course in 2000 and loved it so much that she has barely put her pen down since. She has had short stories and novels published in the US. Her debut novel, *Sugar & Spice*, won Choc Lit's Search for an American Star competition and was her UK debut.

Follow Angela:

Blog: www.angelabritnellromance.com
Twitter: www.twitter.com/AngelaBritnell
Facebook: www.facebook.com/angelabritnell

More Choc Lit

From Angela Britnell

Sugar and Spice

The Way to a Hero's Heart ...

Fiery, workaholic Lily Redman is sure of two things: that she knows good food and that she always gets what she wants. And what she wants more than anything is to make a success of her new American TV show, Celebrity Chef Swap – without the help of her cheating ex-fiancé and producer, Patrick O'Brien. So when she arrives in Cornwall, she's determined to do just that.

Kenan Rowse is definitely not looking for love. Back from a military stint in Afghanistan and recovering from a messy divorce and an even messier past, the last thing he needs is another complication. So when he lands a temporary job as Luscious Lily's driver, he's none too pleased to find that they can't keep their hands off each other!

But trudging around Cornish farms, knee deep in mud, and meetings with egotistical chefs was never going to be the perfect recipe for love – was it? And Lily could never fall for a man so disinterested in food – could she?

What Happens in Nashville

'What happens in Nashville, stays in Nashville!'

Claire Buchan is hardly over the moon about the prospect of her sister's hen party; travelling from the UK to Nashville, Tennessee, for a week of honky-tonks, karaoke and cowboys. Certainly not straight-laced Claire's idea of a good time, what with her lawyer job and sensible boyfriend, Philip.

But then she doesn't bank on meeting Rafe Castello. On the surface, Rafe fits the cowboy stereotype with his handsome looks and roguish charm but as he and Claire get to know each other, she realises there is far more to him than meets the eye.

Can Claire keep to the holiday mantra of 'what happens in Nashville, stays in Nashville' or will she find that some things are far too difficult to simply leave behind?

Celtic Love Knot

Can two tangled lives make a love knot?

Lanyon Tremayne is the outcast of his small Cornish village of St. Agnes. Susceptible to fits of temper and with a chequered past behind him, he could even be described as a bit of an ogre. But nobody knows the painful secret he hides.

Olivia Harding has learnt a thing or two about ogres. She's a professor from Tennessee, specialising in Celtic mythology and has come to St. Agnes to research the legend of a Cornish giant – and to lay to rest a couple of painful secrets of her own.

But when Olivia meets the ruggedly handsome Lanyon, her trip to Cornwall looks set to become even more interesting. Will she get through to the man beneath the bad-tempered façade, or is Lanyon fated to be the 'ogre' of St. Agnes forever?

The Wedding Reject Table

Once on the reject table, always on the reject table?

When Maggie Taylor, a cake decorator, and Chad Robertson, a lawyer from Nashville Tennessee, meet at a wedding in Cornwall it's not under the best circumstances.

They have both been assigned to 'the reject table', alongside a toxic collection of grumpy great aunts, bitter divorcees and stuffy organists.

Maggie has grown used to being the reject, although when Chad helps her out of a wedding cake disaster she begins to wonder whether the future could hold more for her.

But will Chad be strong enough to deal with the other problems in Maggie's life? Because a ruined cake isn't the only issue she has – not by a long shot.

Available as an eBook on all platforms and in audio. Visit www.choc-lit.com for details.

Here Comes the Best Man

Being the best man is a lot to live up to …

When troubled army veteran and musician Josh Robertson returns home to Nashville to be the best man at his younger brother Chad's wedding he's just sure that he's going to mess it all up somehow.

But when it becomes clear that the wedding might not be going to plan, it's up to Josh and fellow guest Louise Giles to make sure that Chad and his wife-to-be Maggie get their perfect day.

Can Josh be the best man his brother needs? And is there somebody else who is beginning to realise that Josh could be her 'best man' too?

Available as an eBook on all platforms and in audio. Visit www.choc-lit.com for details.

Love Me for a Reason

Love doesn't always have to make sense …

When Daisy Penvean meets Nathaniel Dalton whilst visiting a friend in Nashville, it seems there are a million and one reasons for them not to be together. Nathaniel's job as a mergers and acquisitions manager means sharp suits and immaculate hair, whereas Daisy's work as a children's book illustrator lends itself to a more carefree, laid-back style. And, as Daisy lives in England, there's also the small matter of the Atlantic Ocean between them.

But when Nathaniel's job takes him to London to oversee the merger of a small publisher with a large American company, he and Daisy meet again under very different circumstances. Because Daisy works for the publisher involved in the deal, and if Nathaniel does his job, it could mean she loses hers …

Available as an eBook on all platforms.
Visit www.choc-lit.com for details.

You're The One That I Want

What if you didn't want to fake it any more?

When Sarah, a teacher from Cornwall, and Matt, a businessman from Nashville, meet on a European coach tour, they soon find themselves in a relationship …

Except it's a fake relationship. Because Matt is too busy for romance, and Sarah is only trying to make her cheating ex-husband jealous … isn't she?

As Matt and Sarah complete their tour of Europe, they do all the things real couples are supposed to do – from visiting fairy-tale castles in Germany to recreating the scene from *Romeo and Juliet* in Verona. And, of course, for every picturesque destination there's a loved-up selfie and Facebook post to match.

But as their holiday comes to an end, Sarah and Matt realise that they're not happy with their pretend relationship. They want the real thing.

Available in paperback from all good bookshops and online stores. Visit www.choc-lit.com for details.

One Summer in Little Penhaven

Could one summer change your life?

When high-flying American lawyer Samantha Muir finds out she's lost her partnership whilst on an assignment in London, she has a dramatic reaction.

Rather than returning home, she resigns, leaves her business suits behind and jumps on the first train to Cornwall at the encouragement of a friendly stranger.

The village of Little Penhaven, where Samantha eventually ends up, is a world away from her life in Knoxville, Tennessee – and local farmer Cadan Day is certainly a world away from any man she has met before. But could the Cornish village and Cadan play a part in Samantha's summer of self-discovery?

Available as an eBook on all platforms and in audio. Visit www.choc-lit.com for details.

Christmas in Little Penhaven

Have yourself a little Cornish Christmas ...

Wannabe author Jane Solomon is expecting an uneventful Christmas in her Cornish village of Little Penhaven.

But then super fit American gym owner Hal Muir comes to town, and suddenly the holiday season looks set to be far more interesting. Hal is keen on embracing every British tradition on offer, from mince pies to Christmas pub quizzes – and perhaps some festive romance too ...

Introducing Choc Lit

We're an independent publisher creating
a delicious selection of fiction.
Where heroes are like chocolate – irresistible!
Quality stories with a romance at the heart.

See our selection here:
www.choc-lit.com

We'd love to hear how you enjoyed *Christmas at Black Cherry Retreat*. Please leave a review where you purchased the novel or visit **www.choc-lit.com** and give your feedback.

Choc Lit novels are selected by genuine readers like yourself. We only publish stories our Tasting Panel want to see in print. Our reviews and awards speak for themselves.

Could you be a Star Selector and join our Tasting Panel?
Would you like to play a role in choosing which novels we decide to publish? Do you enjoy reading women's fiction? Then you could be perfect for our Tasting Panel.

Visit here for more details…
www.choc-lit.com/join-the-choc-lit-tasting-panel

Keep in touch:
Sign up for our monthly newsletter Spread for all the latest news and offers: www.spread.choc-lit.com. Follow us on Twitter: @ChocLituk and Facebook: Choc Lit.

Where heroes are like chocolate – irresistible!